BOOKED AT THE SUGAR MILL MARKETPLACE

Sugar Mill Marketplace Mysteries Book 1

BECKY CLARK

Foreword

RAT RACE is the prequel novella that bridges Becky Clark's Mystery Writer's mysteries and the Sugar Mill Marketplace mysteries.

Read RAT RACE before you read BOOKED, PLOTTED, and BOUND as it sets the stage for some action that occurs in those early books in the Sugar Mill Marketplace series.

You can buy RAT RACE for 99c or download it for free when you subscribe to Becky Clark's newsletter, So Seldom It's Shameful News.

Subscribers also receive FICTION CAN BE MURDER—the first book in the Mystery Writer's series—as well as some related short stories and a Christmas play.

Dena

"AHOY, THERE!"

The booming sound of a strange man's voice in her used bookstore at the not-yet-opened-for-business Sugar Mill Marketplace startled Dena Russo where she sat on the floor in the far corner behind several shelves. She kicked the stack of books she'd been carefully alphabetizing. Since they hadn't had their Grand Opening yet, it hadn't occurred to her to keep the security gate to Thrice Sold Tales down and locked.

Her feet were afire with the prickly sensation of pins-and-needles from sitting on her legs for too long. Both knees buckled when she pulled herself upright. She grabbed for a shelf, knocking off several precariously leaning books. They'd been threatening to leap at her all morning, every time she added one to its ranks.

She covered her head against the fall-out.

"Who's running this place?" the man boomed again.

She wanted to yell, "Keep your shirt on! I'm trying," but since nobody should be in her store at all at this particular moment, she said nothing. Blood finally circulating through her body again, she made her way from where she'd been hidden in the stacks and peered around the corner.

An elderly man stood scowling, holding a box of books that wobbled a bit, as if they were a tad too heavy for him. Dena could tell he'd once been well-groomed, but now facial hair seemed to be rewilding like a field left fallow for too many seasons. Drab clothing hung off his fragile frame, making it look like he wore Nero Wolfe's cast-off gardening clothes. The booming voice didn't quite match the person she saw standing in the middle of her store.

"Can I help you?" She stepped out from behind the shelf but kept her distance, eyeing the box of books in his arms. Had he carried it in, or was it one of hers he'd picked up when she was hidden behind the shelves? When she bought the bookstore, it included dozens of boxes of inventory, all of it a-jumble, no rhyme or reason to any of it, no labels on the boxes.

She tried to peek at the titles in the man's box, but their angle made them impossible to read.

"Brought these for you to billet here," he said gruffly, thrusting the box at her.

Instinctively, she took one step backward. He thrust it toward her again. She responded with another step backward.

The man grunted loudly and brushed past her to set the box on the front counter. It took him two tries to heave it up there.

Dena jumped aside, consciously keeping her distance. This man gave her an uncomfortable vibe. She knew the other tenants of the Marketplace would come running if she yelled, which made her feel the teensiest bit braver. Assuming anyone was here this early, that is.

Before she could ask again what he wanted, he

gestured at the box he'd just set down. "I'll let you have twenty percent of the proceeds if you billet them here."

"Pardon me?"

"The books." His scowl deepened and he let out an exasperated huff. "They're first edition Colorado histories. All shipshape. Very rare. Very important."

Ahoy? Billet? Shipshape? Dena wondered if she had misheard him and the books were actually first edition naval histories.

"I have no idea what you're talking about." Dena stepped to the box and pulled out the book on top. Dust made her sneeze twice. She looked at two more titles before dropping them back inside. "Are you looking to sell me these books? I'm not—"

"Luckiest day of your life."

Dena's initial assessment of this man hadn't improved any. Even if she was in the market to buy books, she wouldn't buy any from this arrogant, presumptuous person.

"I could go up to twenty-two percent."

Dena couldn't help it and let out a guffaw at his obnoxious cockiness.

His face reddened and she saw him clench his fists.

She backpedaled and tried to moderate her tone. "I'm sorry, but whoever told you I was buying books was mistaken. First," she said, sweeping her arm around all the boxes stacked everywhere, "I have plenty of books already." She silently added, *and I wouldn't buy garage sale cast-offs from a grump anyway.* Without explaining that she didn't have the time to investigate his claims that these were rare first editions, she also didn't even know if her customers would be into that. Or if she'd even have any customers. "I don't have the capability to track consignment sales. I'm sorry."

"So, I schlepped ten miles for nothing."

"I guess you did." The gall of this man to get mad at her for his faulty assumptions.

She took three giant steps away from him in the direction of her back door as he picked up his box of books.

As he marched with them out of the bookstore he bellowed at her, "You'll be sorry!"

There were four outside doors to the large Sugar Springs Marketplace, one at each corner. After allowing plenty of time for him to leave her store and then exit the building completely, Dena made her way around the entire promenade, making sure each was locked. The two emergency exit doors centered on the north and south sides were locked as well.

She pushed the code to lower the security gate down from the ceiling, closing off her bookstore from any further intruders. The security gate moved silently, but much too slowly for her taste. When Norbert Wallace, her landlord, had showed her how it worked, she'd asked him, "What if I needed to lock that down in a hurry?" He'd laughed and said, "This is Sugar Springs. Nothing happens in a hurry here." He had completely missed her point, but she let it go. She didn't want to get labeled a worrywart right out of the gate.

However, at the risk of being labeled a worrywart, she would revisit this with Norbert. Along with everything else.

"How'd he get in, anyway?" she murmured. Since the Marketplace wasn't open for business yet, the outside doors were supposed to remain locked. She got that old prickly feeling. That feeling that said some nebulous thing was wrong, but what and in what way, you simply didn't know. And if you didn't know, how were you supposed to guard against it?

Dena

DENA STEPPED through the back door of her bookstore into the common area for the downstairs tenants of the Marketplace. She glanced at the whiteboard where someone had written, "11 Days to Grand Opening." Dena picked up the red dry erase marker and drew a smiley face underneath. By the time she finished, however, it wasn't smiley; it was terrified. Big eyes, every tooth showing, flames shooting out of the top of its head. Exactly how she felt.

Balaam, Evelyn and Max's charcoal colored Persian cat, glanced up at the whiteboard. He hissed at it, then turned and hissed at Dena, before sauntering away. He hissed at people the same way janitors mopped floors, like it was his job.

An unnamed dread had gripped her ever since she picked up her life and moved it from Santa Fe, New Mexico to the tiny Colorado town of Sugar Springs. And the confrontation with that mystery man hadn't helped to lessen it any.

She'd been telling herself over and over that just

because trauma sent her running off to Santa Fe twenty-some years ago, and now had chased her back to Colorado, there was no reason to worry. What were the odds something bad would happen here too? She'd explained this to herself so often in the past couple of months she felt like one of those internet videos that kept playing on a nonstop loop even when you desperately wanted it to stop. And this was nothing cute like that dancing kitten. Not cute at all.

Of course, deep down she knew that dread had a name. She called it "Whoosh." As in the sound of her life savings whooshing away. The sound of blowing her dry, desiccated body— whoosh—up into the atmosphere like so much useless shredded money. If she couldn't sell enough used books to make this new endeavor of hers profitable, and soon, that's exactly what would happen, to both her and her money.

She erased her terrified stick figure and replaced it with a normal smiley face. If she could pretend all was well when she spoke to her adult children Charlee and Lance, she could do the same with the other tenants, right? Maybe if she pretended hard enough, she'd soon believe it too. Maybe there'd be no whooshing.

She had eleven days before the official beginning of her third act. The first act of her adult life was happily raising a son and daughter as the wife of a police-officer-turned-detective. Her second act was a satisfying career in Santa Fe as an insurance executive. This third one would be as the sole proprietor of Thrice Sold Tales, a used bookstore here at the newly renovated Sugar Mill Marketplace.

Dena crossed the large rectangular-shaped common area to grab a ream of printer paper. The vendor area was centered in the Marketplace, hidden from shoppers, but accessed by all the downstairs tenants from a back door in each of their shops.

Right now there were three empty shop spaces on the west side of the new Marketplace, but the far southwest corner would be home to *Zoet's Chocolate Shop*. The owner, Hugo Dekker, pronounced it "zoot" and told them it meant *sweet* in Dutch. Hugo had a slight indecipherable accent that certainly could have been Dutch, for all Dena knew.

On the southeast side of the Marketplace, directly opposite the vendor room from the chocolate shop, was *Step Into History*, a fun place where you could dress up in period clothing and get your photo taken. It was owned by Evelyn and Max Milligan, an eighty-something couple Dena had met when she and Charlee had scoped out the town a couple of months ago over the long Thanksgiving weekend.

Next to them was Skyler Olsen's *Really Grate Cheese* shop, then Dena's bookstore, then the *Sugar Springs Bakery*, owned by Kober, who Dena and Charlee had also met on their reconnaissance trip. Dena still wasn't sure if Kober was her first or last name, but it was the only thing anyone ever called her, and it seemed too late to ask for clarification now.

The vendors could lock their back doors into the vendor room, but it had become habit for all the tenants to roll up their security screen covering the fronts of their shops, walk through, unlock their back door and leave it open for ease of access to the vendor room. After all, that's where the communal printer and coffeepot lived. There was also storage space, some tables and chairs where they could take a break or eat lunch or even spread out with a task that needed more room than their shop could manage. On the south end, they even enjoyed their own restroom, hidden from the public. Opposite, on the north end, there was a set of stairs up to the second-floor vendor area, a duplicate of the one on the first floor, except for the fact it was empty of tenants for now.

Norbert Wallace, her landlord and the owner and developer of the Marketplace was starting slowly, trying to fill the first-floor shops first.

The Marketplace had a huge rectangular-shaped footprint. The building was beautifully restored from the busy, thriving sugar mill it once was. It was situated near the Arkansas River, which flowed along the edge of Sugar Springs, forming a natural town boundary. Over the years the market for sugar processed from beets fell out of favor with the consuming public, and the mill was abandoned. Unfortunately, it had been the main industry in the community. Most everyone had something to do with the sugar mill, whether it was growing or harvesting the beets, processing them, or running a business to support them.

Sugar Springs began to dismantle itself. That is, until Evelyn Milligan herself rallied the town to pursue a couple of ideas in an attempt to save their community. As a resident of Sugar Springs for her entire life, which Dena knew had to be close to eighty years, people listened to her. The first two ideas—building a regional park along their riverfront to draw in tourists or luring a college to build an extension campus—didn't quite work out, but Sugar Springs did gain a serenely majestic and updated river walk from the community's efforts.

Then one day Evelyn and her husband Max were out walking near the abandoned mill and, as she explained it, the mill magically transformed before her very eyes into something retro yet new, a unique shopping mecca full of artisanal and interesting stores and restaurants.

Unfortunately, she and Max didn't have the money to

realize her vision, so she turned to the town to create some kind of co-op. That fizzled out, despite enthusiasm from the town leaders and citizens at large. Turns out Max and Evelyn weren't the only ones under-capitalized.

But in stepped Norbert Wallace, real estate developer from nearby Colorado Springs. He opened an office and rented an apartment in town and before anyone knew what had happened, he had drawn up plans and created a huge sketch of his vision. It hadn't matched Evelyn's, which irritated her, but when she saw his architect's final design, she told Dena she had gasped at the beauty and attention to detail.

They kept the original decorative brick façade of the sugar mill, using the least damaged part of the main building. Much of the mill was unsalvageable and unsafe, but after an intense power washing of the red bricks, what remained was stunning, jutting up two stories, with the ornate façade even taller than that. Landscaped parking surrounded all four sides, disguising it from looking like a sea of concrete and cars, with public entrances diagonally on each corner.

When a shopper entered the Marketplace, there was a wide promenade traveling the entire rectangular perimeter. Each shop had a large, inviting entrance that was locked down each evening with a hidden security gate that rolled down from the ceiling. The promenade had comfy overstuffed armchairs and bistro tables scattered around, allowing weary shoppers to rest, eat, or simply gather with friends in a charming and accessible setting, a description that could apply to the town of Sugar Springs itself.

Broad, friendly staircases and elevators on the long sides of the Marketplace offered access to the future second-floor shops, either eight large ones like on the first floor, or sixteen smaller ones, or some combination of both. Norbert was playing it by ear, waiting to see how soon the Marketplace could turn a profit and become destination shopping for the region.

Dena, and all the Marketplace tenants, hoped they'd turn a profit quickly. She didn't know the particulars of anyone else's finances, but she certainly didn't have a lot of financial wiggle room. She'd had a large whoosh of cash sunk into this endeavor just after Thanksgiving when she'd decided on the spur of the moment to buy the bookstore and sign the lease at the Marketplace. At the time, it seemed a perfectly sensible thing to do, after all, who doesn't love to buy used books? But about eight minutes after all the paperwork was signed, she began to worry.

What if the good citizens of Sugar Springs didn't actually love to buy used books? What if they did want to buy used books but she didn't choose the right ones to sell to them? What if she priced them too high? What if people only wanted new books? What if she bought too many mysteries and this was a romance reading town? What if there was some clause in the town charter that banned reading, like some bizarro blue law like no dancing in "Footloose" and nobody told her? What if, what if, what if?

She could fill a library with her *what ifs*. They kept her up at night and even when she could sleep, they woke her in the wee hours, chasing her around her newly-built shelves and flinging pages of books at her until she was forced out of bed for a calming cup of chamomile. Or a shot of tequila.

———

Still a bit spooked by the unexpected man in her store, Dena decided to take a break from shelving books and work in the vendor room instead. She'd been avoiding the marketing and promotional activities she needed to do. At least she understood how to alphabetize books. Marketing and promotion for a bookstore was a tad out of her wheelhouse.

She loaded paper into the printer but was having trouble closing it back up again when Kober and her four children came in the vendor area through Kober's bakery door, all of them talking at once. The kids were noisy, but Kober out-noisied them all.

Last week, out of curiosity, Dena had downloaded a decibel meter app for her phone. She activated it while Kober told a funny story in her regular voice to the tenants as they all gathered at lunchtime. Kober had registered an impressive 78, just under that of a leaf blower.

As they all shed their winter wear, Kober shouted to her kids in a stern voice, "If any of you lot get in my way today, I will squash you like a bug. I have seventeen thousand things to do today, and refereeing fights or taking anyone to the hospital are definitely not on my list." Under her pink puffy parka, Kober wore neon-colored leggings in a zigzag pattern with a paisley print tunic.

Dena knew Kober was more bark than bite—or hoped she was, at least—and her children offered noncommittal waves. They'd obviously heard threats like this before. Probably multiple times just this morning.

The ten-year-old twins, Lincoln and Leo, raced their brother Wyatt—two years and forty pounds bigger and faster—to the ping-pong table. Wyatt got there first and snatched up a paddle. "I'll play you both!" he shouted, and the game commenced.

Balaam sat nearby, tail curled genteelly around his feet, hisses primed on his stern puckered mouth and ready to be deployed at the slightest provocation. You know, like someone glancing his way, or attempting to pet him, or breathing.

Today the ping pong table was centered in the vendor room near the south end, with the printer on a stand near it. It seemed to migrate around the room, perhaps as the players finagled the optimum playing location. Every item and every person were trying to find their appropriate place at the Marketplace.

The twins and Dena performed a wary dance around each other while Dena fought with the paper tray.

Jain, Kober's sixteen-year-old daughter, sighed at her brothers. As haphazard as Kober always looked, Dena had never seen anything but an easy flawless style from Jain. She'd told Dena she mostly shopped for used clothing and Dena had been surprised because Jain was always "put together," the highest compliment her own mother had ever offered another woman.

Dena couldn't help but wonder if Jain's classic outfits and symmetrical tendrils were the equal and opposite reaction to Kober's outlandish clothing style and mass of curls pushed up and out of her way on the top of her head.

What was she thinking … *of course* it was a direct effect. Kober and Jain were smack-dab in the middle of that age old mother-daughter dance called *I Will Not Turn Into My Mother*. Dena couldn't help smiling when she thought of Charlee, her own daughter, doing everything possible to be anyone but Dena. Mostly it manifested in her wearing high heels instead of the flats Dena usually wore. The fact that Dena chose them because otherwise she towered over everyone was a particular clearly lost on Charlee at the time. When Charlee realized high heels were mostly uncomfortable and always impractical in high school, she decided to differentiate from her mother in other, less blister-inducing ways.

Jain gently took the paper tray from Dena's hands and expertly slid it in, like a hot knife through butter. Then she and Dena switched the location of the printer stand with one of the round tables. When they were satisfied with the rearranged furniture, Jain smiled at Dena with a nod toward her brothers slamming ping pong balls at each other. "Boys, amirite?"

"You am," Dena said with a return smile. "Thanks." She gestured at the printer. "Apparently that thing and I are not friends, but I have no idea how I offended it."

"Jain, c'mon! They're killing me!" Wyatt called to his sister. He was a plumper version of his siblings, thick curly hair instead of straight, a mini-version of their mother.

Jain hurried over to the ping pong table and picked up the fourth paddle.

"No fair!" the twins cried in unison. One of them—Dena still hadn't figured out which was which because they were identical, sandy-haired, and constantly in motion—grabbed the ball and turned to Kober. "Mo-om! Tell her to—" His words skidded to a stop when he saw his mother's face as she looked up from her phone. "Never mind!" he said. The game resumed just as noisily but not until Wyatt had switched places with one of the twins.

"Looks like you had a come-to-Jesus moment with…" Dena cocked her head at Kober and guessed, "Lincoln?"

"Leo."

"How do you tell them apart?"

"Leo has that mole on his chin. Like a leo-pard."

Dena squinted at him, but he was a blur of activity and she couldn't make it out.

"And luckily, Lincoln conked his face on the coffee table and ended up with a scar on his lip. Li-ncoln, Li-p. I used to color it in with a marker to make it easier to see. I quit doing it when he was old enough to tell me which one he was."

"Yeah, that was lucky," Dena said dryly, failing to keep the judgment from her face.

"You know what I mean. You had a boy and a girl, life was simple for you."

Dena guffawed. "Simple?" She thought about all the trauma her family—especially her children—had suffered over the years.

Kober's voice brought her back to the present. "It's their last day of winter break. Not gonna lie. Ready to turn them back over to their zookeepers, er, teachers."

"At least Santa brought them the ping pong table for when they come here."

Kober leaned in and spoke quietly, even though the kids wouldn't have heard her if she'd shouted. "I told them it came with the lease, not that Nic and I bought it. He figured the kids would end up here a lot, now that I have the bakery, but we didn't want them lording it over anyone or thinking we were rich."

"You and your husband lied to them?" Dena again tried not to sound judgy, knowing that she'd told her kids more than a few lies over the years. But those were to protect them from bigger truths, not something small-scale, like their family could afford a two-hundred-dollar ping pong table.

"Lie is a pretty strong word." Kober bent to retie her ankle boot. "I prefer to call it an embellishment of the truth. I mean, I *don't* want them lording it over their friends or going around bragging about how rich we are, so what's the harm?"

"Why not just tell them not to get smug about having something other people don't?"

Kober rolled her eyes and headed through the door to the bakery. "Your kids were clearly less feral than mine."

As if to punctuate her statement, Wyatt yelled, "In your face!" and slammed a shot right at Jain's face. She raised one hand and caught the ping pong ball with ease. She glared at him as only a big sister can, then casually opened her backpack, dropped in the ball, and withdrew a book. She dragged a chair close to the ping pong table, then sat with her ankles crossed on the table. The boys shrugged and raced out of the vendor room into the promenade.

Dena tipped her chin at Jain, then at the door the boys had disappeared through. "Nice."

Jain shrugged. "Yeah. Sometimes they need redirection. Or some tough love. Or a metaphorical smack upside the head."

Dena laughed. "Don't we all?" She pushed buttons on her laptop until the printer whirred to life. When she looked hopefully at the paper spitting out, Dena muttered, "Back to the drawing board."

She returned to the round table she'd been working at, trying to design a Grand Opening flyer. Remembering she only had eleven days to make the readers of Sugar Springs flock to her store and fall in love with Thrice Sold Tales, she winced at what she saw on the paper in her hand. She couldn't think of a good hook, the design looked like the artwork of a three-year-old, and she had made a typo in both the name of her bookstore and the opening date.

In addition, now she hated, despised, loathed, and detested the name of her bookstore. When she chose it, she'd done her research and seen a plethora of used bookstores called Twice Sold Tales and knew it was a play on the title of Nathaniel Hawthorne's short story collection called "Twice Told Tales." But thrice? Yes, it set her apart from the other stores, but she wanted to slap herself upside the head. First, nobody said thrice. Not ever. Unless they were being sarcastic or were time travelers from the Middle Ages. Second, since when did used books get sold three times? Maybe once in a while, sure, but not regularly. And even if they did, was that such a good thing? Did people want books that had passed through that many hands?

Dena was staring forlornly at her computer screen when Skyler came in from her cheese shop holding a stack of papers.

Her honey-blond tousled curls bounced merrily around her face, as perky as she was. She greeted both Dena and Jain, who gave a wave without looking up from her book.

"I came to ask if you wanted me to deliver any of your Grand Opening flyers. I'm getting ready to take mine around town." Skyler stood much too close to Dena and waved her stack of papers around.

Dena scooted the tiniest bit away from Skyler as she accepted the top sheet of paper Skyler held toward her. She glanced at Skyler's cheese shop flyer and groaned. "I don't even have mine yet. Yours are fantastic. Mine look terrible."

"I'm sure they don't. Let me see."

Dena turned her screen so Skyler could see.

"Oh. Hm."

"See? I told you." Dena rested her chin in her hand. "Why do we each have to make our own, anyway? Why didn't we make one flyer with all of our info on it? We're taking them to the same places, after all."

Skyler stared at her. "You're a genius!" She yelled toward the other shops. "Kober, Evelyn, Hugo … you guys here?"

"Son of a custard pie!" Kober yelled back. "You made me spill!"

Hugo hurried in. "What is it, Skyler? Is everything okay?"

"Everything's fine. But Dena had a great idea. Why are we all making our own Grand Opening flyers? Why don't we just make one with all our stuff on it. We could have all our logos on it."

Evelyn, wearing a mint green cardigan over matching elastic waist pants, shuffled over and sat in the chair opposite Dena.

Dena was itching to someday be in a position to take a peek in Evelyn's closet. She had never seen her wearing anything but sherbet-colored polyester pants and a matching knit cardigan over a plain shell, almost always white. Dena secretly hoped she owned nothing else.

"We were supposed to make a flyer?" Evelyn glanced at Hugo, then Dena.

Kober hurried through her door to the vendor area, already covered in flour. She used her forearm to push her sinking tower of hair back where it belonged. "Flyers? What flyers?"

Skyler handed each of them one of her flyers. "We should all be on here."

Kober sidled further away from Skyler until none of their body parts touched.

"Did you make this?" Hugo said, admiring it. He remained where he was, touching shoulders with Skyler.

Skyler blushed. "I did."

"Well, if you don't mind," Dena said. "I don't want to steal your idea, but maybe we can have our logos and a coupon or something for each of us. Or we could do that thing where every shopper has to visit each of our businesses to be in a drawing for a prize, maybe answer an easy question about each one—"

"Or maybe buy something from each of us." Max's

gruff growl of a voice belied what Dena had come to know was his soft marshmallow interior. He stood behind Evelyn's chair and lightly rested his hands on his wife's shoulders.

"Now, dear." Evelyn reached up and patted his hand.

"That would be great, Max," Dena said, "but I don't think we can require people to purchase something to be in a drawing."

"Who said anything about a drawing?" Max grumbled.

"Dena did, dear. Now, hush up."

They discussed what they might give away, or include in their coupons, and whether they wanted to do a grand prize. While they brainstormed, Skyler ran for her laptop, sketching revisions to her flyer as they spoke. When they had bandied about plenty of ideas, she showed them the finished product, a fun and funky flyer, bound to garner attention. They all agreed it was perfect, even Max, despite the fact it didn't require anyone to purchase anything.

"It's beautiful, Skyler," Dena said. "I'm sure it'll bring everyone to the Grand Opening."

Hugo made a noise in his throat and everyone turned toward him.

"Don't you like it?" Skyler glanced at her flyer with a critical look. "You're right. It needs—"

"It's great. Your flyer is great," Hugo said. "I just don't think anyone's going to come. Or at least not enough people to matter."

"What are you talking about?" Skyler's voice pegged up two notches. "You don't think anyone will come to our Grand Opening?"

"I think with all of Norbert's construction and permit delays, opening *after* Christmas sealed our fate."

"You're such a pessimist, Hugo." Evelyn *tsked* him. "We're not just about Christmas shopping here. Besides, we're going to take advantage of the long Martin Luther King holiday. People will come and maybe stay the whole weekend. They wouldn't do that at Christmastime."

Dena didn't necessarily share Evelyn's optimism. They were all furious with Norbert, not just for his delays, but for a million additional problems he had created, making life —and the Grand Opening—difficult for all of them. She still couldn't believe he'd made a math error on her lease showing her shop was double the actual size, effectively doubling her rent and tax burden, and after numerous requests still hadn't sent over the corrected paperwork.

He had also refused to sign for Evelyn and Max's big photo screen backdrops when they were delivered because he didn't want the liability. They were forced to rent a truck and drive to Denver to pick them up themselves.

And Norbert wouldn't allow Hugo's very expensive sign even though it was completely up to town code. He simply said it didn't fit into his vision for the Marketplace, which he never articulated to any of them.

There were continuing problems with the electricity in the Marketplace, mostly affecting Kober, causing her oven to work unreliably, which might prove disastrous for the prospects of a new bakery. During some of Kober's more colorful and loud tirades, however, Dena had entertained the very real possibility that she simply bought the wrong kind of oven and had jumped on the bandwagon to blame Norbert for that, too. Dena had come to realize over the last few weeks that Kober wasn't always entirely truthful and tended to melodramatically exaggerate everything.

Dena had also overheard Skyler leave a zillion increasingly frantic phone messages for Norbert to return her calls, which he'd obviously been ignoring.

It wasn't just Dena who seemed to be freaking out a bit as the Grand Opening drew near.

Hugo's pessimism wasn't entirely misplaced, but it was too late to do anything differently. They were all much too deep in the Marketplace to back out now. Even though she leaned uncomfortably close to Hugo's pessimistic opinion, Dena activated her optimistic face. "Skyler, Hugo is just worried, but it's all going to work out. Trust me, we're all suffering from a temporary case of the jitters. Everything will be perfectly fine on the day of the Grand Opening. We'll all forget what we were even worried about. We just need to get through the next eleven days." Dena felt her cheeks begin to quiver at the tight way her face was set. If her grandmother's curse came true and she froze this way, she knew she'd have to wear a paper bag over her face to keep from scaring young children. She drew her hand down over her mouth, ending with a pull and a pinch of her bottom lip. "You go get those flyers finished up and I'll help you put them around town. But first I have to make a banner for my new FacePlant business page."

Social media was the bane of Dena's existence and the last thing she wanted was to feel like she had to constantly shill online for her bookstore. When she had whined to her daughter, Charlee, the next thing she knew, she and her tech-savvy boyfriend Ozzi had convinced Dena over a video chat that a social media presence was an absolute necessity for Thrice Sold Tales. They showed her how to set up her FacePlant page and then began talking about the best ways to scale her site. That's when Dena became overwhelmed and lied to them, saying she totally understood what they were telling her even though they were using phrases that included words like *integration*, *synergy*, *sliding into DMs*, and *getting ratioed*. They even admonished her not to *weird flex*. She assured them she wouldn't, but since she had no idea what it meant, she became worried she might have already flexed weirdly.

Skyler continued to tap the keys of her laptop, adding artistic bits here and there to the flyer, and changing the font to find the most impactful, easiest to read style. Dena envied her effortless design skills as she stared at her own mishmashed banner she'd created for her FacePlant page.

Max and Evelyn began playing ping pong, the gentle, rhythmic *plonks* soothing and hypnotic after the kids' raucous thumps and worrisome crashes. Hugo leaned against the wall watching them, but Dena noticed him sneaking glances at Skyler. She hoped he felt guilty about worrying her.

After an eternity of working on the internet banner, Dena sighed loudly and melodramatically, lobbing a well-deserved expletive at her screen.

"What's that, dear?" Evelyn paused the game.

"Computers are evil," Dena said a bit too loudly.

"Pish." Evelyn served to Max. "Game point." She kept her eye on the bouncing ball as it pinged and ponged back and forth, but addressed Dena. "Computers are just ones and zeroes, they don't know from good or evil."

"The opposite from people," Max said, concentrating on the bouncing ball. "People are constantly battling against angels and devils."

"All I know is that I'm constantly battling against technology. Angels and devils I understand." Dena let her mind drift back to Santa Fe and her ordeal with her friend Georgia and that ex-con, glad the dreadful event was far behind her in life's rearview mirror.

"You just need to make the forces of evil work *for* you rather than against you." Evelyn made it sound so easy.

Kober spoke in her thunderous voice, making Dena jump. She hadn't realized Kober was in the vendor room. "Everything has good and evil all twisted up together—"

"Like people," Dena interrupted.

"I was thinking more like sourdough toast."

At everyone's blank look, Kober explained. "Sourdough toast is delicious, but not when it's spread with vegemite. Cake is good, but with sugar-free frosting it's terrible. Brownies are good, but with walnuts they're truly evil … don't get me started." Kober turned toward the door to her bakery and sniffed. "That darn oven!" Except she didn't say *darn*.

Evelyn set down her paddle, trapping the orange ping pong ball under it, ready for the next player. "Better luck next time, my friend," she said with a cackle to Max.

Max waggled his ping pong paddle at Jain. "Care to beat an old man at this ridiculous game?"

She smiled and jumped to her feet, sticking a bookmark in her thick novel. "Go easy on me," she said.

"Not a chance."

Evelyn shuffled over to see what Dena had come up with. "Oh, dear. That's awful."

Hugo hurried over to look at Dena's screen. "You've stretched that photo like it was saltwater taffy."

"Plus, it's a terrible picture of your store. Sit tight." Evelyn hurried through the door to her photography studio. She returned almost instantly with her camera before disappearing through Dena's back door into the bookstore. "Dena! What's your code?"

Dena and Hugo followed her into the bookstore. "My code for what?"

"Your security gate. It's making shadows." Evelyn waved at the front of the store. "Why's it closed anyway?"

Dena told Evelyn and Hugo about the man who came in earlier. "He gave me the creeps so I locked everything up. We need to be more conscientious about leaving those outside doors locked."

"The workmen won't like that," Hugo said gloomily.

"*You* can ream them out when they forget. I still need base-boards installed."

Dena glanced around uneasily as she punched in her code to roll up her security door. She needed baseboards too. And some touch-up paint. And her sign hung. Maybe she'd just take it upon herself to check the doors more often.

Evelyn assessed the bookstore in the better light. "Now if I can just figure out how to work Max's fancy camera." She pointed it around, finally shooing Dena and Hugo back to the vendor room.

A few minutes later she stood between Dena and Hugo with her camera's screen angled so they could both see, slowly sliding through the photos revealing the shots she took from different angles around the bookstore.

Hugo pointed. "That one."

Evelyn nodded. "That's what I thought too." She poked Dena in the shoulder. "Scoot."

"You don't have to tell me twice. Work your magic." Dena stood up and wandered over to watch Jain and Max play, allowing Hugo and Evelyn the space to huddle around her laptop.

Jain's long loose brown hair bounced around her face, at one point covering it completely so it blinded her when she had to dive to return a shot. The point went to Max.

He laughed at her. "Try going bald, maybe you'll have a chance of beating me then."

Jain waggled her head around then pulled a scrunchy from her wrist. In half-a-second she had her hair in a high ponytail. "Do your worst," she challenged.

"Who's winning?" Kober asked Dena, plopping a bunch of jumbled papers on one of the tables.

Dena saw the glee on both Jain's and Max's faces.

"Both of them." She gestured toward Kober's papers. "What's all that?"

"Spreadsheets. Which are the most important, you think? Profit and loss, expense reports, or inventory management?"

"You're asking the wrong person."

"What do you use?"

"Um … pencil and paper and lots of hysterical calls to my accountant?" Dena gestured at Hugo and Evelyn, heads bent over her computer. "I'm not very techy. Maybe you've heard?"

Kober laughed. "You don't say."

Evelyn called Dena over and showed her what she and Hugo had done.

"Oh my gosh! You guys! That banner is beautiful. Thank you both so much."

"Just remember when your frustration boils over… computers aren't good or evil. Save your anger for evil people, not machines," Evelyn said.

Dena went into the bookstore to give them each a set of notecards she'd seen in one of the boxes, as a small token of her thanks. Out the large Marketplace window across the promenade from the front of her shop, she caught movement in the parking lot. A flash of winter sun on Norbert Wallace's car stabbed her in the eye as he swung into a parking space. Good, she thought. I bet he's brought my new lease. He better have, anyway. If he knows what's good for him.

Dena returned to searching the stacks of boxes scattered around the bookstore. It took her some time to find the right large box filled with small boxes each holding a dozen notecards and matching envelopes she planned to give to Hugo and Evelyn. When she returned to the vendor room, however, everyone was gone, presumably back to their own work.

She slipped into the back door of Hugo's chocolate shop, almost swooning at the aromas swirling around her. Chocolate, vanilla, cinnamon, and something she couldn't identify, maybe lavender? She thanked him again, pressing the box of stationery into his hands, then hurried across the vendor area to do the same for Evelyn. She didn't want to miss Norbert when he came to give her the new lease. She'd sign it right on the spot and be done with it.

When she came through Evelyn's rear door, Dena saw Norbert heading up the stairs at the other end of the vendor room. He struggled with a heavy toolbox so dented and paint-chipped it reminded Dena of one her grandfather had used when she was a young girl. She called to him, "Norbert! Did you bring my new lease?"

He didn't respond.

She called out louder and hurried up the stairs behind him. "You can run, but you cannot hide!" Dena was trying to be playful and charming, but realized she sounded shrill and threatening instead. She shifted tactics and tried for a more businesslike tone. "You *must* get this lease situation resolved, Norbert. The Grand Opening is coming up fast and I need to have all my little ducks in a row. And one of those little ducks is my lease. You know, the one you screwed up."

She had learned the only thing Norbert responded to involved a commanding tone and attitude, bordering on hectoring, since that was how he acted most of the time. A little taste of his own medicine.

Norbert had given her grief when she and Charlee had first visited Sugar Springs, practically demanding that she come back to talk about leasing space for her bookstore with a male chaperone. Until she put him in his place, that is, much to the delight of Charlee and Norbert's assistant, Audra. The two of them were both young enough that Dena wanted to show them how to deal with a misogynistic bully, something she'd had some experience with over her fifty-nine years of womanhood.

Today, however, was different. He was ignoring her and she was too busy to be articulate. She stomped up the last few stairs and into the second-floor vendor area, telling Norbert exactly what she wanted, lobbing a few *you betters* and *or elses* so he knew she meant business, even though she cringed and felt like a bully. He didn't seem to care, though, and continued setting up his ladder and organizing his tools for the job at hand.

He must have wearied of her threats, or maybe he finally noticed she was there, because he said, "I'm busy troubleshooting Kober's electricity problems. Now take your pretty little butt back downstairs so you don't make me electrocute myself."

Dena took a deep breath before letting loose with the furious tirade she felt bubbling up inside her.

Before she could begin, though, he waved her away like he would a buzzing mosquito. "Don't get your undies in a bunch, missy. I'll stop by before I leave and you can tell me exactly what the problem with your lease is."

"I've told you a million times—"

"Scoot out of here. I've got man's work to do."

Dena didn't know if he was serious or simply baiting her, but she was too angry to stay and find out. She left a trail of loud invectives in her wake as she made her way back down the stairs.

Some day that man's shocking amount of luck will run out, she thought angrily.

Skyler

SKYLER SAW Norbert go upstairs too. As soon as she finished ordering her first batch of organic crackers, cheese straws, and nori chips from the online supplier who appealed to her—and her wallet—the best, she hurried up the stairs until she stood shoulder-to-shoulder with Dena who had stopped about halfway down.

Skyler's blue eyes widened when she felt the fury emanating off Dena. She was a welder's torch in a blast furnace on a one-hundred-degree day.

"If you're going to see Norbert, don't bother," Dena said through tight lips. "He's … indisposed."

Skyler stood in the center of the stairway, nervously looking back and forth between the door Dena had just slammed, and Dena herself. Dena wasn't moving, reminding Skyler of one of the dairy herd her parents raised. If the cows didn't want to budge, nothing you could do would make them. She flushed, embarrassed she had compared Dena to a stubborn bovine. At least she hadn't said it out loud. "It's probably just as well," Skyler said. "He gives me the creeps anyway. Always calling me *girlie* and *blondie*, like he's talking to a child, or worse, some bimbo. I'll talk to him when we're not alone."

"What do you need to talk to him about?" Dena asked.

"Everything. Nothing. I'm rethinking my paint colors. I'm wondering about my decision to only use local cheese. I'm worried about my logo. I'm—"

"What can Norbert do about any of that?"

"I guess I just need validation."

"If he calls you *girlie* and *blondie*, I don't think you want to know what he thinks."

Dena made a show of forcing herself to calm down. Skyler assumed it was because she seemed so needy and Dena felt sorry for her. If only she could get Norbert to do the same.

"If you want my opinion, I think your space looks great —you're very artistic—and only using locally sourced cheese sounds like a real niche. A clever business move." Dena made a move to her left in an effort to make room for them both to go down the rest of the stairs.

They moved awkwardly, trying to descend side-by-side when the staircase wasn't quite wide enough. Dena held tight to Skyler's arm all the way to the bottom.

At the bottom Skyler stopped and turned toward the top of the staircase, her face defiant. "No. I'm a business-woman now. Sometimes I must do unpleasant things. Like make sure my landlord knows what happens when people ignore me."

Dena stared at her for a bit and Skyler almost lost her nerve. But Dena let go of her arm and shrugged, saying, "It's your funeral," before going back to the bookstore.

<h1 style="text-align:center">Dena</h1>

DENA FINISHED SETTING up her social media for the bookstore, hoping she wasn't getting ratioed or flexing weirdly in cyberspace. Or wait, did Charlee and Ozzi say those were good things or bad? Dena couldn't remember. As she tried to stretch the kink from her neck, she realized Norbert hadn't come to talk to her yet. She walked from the front of her shop across the promenade and looked out the big window. His car was gone.

She saw Kober's kids walking across the far side of the parking lot, probably going home for lunch. A pang of anxiety stabbed her, but she shook it off. They'd be fine, the four of them together like that.

Dena had become much jumpier since what happened in Santa Fe, even though as a woman and a cop's wife, she'd prided herself on how situationally aware she was. Much more so than her friends. Some things, however, were simply less obvious and couldn't be predicted, she thought sadly as the events flashed through her memory.

The kids turned the corner and disappeared from view.

Once again, she told herself they'd be fine. This was Sugar Springs, after all, not Santa Fe, not Denver.

The public didn't have access to the Marketplace yet so Dena didn't worry about locking up when she grabbed her coat and purse and angrily marched off toward the exit. She paused briefly when she thought about the man with the box earlier. She wondered if she should lower her security gate again, now that Evelyn had taken those pictures. But she was in a hurry and that gate lowered so slowly. Besides, even if someone did get in, she reasoned, there's nothing terribly valuable. She remembered her laptop locked in her desk drawer, then made a quick lap around the promenade checking the locks on all the outside doors before making her way to Norbert's office to give him a piece of her mind.

She hoped the frigid January air would cool her down before she got there. Odious as he was, he was also her landlord, and she shouldn't push him too far.

Dena opened the door to Wallace Development at the same time she saw the *Back in 5 minutes* sign and was surprised the door was unlocked and opened easily.

This really was Sugar Springs and not Santa Fe or Denver, she thought. She smiled to herself, thinking of her locked up laptop, and stepped inside. She wrinkled her nose against the reek of cigarette smoke that permeated the walls and carpet, which she and Charlee had both noticed that very first time they'd visited. Woe to any future tenants of this office.

"Hello? Anyone here?" It was obvious that neither Audra nor Royce, Norbert's other employee, were working in their usual places since their two desks were right there when you stepped inside. Dena passed the desks and poked her head into an open doorway. She found nobody in the break room, but the coffee pot was still on. Dena pushed the button to turn off the warming plate, since the pot was empty. "Hello?" she called again. "Norbert?"

A few steps down the hall offered another open door, Norbert's office. Dena stuck her head in, even though the light was off. Nobody there either. Dena leaned against the doorjamb, staring into the dimness. This office was dark, with its wood paneling, mahogany furniture, and chocolate color carpet. Early afternoon light on the opposite side of a building in January didn't help to brighten anything up. She was struck again by the understated elegance of Norbert's office. Norbert had plenty of faults, but bad taste wasn't one of them.

She stared at the framed poster-sized photograph of a nondescript city skyline with the Albert Camus quote written underneath in stylized lettering, as she did every time she saw it. "To be happy, we must not be too concerned with others."

She still hadn't puzzled out what message Norbert was trying to send with this artwork. Was it his daily reminder that people were unimportant and he should mess up their leases? Or did it mean he should be true to himself … and mess up their leases.

She debated whether to wait for someone or to leave. If she stayed, theoretically it would only be for five minutes, according to the sign on the door, and the clock was already ticking. Whoever showed up first—Norbert, Audra, or Royce—would be able to deal with her lease situation, she assumed. She wouldn't leave until she had the corrected copy in her hand. But if she left now, who knew how long this would go on?

She checked the time and decided to stay, continuing to lean against the doorframe. It was so calm and peaceful back here, despite the cigarette stink. Her eyes grazed across Norbert's normally neat desk, papers and file folders scattered all over it. "No wonder he hasn't dealt with my lease yet. It's probably buried under there," she muttered with irritation.

She straightened up. Yes, it probably *was* buried under there.

She took a couple of tentative steps forward, craning her neck to see if any of that mess looked like a lease. Specifically, her lease.

Dena glanced back at the doorway, then edged forward a couple more steps until she stood at the corner of Norbert's desk. Craning her neck again, she saw paperwork that appeared to be a lease. Or at least it was several pages stapled at the top like her copy of the lease. She reached out one hand to slide a folder marked *Contractors* off the top of the pile.

As she bent closer to read the stapled papers, a voice said, "What are you doing in here?"

Kober

KOBER LISTENED to her children playing ping pong in the vendor room while she remained on hold—again—with the oven manufacturer. Barely listening to the hold music—occasionally interrupted with the ridiculous message that her call was important to them—she hoped her kids weren't bugging anyone, but who was she kidding? Of course they were bugging the other tenants; they were kids and that was their job.

The other tenants had been doing their jobs as well. Dena was fighting yet another unwinnable battle with her computer. Skyler was obsessing about something inconsequential. Hugo was doing his Eeyore impression. She didn't hear the boys and glanced into the vendor room, phone still plastered to her ear.

Max and Jain were playing ping pong. At least Kober was confident Evelyn and Max tolerated her kids and maybe even got a kick out of them. Whenever they talked to her children, Kober remembered they had at least one adult son of their own. You could always tell when adults had never been around kids regularly because their conversation always sounded stilted, like they were chatting with some foreign ambassador from a distant galaxy. Evelyn and Max never spoke at length about their son, but when he was mentioned, Kober sensed it was a sticky subject because they were either wistful or prickly about him and quickly changed the subject.

The boys must be off practicing their newly-discovered love of parkour, or as she referred to it, Emergency Room 101. Luckily, the twins were pretty good at it and as long as she didn't have to watch them hurl their bodies off, over, and around things, they were all happy. Wyatt was especially happy witnessing his younger brothers' wipe-outs, but had the good sense not to tell Kober about them anymore, since the last time he regaled her with the particulars, she hollered at him instead of the twins. Life was so unfair, Wyatt had complained, but Kober had a hair-trigger shoot-the-messenger attitude she barely controlled. It was one of her many charms, she thought ruefully.

She knew it wasn't Wyatt's job to keep his brothers from doing dumb stuff—if that was even in the realm of possibility—but it did seem that someone should have gotten yelled at. Poor Wyatt had the misfortune to end up nearest in proximity to her that day and ended up strafed with verbal shrapnel. She knew her twin daredevils weren't afraid of anything, not even her wrath. Not that Wyatt was afraid of her either, but it was a mother's duty, right? Somebody had to get yelled at. Plus, that whole life being unfair thing.

Today she'd decided to trust the universe with this one; she had bigger things to worry about than her ten-year-olds' love of extreme sports.

She tapped her foot to the hypnotic tones of Metallica rendered harmless by a string quartet. She had almost forgotten how angry she was until some overly unctuous customer service representative finally answered the phone.

"This is Finlayson. May I have your name and account number?"

His voice slithered out like an oil spill and it was all Kober could do not to wipe it out of her ear. Who named their kid Finlayson for heaven's sake? His parents must have had grandiose plans for him. Maybe a barrister in Ye Merry Olde Regency England. Or maybe as the head butler at Downton Abbey. Perhaps as an AKC registered poodle. Probably not as a customer service representative for an appliance manufacturer.

"I've given my name and account number to three different people in the last fifteen minutes. Why do you ask for it if you don't do anything with it?"

"Ma'aaam, I understaaand the nature of your frustraaation, but it would be my honor to solllve the problem you are contaaacting us about todaaay."

This time Kober couldn't help herself. She switched the phone to her other side and wiped Finlayson's voice from her ear. "Finlayson … sir … if you truuuly understoood the nature of my frustraaation, you wouldn't ask me for the thousandth time for my name and account number!" Kober shouted the last few words at him, but Finlayson remained silent long enough that Kober knew she would indeed be reciting her name and account number yet again.

After she did so, Kober heard Finlayson tap some keys. "Aaah, theeere it is. And what might I dooo for you today, Mrs Bertoletti?"

"Wait. Seriously? There's nothing in my file about this problem?" Kober hoped her voice was like a knife that had the ability to stab Finlayson directly in his ear.

"A problem you saaay? I'm not seeeing anyth—"

Kober hadn't been holding things together very well for several weeks, not since her husband Nic convinced her to get this stupid top-of-the-line commercial oven. Deep down, she knew it was too much oven and much too expensive, especially when she was just starting out—and she'd told him this—but he'd talked her into it, telling her it was an excellent investment. And it probably would be, if she could get it to work reliably. Sometimes it would heat properly, sometimes it wouldn't. There was no rhyme or reason to its fluctuating temperament, but she knew there was no way she could run a bakery with it as her cornerstone. She hadn't even been able to determine if it was the oven's fault, or if it had something to do with the wiring in the Marketplace. She knew it was one or the other, though, and maybe even both, and she was going to get it fixed, even if it killed her. Or someone else.

She knew none of this was Finlayson's fault. But he was unlucky enough to be the one she was talking to. Just like Wyatt, he was bound to get hit by some erratic shrapnel.

Kober explained the problem for the umpteenth time, but Finlayson offered no solutions, even when she gave him an easy one. "Send me a new oven that works!" Instead, he murmured that he understood the nature of her frustration, then connected her with his supervisor.

While she waited on hold yet again, Kober pulled a loose thread at the hem of her favorite paisley tunic, almost as loud as she was. As she worried that the loose thread signaled the demise of this shockingly comfy top, she noticed the color combination she'd thrown on this morning. Paisley over neon zigzag leggings. No wonder everyone shaded their eyes when she walked in the vendor room. She slapped her forehead. That must have been what Jain meant when she said something about the International Space Station when they were leaving the house this morning. Kober thought she meant it as a compliment, like she was out of this world, when in reality she probably meant that Kober's outfit could be seen from space. Pfft. She couldn't be bothered with what other people thought about her personal style. "If you're comfy and you know it, clap your hands," Kober sang to herself.

"This is Helen." A molasses-voiced woman finally came on the line, her words even slower and stickier than Finlayson's. Kober wondered about their hiring practices. This company definitely had a type. "May I have your name and account number?"

"Son of a marshmallow!" Kober held the phone at arm's length, yelled again, then unloaded the nature of her frustration at Helen who had the exceptional common sense to remain silent. She ranted at Helen, detailing the problem at least three times, each one louder and more colorful than the last, ending with a nonspecific threat that she hoped came through loud and clear. "It's *obviously* a known *safety* issue and I won't be *responsible* for the full-blown *explosion* that's *bound* to happen the next time I try to bake my freaking *lemon poppyseed cupcakes*!" But she didn't say freaking.

As Kober caught her breath, Helen's voice dripped in her ear. "I understand the nature of your frustration, ma'am. I'll submit a ticket to the maintenance department. And for future reference, you can do that yourself directly from the website. Please hold to complete a short survey about our customer service today."

If her husband Nic hadn't pushed her off this metaphorical cliff, Finlayson and Helen probably would.

Kober had been trying to keep her worries from seeping into her relationship with her children, but they'd figure it out as soon as they saw she wasn't ready for the Grand Opening. She had less than two weeks—eleven days, according to the white board—to get a new working oven delivered and installed, and to learn its idiosyncrasies so she could make every type of delicious goodie, from sturdy brownies and oatmeal cookies to delicate cream puffs and souffles.

If she didn't get a working oven, she could barely afford to replace it with a toaster oven from the thrift store.

Since she had no desire or ladylike vocabulary left to take Helen's customer service survey, she dialed Royce over at Norbert's office. "Hey, it's Kober. I need some advice. What's the best way to approach Norbert about renegotiating my lease? I think I just want half the space, not this whole thing."

"I can't help you."

"Can't or won't?"

"Just suck it up and pay your rent. That's what you promised and that's what you need to do."

"What if I can't?"

"That's between you and Norbert." Royce chuckled. "In the words of Shakespeare, *cry havoc and let slip the dogs of war.*"

"And in the words of Ricky Ricardo, you've got some 'splainin' to do. Are you really just going to spout Shakespeare instead of helping me get out of this lease?"

"My hands are tied, Kober."

"They are not," she snapped. "You're just sitting on them."

"Be that as it may, I am not going to risk getting on Norbert's bad side just because you bit off more than you can chew. Not my problem."

"I'm making it your problem. And Norbert's. I will get out of this lease if it's the last thing I do. You will rue the day you got in my way." In her fury, Kober constricted all the muscles in her face.

Royce was quiet for a moment. "You are the angriest, most melodramatic woman I've ever met. But if you're done twirling your mustache, I have work to do. And the next time you feel like ranting and raving like a lunatic, you should make an appointment to come over here so I can record it for my SplishSplash page. I need something to go viral."

Kober could see Royce's smirk through the phone. "Fine. Then set up an appointment for me. Make sure to clear your schedule and remove any sharp objects from your desk."

Royce laughed but Kober knew he wouldn't have if he could have seen her face. "Funny, but that does not make me want to add you to my appointment book."

"I'll bring lunch."

Royce mulled that over. "Including one of your chocolate lava cakes?"

Kober mulled *that* over. She already had some mini-cakes in the freezer. "Fine."

She heard him shuffling papers. "I'm swamped until Friday. Make it early so I can eat before I hit the road. Driving to Gunnison for the weekend. Say eleven-thirty?"

"Are you kidding me? Not until Friday?"

"Take it or leave it."

"Fine."

"Fine."

Royce disconnected and Kober took two aerobic laps around the promenade before her temper moderated and her vision cleared. "Does everyone get that angry on the phone or is that simply my albatross," she grumbled. When she rounded the corner near the chocolate shop, her phone rang.

She checked the caller ID and scowled. "Finally," she said crossly. "You got my message?" She listened for a few moments, her face tightening once again, lips turning white, before bellowing, "This is all your fault! Has this been your plan all along, to ruin everything completely? Well, you are *not* going to take me down with you. I will get out from under this lease if it's the last thing I do…. I don't care about the contract…. Don't you *dare* threaten me! … Fine. I'll give you the chance to fix it, but you better fix it before I fix you!

Evelyn

"MAX, THESE JUST AREN'T … GOOD." Evelyn had been looking at the photos Max had taken of her during their practice shoot with the new studio camera and lighting. She shuffled through the lot of them again, from the beginning, still wearing one of the schoolmarm dresses. The Velcro had come loose and the garment drooped forlornly off one of her shoulders.

She'd been eager to try on some of the costumes to see how they'd look on film. She was pleasantly surprised that so many of the outfits truly were one-size-fits-all, as advertised. She was tiny and Max teased her that if she kept shrinking, she'd fit in his pocket. But she'd also cajoled Kober, who was taller and plumper, to try on some of the dresses that came in the other day. She silently blessed the person who invented Velcro.

Ideally, no customer would have to disrobe in the studio, although she had created a small, curtained area in the corner, just in case. The dresses were roomy enough to go over most attire, although maybe not a bulky turtleneck sweater. And if men came in wearing a summertime tourist's favorite outfit of cargo shorts instead of jeans, the leather chaps and boots would cover bare, hairy legs. The pirate costumes had billowy black pants with wide Velcro waistbands, fully adjustable from children to large adults. If they were too long, they could simply be tucked into the tall "boots"—which were really just realistic looking spats that pulled up over their shoes.

She'd been worried about the length of some of the dresses too, but they draped gracefully, and she'd already decided the floor wouldn't be in any of the photos. If three yards of fabric pooled around some short woman's ankles —like it did around hers at the moment—nobody would be the wiser.

She chose the Old West tableau for today's practice photo shoot, thinking it would turn out to be popular with the tourists visiting Colorado. Evelyn and Max had acquired tons of props including generic-looking crates, fake bales of hay made from sturdy plastic, rough-hewn wooden benches, a couple of recreations of one room schoolhouse desks complete with inkwells, and a velvet settee, appropriate for both the Genteel Schoolmarm outfit as well as the Saloon Gal. Dusters, chaps, cowboy hats, boots, and long guns for the men and boys; modest or sassy outfits for the women and girls, depending on which direction they wanted to go.

"They look okay to me." Max accepted one of the photos she held out to him.

She pointed at different areas of the photo. "You can see the floor here. The set isn't centered. I'm not even in focus."

"Sounds like a personal problem."

"Max, I'm serious. Do it again. We can't charge people for photos like this."

They worked on different scenarios, giving Evelyn a

chance to try on almost all the other costumes and create just the right look with the props so they wouldn't have to rethink it every time.

She had doubts about the skimpiness of the caveman outfits, but the togas, the Renaissance outfits, the Roaring Twenties flapper dresses and tuxedos, and the poodle skirts and leather jackets were all ready to go.

She took notes and made sketches and diagrams about all of it while Max dealt with the photography aspect.

When they'd gone through several scenes, they sat down to flip through the new batch of digital photos together.

"You're awfully quiet." Max tapped his foot.

"Oh, Max. I really thought you'd be good at this! What are we going to do?" Evelyn placed one hand low on her belly to try to quell the quiver she felt beginning to roil.

Balaam wandered in and took one look at Evelyn before jumping to her lap and hissing at Max.

"Hello to you too, Devil." Max made a face at Balaam.

"Don't call him that," Evelyn said for the millionth time.

"You named him after the devil of avarice and greed. Not me."

"Well, I didn't know that at the time, did I?" Evelyn stroked Balaam's silky soft fur, trying to calm herself while staring at the Greek Forum tableau in front of them. She fought to control the anxiety threatening to bubble to her surface. She reached for the bottle of chewable antacids.

Balaam and Max took the opportunity for a stare-down. Balaam's copper-colored eyes versus Max's watery blue.

Max lost, blinking hard three times before rubbing his eyes. "Pretty sure he just saw my ancestors."

"I don't know why you go toe-to-toe with him. You

always lose," Evelyn said absent-mindedly, chewing the antacid. "But we have more important fish to fry."

Balaam broke eye contact with Max and looked up expectantly at Evelyn.

She lifted him off her lap and stood. "Metaphorical fish. Sorry."

Balaam flicked his tail at her, posturing that he already knew there would be no fish in his immediate future, and strutted away.

Evelyn repeated, "We can't charge people for photos like this."

"I can fix them. Watch." Max loaded the last few photos he took onto their computer. Evelyn peered over his shoulder as he worked in the Photoshop program he'd recently downloaded. He used the online cutting tool to trace around Evelyn's face in one of the photos. His hands shook and he was left with a jagged perimeter. He typed "famous photos" in his web browser and dragged Evelyn's face into the first photo that popped up. After several more clicks of his mouse, Evelyn's jagged face appeared next to Jesus in Leonardo da Vinci's Last Supper painting.

"Max, you can't do that. We'll get arrested and then we'll go straight to hell." Evelyn raised her voice and heard the hysteria in it. Their entire business plan was on the line and Max was absolutely and perhaps willfully oblivious to their plight. She stomped across the room, clawing at the schoolmarm dress until she was free of it. Yanking a hanger off the rack, she roughly hung the dress, pinching the Velcro at the neck so it wouldn't slide off.

Max cocked his head, assessing his work. "Nobody will ever find out. We can make it look completely natural," he called to her.

"The aftermath will look like something out of a horror movie. Everyone will know. We'll be drummed out of town." She shouted across the studio to him. "*Then* we'll be arrested and sent straight to hell to burn for eternity."

Evelyn grew increasing worried about her husband's mental health as she watched him place her head on Taylor Swift's body, as a passenger in Jeff Gordon's race car, and as Scarlett O'Hara, face upturned millimeters from Rhett Butler's on the *Gone With the Wind* movie poster.

When he made moves to replace Rhett's face with hers too, so it looked like she was going in for a passionate kiss with herself, her voice hitched up a notch. "You can't do this, Max," she said firmly. "Even if you were any good at Photoshop—which you are decidedly not—we couldn't deceive people this way."

"You're missing the big picture, Ev," Max said excitedly. "This way we don't even need a studio. We can do all this online. People just upload a photo of themselves, and I can put them in any photo they want. We can triple the size of our offerings! Quintuple, even! All we need—"

Evelyn squeezed his shoulder until he quit talking and flinched. "Ow."

"We are not going to have some online business creating deep fakes."

"What's a deep fake?"

Evelyn pointed at the computer screen. "This. Manipulating reality. Making something completely bogus look real. It's the kind of stuff conspiracy theorists do to stupid people."

"It does look real, doesn't it?" Max said proudly, bobbing his head up and down.

"It does not." Evelyn stood in front of Max and crossed her arms. "Go put on that toga."

"I will do nothing of the kind."

"Well, go put on something interesting and pose yourself. I'm going to take your picture. We've *got* to figure this out."

Max shoved his arms into a tuxedo shirt which Evelyn helped Velcro closed in the back. He then donned a leather jacket, a poodle skirt, and a top hat, before sitting primly on a bale of hay with his ankles crossed.

Evelyn placed a rifle across his lap, adjusted the lighting, adjusted his pose, adjusted the backdrop—she chose the one with the cave paintings—and started shooting. She moved around the space, telling Max to look here or tilt his head there, camera clacking all the while.

When she was satisfied she had plenty of shots, she sat down and flipped through the photos.

Max disrobed and hung up his costume, such as it was. "Well? You're not saying anything." He came up behind her and looked at the photos over her shoulder.

Evelyn silently flipped through all of them again before looking up at him with wide eyes. "They're good, aren't they?"

Max took the camera from her and flipped through them all again before looking up at her. "Leave me out of it."

Evelyn watched in shock as Max stalked out of the studio.

Skyler

SKYLER STARED at her Really Grate Cheese sign. The colors were all wrong, the font too plain, and that tagline? *It's cheddar to give than to receive.* She simply didn't know any more. No, she did know … she hated it.

She wanted to get some input about her cheese samples, but when she poked her head into Evelyn and Max's photography studio, they were in the thick of an argument.

She listened at their back door, long enough to hear Evelyn say, "We'll get arrested and then we'll go straight to hell." Then she heard Max say, "Nobody will ever find out. We can make it look completely natural." Then Evelyn said, "The aftermath will look like something out of a horror movie. Everyone will know. We'll be drummed out of town."

Skyler turned back to the cheese shop and tiptoed away without entering the studio. She couldn't even imagine what they were talking about.

It seemed quieter a bit later, so Skyler returned next

door with her tray of samples. "I hope I'm not interrupting …"

"Not at all, dear," Evelyn said.

Skyler glanced around uneasily.

"What are you looking for?" Evelyn asked.

"Max."

"Oh. He's blowing off steam someplace else. What can I do for you?"

Skyler knew something important had happened because Evelyn still hadn't smiled. She knew Evelyn and Max had been married for an eternity, and she herself hadn't had a relationship that lasted more than eighteen months, so she was uncertain as to whether their arguments were frequent or not. All she knew is that in the short time she'd known them, they never showed any animosity toward one another. Skyler had always felt quite comforted by that, as if it were something she could always rely on. But now she felt wobbly by the vibe Evelyn gave off. She wondered what it might look like for Max to blow off some steam. She hoped it wouldn't be anything dangerous.

"Dear?" Evelyn prodded.

"Oh, sorry. Would you mind sampling some of my cheese? I've lost perspective about everything and don't even know what I like now."

"That is a task I'm very willing to take on." Evelyn finally smiled.

"Thank you so much!" Relieved, Skyler put the tray down and pointed out the selections, a few bites of each. "That's a brie, that's cacio pecora, that's cheddar, that's a green chile jack, that's some queso, and that one is feta."

"Goat cheese?"

Skyler nodded, holding out a tiny fork to Evelyn.

"Pass."

Skyler frowned. "You don't like goat cheese?"

"Hate it."

"Why?"

Evelyn quirked her forehead. "I guess because of the taste. What do you mean, why?"

Skyler dangled the tiny fork. Evelyn caught it before it hit the floor.

"Maybe I shouldn't sell goat cheese."

Evelyn laughed. "Because I don't like it? Even though I've always felt called to the position, I am not technically the arbiter of good taste in the Arkansas River Valley region." Evelyn jabbed her tiny fork into a chunk of cheddar and made excessively dramatic yummy noises as she chewed.

Skyler appreciated her efforts, but nonetheless felt condescended to, perhaps even mocked. She might have lost perspective about that as well.

"Maybe I shouldn't only sell local cheeses," Skyler fretted, feeling her chest tighten.

"Now you're being ridiculous." Evelyn stabbed a hunk of the green chile jack then swiped it through the queso and made even more excessive yummy noises. "Your entire business model was built around advocating for local cheeses. It was an excellent idea then, and it's an excellent idea now." Evelyn jabbed the remaining bites of cheese—except for the feta—and ate them all at once.

Balaam sat at Evelyn's feet and curled his tail around his body. He kept his eyes on Evelyn, but turned his head toward Skyler and hissed.

"Oh, stop that," Evelyn said to him.

"He doesn't like me, does he?"

"He doesn't like anything." Evelyn stared down at the cat. "Well, almost anything." Evelyn pointed past Skyler's head. "Did you see that?"

Skyler turned. "See what?"

"Thought I saw a balloon bouquet being delivered. Wishful thinking, I guess." Evelyn handed the tiny fork back to Skyler. "You know, that feta wasn't half-bad. Maybe it'll grow on me."

A grin formed on Skyler's face.

"That's better, dear. You'll get wrinkles like me if you worry too much."

"What do you worry about?" Skyler asked as she collected her tray.

"You've met Max, right?"

———

Skyler washed the tray and the tiny fork. Her grin had disappeared practically the minute she left Evelyn. She acted like she'd been joking, but *was* she worried about Max? Did it have something to do with their argument earlier?

Skyler jumped when she saw Balaam in the cheese shop staring at her. She couldn't be certain, but he seemed to be licking his whiskers a bit too enthusiastically. And the way he eyed the cheese tray she was washing? He hadn't even hissed at her, she realized. "It would be just like that sweet old Evelyn to tell me something I want to hear, wouldn't it?" Skyler said to Balaam as she swirled her hand in the sudsy water, watching the fluffy bubbles form and pop over her wrist. "But that's ridiculous, isn't it? She'd never lie. Not to me. Not about that. She said she didn't like feta, but then she ate it and liked it, right?" Skyler was unsure now. Skyler glanced down at Balaam, becoming anxious at his scrutiny.

Balaam watched her with his unblinking copper-colored eyes. Skyler accidentally splashed some suds out of the sink causing him to flinch, as if it were holy water and he was a vampire. He plastered his ears against his head and scurried away.

It had never occurred to her there were people in the world who didn't like goat cheese, and the fact that someone who owned the shop right next door to hers might be one of them made Skyler very nervous. "If people don't like feta, what's next? Not liking me? Not liking my shop?" She glanced at her sign with the terrible colors, font, and tagline.

She swirled her hand in the suds a bit longer, but then she had to sit down. She suddenly felt dizzy. The Grand Opening was in eleven days. "I have to get a grip," she murmured. She knew she had a million things to do, and she wanted everyone's opinion on all of it.

If only Norbert would have returned my calls.

Hugo

HUGO WATCHED Evelyn and Skyler from one of the tables in the vendor room. He was at the perfect angle to see Skyler standing with her tray, pointing out sample selections to Evelyn. He couldn't hear their conversation so tried to construct it in his mind. Deep down, he knew it was probably about cheese and the merits of locally-sourced selections, since that was quite often what Skyler wanted to chat about these days, but Hugo wondered if there was the slightest chance Skyler was talking to Evelyn about him.

There was absolutely no reason for her to do so, but as pessimistic as Hugo was, he garnered the tiniest bit of hope where Skyler was concerned.

He rearranged his chair when Skyler returned to her own shop, straining to see her as she stood at the sink. As she swayed from side to side washing dishes, he caught various glimpses of her different poses and daydreamed what it might be like to dance with her.

At their apartment building, he always tried to guess when she'd be doing her laundry so he could be in the laundry room at the same time. She did that same swaying motion when she folded her clothes.

She always seemed glad for the company, so he made a joke once about their "Friday night laundry date." She'd laughed and it suddenly became their thing. Hugo felt chivalrous, like he was protecting her, but from what, he couldn't say. This was the Sugar Springs Village Apartments, after all.

One Friday, though, as he was carrying his dirty clothes to the laundry room, he saw Skyler get into a car with Royce what's-his-name from Norbert Wallace's office.

Hugo hadn't planned on eating out that night instead of doing his laundry, but he found himself in the same restaurant as the two of them. Not wanting to interrupt them, he took a table in the corner by the big fake ficus plant. He didn't know where they went after they ate. He ate as slowly as he could, but they ate slower, laughing and talking and even ordering another bottle of wine. His server was giving him the stink-eye for dawdling, so he paid his bill and left.

Hugo had walked slowly back to the apartment building, taking in the late autumn air on the porch, even though it was much too chilly. He sat outside as long as he could stand it, but never heard Skyler come home.

The next time Skyler went out with Royce, Hugo hadn't even realized she had been with him. Not until she slammed her car door and had stomped up the wooden stairs of their building. Hugo had opened his apartment door and intercepted her.

"What's wrong?" he'd asked a tearful Skyler.

Skyler tried to sidestep him, but Hugo filled the hallway. On purpose. He needed to know what happened.

"Nothing," she said. "Just that Royce Reynolds is not the nice guy he pretends to be."

Hugo wasn't surprised since he'd never thought Royce was all that nice to begin with. But clearly Skyler had and now he'd made her cry.

"What did he do?" Hugo clenched his fists and through gritted teeth asked in a low voice, "Did he hurt you?"

Skyler pressed one hand to Hugo's chest and propelled him out of her way. "I don't want to talk about it. Goodnight, Hugo."

From then on Hugo kept a wary eye on Skyler's comings and goings, with an extra lookout for any sign of Royce around the Sugar Springs Village Apartments. He'd asked her several times about Royce, not directly, of course, but offering many openings for discussion. She never took him up on any of the opportunities.

It was the next time he saw Skyler and Royce together that really bothered him, however. They were on the sidewalk outside Corky's sandwich shop as he was leaving the grocery store. Why was she with Royce after what she had said, after he had made her cry? Her body language was all wrong. She was leaning away from Royce, even though he was leaning in close to her. It was obvious that she was uncomfortable. Then, with a magician's flourish, Royce had produced a flowy chiffon scarf from a gift bag he held. He wrapped it around Skyler's neck and she had pulled to loosen it. They spoke a bit more, then Royce pulled Skyler in for a hug which looked unwelcome to Hugo. Royce crossed the street to go back to work at Norbert's office and Skyler headed the opposite direction, making a bee line right toward Hugo.

She hadn't seen him standing in the shadow of the building so he waited until she was almost there. He pretended to have just emerged from the store, shifting his bag of groceries. "Well, hello there, Skyler." He mentally kicked himself for sounding so unnatural. Surely she'd know he'd been watching her.

"Oh, hi, Hugo."

He fell in step with her.

"Going back to the Marketplace?" he asked. "I got some supplies to experiment with chocolate and peanut butter pretzels."

"That sounds yummy."

"You can be my taste tester."

"I'm actually headed home, I think."

They had almost reached the intersection where they'd go their separate ways. Hugo wanted to delay that as long as possible. "Nice scarf," he said.

Skyler reached up to finger the delicate fabric in muted greens and golds. "Royce gave it to me just now. He said it reminded him of me." She stopped walking and spread the fabric to show Hugo.

He had stared, trying to figure out why a barnyard scene printed on the fabric reminded Royce of Skyler.

"It's a reproduction of Claude Monet's Farmyard in Normandy," she explained. When Hugo didn't say anything she added, "Because I was raised on a dairy farm?"

"Of course. It just doesn't, um, look like a dairy farm to me." Hugo had kicked himself for not making the connection himself.

Skyler shrugged. "I don't think it is. And I didn't grow up in Normandy either, so there's that." She rearranged the scarf around her neck and turned toward home. "See you later."

Hugo longed to go with her, but he already said he was going to the Marketplace. "Yeah, see you," he said glumly.

Hugo experimented with the chocolate and peanut butter pretzels until he perfected them, all the while preoccupied by that scarf. Why had Royce really given it to her? Was it the case of an abusive partner showering his victim with gifts and apologies for his bad behavior? Was Skyler in a bad situation? Her body language screamed that she was uncomfortable with Royce. At least that was how it seemed to Hugo.

By the time he had packed all the pretzel confections away that day, Hugo was sure someone should have a serious conversation with Royce.

"Whatcha doing?"

Hugo practically jumped out of his shoes at the sound of Max's voice, bringing him back to where he sat in the vendor room staring at Skyler in her cheese shop washing dishes. "Wha—?"

Max laughed, then frowned.

Hugo saw him take in the trajectory of his line of sight.

"Just ask her out, boy. She won't bite. Not too hard anyway."

Hugo jumped up and scurried into his chocolate shop, slamming the door behind him.

Balaam

BALAAM SAT behind the door of Evelyn and Max's photography studio near his empty bowl. He had inadvertently scooted it back there with his robust licking, a victorious attempt at cleanliness as he retrieved every last crumb of kibble. He hoped it would miraculously find its way back to its normal resting place so it could be filled again. Soon.

He never saw anyone place kibble in the bowl, but he suspected Evelyn. Max always said she was a good egg, but that didn't make sense because all eggs were good. Balaam just knew that Evelyn was his favorite human. Everyone else was barely tolerated, unless they made some offering to him, preferably in his bowl which didn't require supplication at their fingertips. That always made him feel so servile. Like they didn't realize *they* should be subservient to *him*.

He never refused their treats, however, no matter how pandering they were. He was only human, right?

Balaam stepped to the threshold facing the common

area in back of the shops, licking his whiskers and resetting his clock until his next snack.

The door squeaked open and someone peered into the vendor room. Balaam stared, tail wrapped around his feet, naturally suspicious of anyone who didn't acknowledge his presence. The tip of his tail twitched in anticipation every so often. People often meant treats, after all. But this one kept walking. Never even noticed the regal feline waiting so patiently.

When it seemed they had completely missed their chance to feed him or bask in his aura, he padded after them, across the room, up the stairs to the second floor. He squirted through the door before they closed it.

Balaam sighed at the raised voices, arguing about something he didn't care about since he hadn't heard his name nor did he smell any delicious odors. The odds that they were arguing about who would feed him snacks seemed very low, dropping further with every angry word.

He headed back to the door, only to find it closed. Oh, people. You could never trust them to do the right thing. Like leave doors open. Didn't they realize he was not only lacking thumbs, but also height? How did they expect him to get back downstairs?

He sighed again, this time with a melodramatic flop to the floor. Couldn't they see how inconvenient this was for him?

A loud crash jolted him awake and he shot behind some boxes faster than you could say Mister Mistoffelees.

Dena

DENA DARTED AWAY from Norbert's desk at the sight of Audra staring at her.

"Lucky for you Royce didn't catch you. Dealing with intruders is above my pay grade, but not his. He takes things very seriously around here."

"Don't you?" Dena followed Audra down the hall, away from Norbert's office.

"Yes, but not He-Man seriously."

Dena explained her frustration with Norbert's inaction about her lease. "I know I shouldn't have been in there, but I was hoping he had dealt with it already and it was on his desk waiting to be given to me."

"No worries. Leave it to me. I'll take care of it." She smiled at Dena. "We gals gotta stick together." She began to put her things on her desk. "I guess it's not an excuse, but Norbert is so scattered these last couple of months, trying to get everything at the Marketplace ready in time. I guess I'm a bit scattered too, leaving the door unlocked."

Dena noticed the bag from Corky's Corner. "You know

I've only been in town a few weeks, but it's embarrassing how often I eat at Corky's."

"You know then. It's a huge sandwich. Want half? I'll share. You can fill me in on the deets about your lease. First things first, though." Audra held out the back of her hand to Dena where some tiny blisters had risen. "Will you put some antibiotic cream and a bandage on this? I was trying to be helpful when Corky was grilling my sandwich and got in his way."

"Of course. Does it hurt?"

"Nah, not really. Startled me. Stung a bit at first. I didn't want to say anything to Corky, though. He'd feel terrible if he knew."

Dena was happy to play nursemaid but less than thrilled about eating in the midst of all the cigarette smell. But she was starving, and, well, Corky's sandwiches were worth it. Plus, Dena was trying to get to know more people in town and Audra had offered to help with the lease. She could overlook a bit of stale smoke.

Audra was one of the first people Dena had met in Sugar Springs, that day she and Charlee visited over Thanksgiving weekend. She'd seemed impressed that Dena was able to put Norbert in his place. Maybe she invited her to share her sandwich so Dena could give her some pointers or something. After all, Dena was older than Audra and had met her fair share of jerks like Norbert. But still … that cigarette smoke.

As if she read her mind, Audra said, "I'm sorry about how this place must smell. I'm so used to it I forget. At least until I see people wrinkle their noses."

Dena blushed. "I thought you couldn't smoke indoors in Colorado."

"Rules don't apply here in Norbertland. We run amok like we're Lost Boys in Captain Hook's lagoon."

Dena laughed. "But I bet he'd be all over me if I started smoking in my bookstore."

Audra found two plates in the break room and placed half a Reuben sandwich on each plate. "You want the pickle or the chips?"

"Whichever you don't want. Either is fine with me."

As Dena watched Audra organize their lunch, she realized that, as a smoker, Audra was not only unaware of the stench of cigarette smoke that clung everywhere, she didn't even notice all the tiny ash burns on her blouse when she had gotten dressed that morning. They were practically invisible, but as Audra turned this way and that, the light caught the flaws in the polyester fabric.

They sat at the table in the break room and dug into their food. Dena bit into the crunchy dill pickle.

Audra swallowed a big bite of her sandwich, wiped her lips with a paper towel, then said, "Let's get to know each other better with a game of Best/Worst." She pointed a potato chip at Dena. "Worst boyfriend."

"Oh, easy. Guy who stalked me and tried to scam me. You?"

Audra cocked her head. "I will need more information about that at some point."

"Duly noted."

"For me, it was a guy who really had a crush on my older sister and was using me to get closer to her."

"Ugh."

"Indeed. Best boyfriend, then."

"Again, an easy one," Dena said. "Guy I married."

"Aw, sweet."

Dena wondered if Audra noticed she wasn't wearing a wedding ring. If so, she didn't let on. It wasn't a secret her husband had died, but when people found out, Dena didn't like the sorrowful look in their eyes, even twenty years after the fact. That sorrowful look became even more pitying when they heard he was a detective killed in the line of duty. It was easier not to bring it up at all, if she could avoid it.

Audra finished chewing. "For me it was a rich, handsome guy I met through a friend. He showered me with expensive gifts. I sold them on eBay whenever money got tight. Really saved my life a couple of times."

"What happened to him?" Dena asked.

"Nothing too dramatic. We had fun for a while, but ultimately wanted different things out of life. Plus, there was an age difference. It was all very mature and amicable."

Dena nodded, picturing their experience. "Worst boss."

Audra wrinkled her nose. "I seem to attract lots of those. But the guy who sticks out most harassed me on a road crew I worked on. He really went all out to make my life miserable. Gave me a bogus proficiency test in front of all the guys. Made me drive all the heavy machinery. Joke was on him when I did it all perfectly. That shut him up." She stared into space for a moment. "It was probably a blessing in disguise since all the guys gave me the teensiest bit of respect after that." She got a pensive look on her face, then shrugged. "Still must be stuck in my craw, though, since he was the first thing to pop into my brain."

"He-man woman haters tend to do that." Dena thought for a bit. "My worst boss was the regional manager at the insurance company I worked at in Santa Fe. He knew absolutely nothing about insurance and didn't even try to learn."

"Then why—"

"Nepotism hire. I ended up having to do his work and mine. 'Bout near killed me."

"What happened to him?"

"He cheated on his wife. The boss's daughter." Dena laughed. "One day my job sucked, and the next it didn't. I got promoted and finally got paid for doing his job."

Audra lifted her bottle of water in salute.

Dena tossed out the next category. "Best boss."

"Hands down, the state wildlife ranger who encouraged me to become skilled in bird identification so I could lead ranger tours. I loved leading those tours."

"In high school I worked at a fabric store," Dena said. "The assistant manager was an older woman who let me work the cash register on all her shifts, even though the store manager said I was too young. She taught me so much. Not about fabric or the cash register, mind you, but about how to be assertive and demand agency and respect."

"Wow," Audra said. "You were a precocious kid."

Dena snorted. "Oh, I didn't realize that at the time. I just thought she liked me as much as I liked myself. Which was a lot, in case you couldn't tell. I didn't truly grasp the importance of what she did for me until I had teenagers of my own."

They chatted about other Best/Worst categories, including apartments, teachers, outfits, and cars until their plates were empty except for crumbs. Dena cleared the table, while Audra threw away the trash.

"This was fun. Thank you for the sandwich, but I've got to get back to the Marketplace," Dena said. "I am so not ready for the Grand Opening. At least you helped me forget about it for a little while." Her face clouded.

"Don't worry," Audra reassured her. "I'll figure out what's going on with your lease and get it sorted out. Cross that item off your To-Do list."

"Thanks so much, Audra." Dena buttoned her coat

and tugged on her gloves. "It's nice to have a friend in town."

"It really is. I'm glad you stopped by to break into Norbert's office."

———

Dena hurried back to the Marketplace, braced against the cold January afternoon, but warmed by Audra's friendship and the fun lunchtime. She couldn't remember the last time she enjoyed someone's company like that. Someone who wasn't Charlee or Lance, that is. But by the time she had removed her coat and gloves, she was angry again. "It shouldn't be up to Audra to fix Norbert's mistakes on my lease," she said to a box of books she still had to shelve. It was just like that annoying nepotism hire all those years ago. She kicked the box.

Dena went through her back door into the vendor area to hit the restroom before tackling more boxes of books. She stepped left toward the restroom, which was at the far end of the room, but noise to the right made her turn the opposite direction.

Kober was breathing hard at the bottom of the stairs up to the second-floor vendor area, like she had just run down them.

"Are you okay?" Dena asked.

Kober waved away her concern, then used her hand to tidy the mass of curls threatening to slide down from the top of her head. "Just had a … hard talk with someone."

Dena thought about Norbert up there earlier. "Who?"

"One of my kids."

Dena knew this was a lie because Kober yelled long and creatively at her kids without breaking a sweat. This was clearly different.

By the time Dena had come out of the restroom, Hugo and Skyler were playing a raucous game of ping pong. Evelyn and Max had chosen sides and loudly cheered each point earned. She found their game irritating. And her irritation irritated her. How was she the only one not prepared for the Grand Opening? Plus, she was still angry about Norbert. She slipped into the back of the bookstore, but the cheering and laughter and incessant *plinks* and *plonks* continued to irk her. She knew she was being petty and unreasonable. Her co-tenants were just taking a break and enjoying a short respite.

She thought about taking a power-walk around the promenade to calm herself, but knew there would be workmen all around she'd have to dodge. Instead, she decided to head up the stairs to the second-floor vendor area. Either Norbert would be working up there and she could confront him, or it would be empty and she could be alone in the quiet for five minutes.

She was fine with either scenario.

Barely opening the door at the top of the stairs, she gasped when something rushed her. She braced herself, using the wall for support. An angry hiss made her look down. Balaam was on the third step down, stopping to collect himself, before haughtily gliding down the rest of the way.

Dena rolled her eyes at his back. "You're lucky I came up here, you little stinker. Otherwise you might miss a meal, heaven forbid."

Balaam swished his tail at her.

Dena opened the door again, this time all the way. Her nostrils flared at the odor of smoke. She rushed in, searching for the source. The skylight let in plenty of sunshine, enough for her to once again assess the disarray of the room. It had been a mess the entire time Dena had been at the Marketplace, full of storage boxes, piles of fixtures waiting to be installed, power tools, stacks of broken drywall, and pallets of unidentifiable construction materials with no other home. She pawed her way around, nose sniffing for the source of the smoke like a bloodhound.

The electrical box had its cover off and it seemed to Dena the smoky smell was stronger there. She didn't see any flames, though. The ladder Norbert had been standing on earlier was tipped over. She pushed aside stacks of boxes in order to see if he'd fallen. He wasn't at the end of the ladder, but Dena searched further and found him sprawled awkwardly on the floor about eight feet away.

"Norbert! Are you okay?" She shook him, probably too energetically in her panic. He didn't respond. Shook him again. No response. She placed two fingers on his carotid artery, but felt no pulse. She scrambled to her feet to get back to the bookstore to call 911.

As she hurried from the room, time seemed to slow down. She took in the angle of the fallen ladder in relation to where Norbert sprawled on the floor. There was no math involved, no tangents or extrapolations, but he seemed too far from the ladder to have fallen off it. It looked like he launched off it. Regardless, would falling— or launching—off a six-foot ladder be enough to cause someone's death? Dena remembered Norbert's joke about getting electrocuted. Is that what happened? It would explain the smoke she had smelled. They may never know, though, if Balaam was the only witness.

Halfway down the stairs Dena stopped short. Is this why Kober was out of breath at the bottom of these stairs? Did she have something to do with this? Did she push him? Was her hard talk with Norbert?

Time sped up again, seemingly faster than normal.

Dena flew through the doorway into the first-floor vendor room. The ping pong game had ended. Nobody was there, just Kober leaning on the back door of her bakery furiously scrolling through her phone. Dena didn't even think she was looking at it because Kober cut her eyes at Dena without moving her head. She knew what I found up there, Dena realized, and was gauging my reaction.

As Dena ran past her to the bookstore next door, she couldn't help but cry out, "What have you done?" She didn't stop running until she locked her back door and called 911. With her phone nestled in between her neck and shoulder, she pushed the electronic button to lower the security gate in the front of the store. "Hurry up, hurry up." By the time she explained the emergency to the dispatcher and was assured help was on the way, there was banging on the bookstore door from the vendor room.

Dena heard the other tenants' voices, all talking at once. Their voices were an indistinct buzz, until she heard Kober shout very clearly, "Dena! What did you do to Norbert?"

Kober

IT TOOK Kober a moment to process Dena's words as she'd rushed past her. But when she did, an icy blast zigzagged up and down her spine. She shot up the stairs to see exactly what Dena had seen. She barely glanced inside the second-floor room before thudding back down the stairs, shouting to the other tenants. "It's Norbert! He's upstairs! I don't know what happened." She ran past Evelyn and Max. "I think he's dead."

Even though Kober still had her phone in her hand, she banged on Dena's back door asking if she'd already called for an ambulance.

Evelyn

EVELYN RAN BACK to the photo studio to call 911. Why hadn't Kober called? Her phone was right there in her hand. And what had Dena been yelling about?

When she was reassured an ambulance was on the way, Evelyn went back out to the vendor room. Kober was still there, banging on Dena's door.

"Dena! What happened?" Evelyn elbowed Kober out of the way to open the door, but the knob wouldn't turn. Evelyn glanced around the room, eyes wide. She saw Max come in from the other direction and hurried over to him. He put a comforting arm around her shoulder.

"Kober, what is going on?" Evelyn asked. "You found Norbert?"

"No!"

Kober answered too quickly and too loudly, Evelyn thought. She reached for Max's hand and squeezed it tight. "What is happening?" she whispered.

"It's bad," Max whispered back. "I think it's real bad."

Hugo

WHEN ALL THE RUCKUS BEGAN, Hugo sprinted across to the cheese shop, but Skyler wasn't there. He hurried back to the vendor room. "Kober, what're you yelling about?"

"Norbert's upstairs dead!"

"Dead? How do you know?" He glanced behind him to the stairwell, but his vision narrowed to pinpricks of light. How did she know, he asked himself again. He braced one hand on the wall next to him because he felt his knees weaken. He took deep breaths until his vision cleared.

Skyler had materialized at his side and he wondered how long she'd been there.

"Are you okay?" she whispered. "What's going on? Why is she so riled up?"

"She says Norbert is upstairs, dead."

Skyler recoiled from Hugo and his words.

Their eyes met.

Hugo recoiled from her too.

Skyler

SKYLER HAD NEVER BEEN SCORCHED with a look like that before. Hugo blazed at her with saucer-sized eyes, staring and staring until she thought he'd burn a hole straight through her.

She broke away from his gaze, glancing at the floor, then up at the other frantic tenants. What had they seen? What did Hugo's stare mean?

Chancing another glance at him, she saw he was still gaping at her. She narrowed her eyes at him, which finally seemed to break the spell. His face crumpled and Skyler thought he might start crying.

"Keep it together. Norbert's not dead. He can't be. Somebody's just overreacting."

"They're not," Hugo stammered.

Skyler jumped. She didn't realize she had spoken out loud.

She moved away from Hugo, closer to the safety of Max and Evelyn as she waited to see what was going to happen.

Dena

DENA DIDN'T COME out of her locked bookstore until she heard the police and EMTs arrive. She unlocked her door into the vendor room, but stayed close to it. The other tenants were standing around the vendor room. Kober by the stairway. Max with his arm around Evelyn over by the back of their studio near the restroom. Hugo and Skyler on opposite sides of the ping pong table.

They all stared at her when she entered the room.

Dena recognized Sheriff Keisha Johnson and her deputy, Vincent Chavez. She hadn't technically met either one of them, but she'd seen photos of them on the Sugar Springs town website.

They were talking in low voices when Dena approached.

"Chief Johnson, I'm Dena Russo. Can I have a minute?"

Johnson and Chavez shared a look. Then the sheriff said to Chavez, "Go up with the EMTs." When he'd stepped away, she turned to Dena. "Of course."

Dena glanced around to make sure everyone was out

of earshot before speaking. She leaned close to the sheriff and spoke quietly. "I think Kober had something to do with Norbert's death." Dena lifted her chin toward Kober, in case the sheriff didn't know which one she was.

Kober saw Dena's movement. "What are you saying about me?" she bellowed, rushing over to them.

The sheriff stiffened and stepped in front of Kober, who stopped short.

"If she's telling you I had something to do with this, she's lying!"

Dena tried to keep her voice steady. "Kober, if anyone's lying, it's you. You've probably already told a hundred lies today. Just to me this morning, you've said you lied to your kids about the ping pong table, that you didn't know where the extra ream of printer paper was, that you didn't use the last coffee filter, that you took that class about collecting sales tax when it's obvious you didn't...." Dena paused. "And that you were yelling at one of your kids when I know full well you were yelling at Norbert."

Sheriff Johnson cocked her head at Kober but didn't say anything.

Hugo stepped toward them, but kept a wary distance from Kober. "I heard all kinds of yelling today. Even Evelyn and Max were arguing."

"Don't get us involved in this," Max warned, tightening his arm around Evelyn.

"I heard you too," Skyler said in a shaky voice.

"I'm just saying, Max," Hugo continued. "I didn't even hear what you were fighting about. But I heard Kober loud and clear. She said, 'Don't you dare threaten me.' And, 'Fix it or I'll fix you.'" Hugo narrowed his eyes at the sher-iff. "And 'men are pigs.'"

Kober took a threatening step toward Hugo, but Sheriff Johnson stopped her. It didn't stop Kober from shouting at Hugo, though. "You don't know what you're talking about!"

The rest of the tenants stared at Kober. Dena nodded but backed away from her and the sheriff.

Sheriff Johnson glanced around the room without speaking, assessing each of them and the situation. When her gaze landed on each tenant, to a person, they looked at the floor. Even Dena. Police scrutiny was scary, even when you hadn't done anything. Everyone in the world got nervous when a police car pulled up behind them in at a stoplight and were relieved when they turned a corner.

Sheriff Johnson strode to the bottom of the stairs and called up. "Chavez! Can you come down here please?" When he was on the bottom step, she leaned in and whispered something, to which he nodded.

The sheriff stepped toward Kober. "I'd like you to come to the station with me for a little chat."

"A little chat? Am I under arrest?" Kober's eyes widened. "Are you going to believe what that dinky pipsqueak said?" She pointed a shaky index finger at Hugo, then at Dena. "And her? They don't know what they're talking about."

Evelyn stepped forward. "Keisha, do you really have to arrest her? I think this must all be a misunderstanding of some kind."

Sheriff Johnson patted Evelyn's shoulder. "Nobody's being arrested, Evelyn." Addressing the room she said, "Kober and I are going to the station. Deputy Chavez will be staying here and taking your statements. I'd like you to cooperate with him so we can get this done as expeditiously as possible. Will that be okay with everyone?"

It didn't seem to Dena like that was a real question that needed to be answered, but everyone, Dena included, murmured an assent.

"Good. Thank you. Grab your coat, Kober. It's chilly out there." Sheriff Johnson followed Kober into the bakery. They returned to the vendor room with Kober carrying her purse and bundled up in her pink puffy parka.

They left through the emergency exit at the restroom end of the room. Kober became more distraught with each step. Before they reached the exit, Kober turned and yelled to the other tenants, "I didn't do anything! We have to figure this out before the Grand Opening. The PR won't be good for business!"

Dena's thoughts turned from Norbert to the reality Kober alluded to. While she was far from convinced Kober didn't do anything, she was absolutely certain Kober was right about the bad PR barreling toward them and the Marketplace. As sad and scary as it was when someone died, especially if there was some kind of foul play, there were still practical considerations to attend to.

Dena was relieved that the police and EMTs were here to handle everything.

Deputy Chavez set a chair for each of them evenly spaced around the room, near the back doors to their shops. Dena sat nearest to him, then Skyler, then Evelyn and Max in the back almost directly behind the ping pong table, but separated from each other by several feet, then Hugo on the other side of the room. Chavez placed two chairs side-by-side near the stairway where the paramedics were still working upstairs, leaving extra space for them to come back down. He stood with one hand on each chair and began explaining what was going to happen.

"For heaven's sake, Vince. Slow down. I can't understand a word you're saying," Evelyn scolded.

Deputy Chavez began again. Dena could see it took all his effort to slow down his speech. If a normal person spoke at one hundred percent speed, Sheriff Johnson spoke at fifty percent and Deputy Chavez at two hundred. Their conversations at the police station must be challenging.

"I will take statements from each of you up here in these two chairs. The rest of you will chillax in those chairs I set out for you by your doors. No more talking, please."

Chillax did not seem like an important enough word for what they were doing, but Dena took her place as directed and tried her best, under the circumstances, to chillax.

Skyler raised her hand to speak, as if she were in elementary school. "Excuse me, Deputy Chavez, but are we … suspects?"

Chavez turned his dark brown wide-set eyes on her. "Should you be?"

"I don't—I mean … no?"

"Get off it, Vince," Max growled. "You know as well as I do that Norbert Wallace was trying to squeeze a penny from both ends and instead of hiring somebody who knew what they were doing, got himself zapped. Now don't get all high and mighty with us, trying to pretend this is anything different."

"You might be right, Max, but it seems I'm wearing a sheriff's department uniform, not you, so we'll just do this my way. I think Keisha, er, Sheriff Johnson left me in charge here."

"Max didn't mean anything, Vince," Evelyn said soothingly. "And it seems like Dena had an intruder in her store this morning. Maybe you should be talking to him."

"An intruder?" Deputy Chavez turned toward Dena for clarification.

Dena nodded.

"Did you recognize him?"

"No."

"Could you give me a description?"

"An older man, never smiled, unshaven—"

"Sounds like Max." Hugo eyed Dena suspiciously.

"For heaven's sake, I'd know if it was Max."

Chavez wrote it all down. "Anything else?"

"He was quite thin. And he wore shabby clothes." Dena made it a point to ignore Hugo and address the other tenants. "We need to make sure that the Marketplace doors are locked. Only people with a key should be able to get in here if we're not open. That would only be us, Norbert's office staff, and the construction foreman."

"And the sheriff," Chavez added.

Evelyn walked over to the deputy and adjusted her eyeglasses. "That looks like a new uniform. Funding finally came in? Looks spiffy."

Chavez tugged on his sleeve. "Cut's a little slim for me, I think, but Carmela likes it."

"How is Carmela, anyway? Haven't seen her at the Sugar Springs Sirens lately. Nobody screams *Bunko* like your wife."

"She's just fine, Ev. I'll tell her you said hi."

"And get her back to Bunko Night toot sweet. We miss her."

"I'll let her know."

Deputy Chavez beckoned Dena to join him. He pulled a small notebook from his shirt pocket and spoke to her.

"Pardon me?"

Deputy Chavez sighed and repeated himself slower. "State and spell your full name and address."

When they got the basics out of the way, he asked, "Now … walk … me … through … your … day … today."

Little too slow, dude. Dena led him through the highlights of her day—what time she got to the Marketplace, talking to Norbert upstairs, that kind of stuff—but when she got to the part where she returned after lunch, they were interrupted by one of the paramedics.

Deputy Chavez stood. The two of them whispered together at the bottom of the stairs until the paramedic went back up. Chavez stepped away and pulled out his phone, speaking with Sheriff Johnson. Dena only caught two words: *electrocuted* and *coroner*. Relief coursed through her. Nobody killed Norbert. It was just an accident.

When Chavez sat back down and picked up his notebook again, Dena nodded knowingly at him. "Norbert didn't want to talk to me right then because he said he had to concentrate so he wouldn't get electrocuted. I smelled smoke when I went up there."

"Why'd you go up there, anyway?"

"I told you, I wanted to talk to him about my lease."

"No, the second time, when you found his body."

"Oh." Dena quickly glanced around the room at her fellow tenants. "It was noisy down here so I went up there for some peace and quiet."

"Why not go out and sit in one of those comfy chairs in the promenade?"

"I didn't think I'd be alone out there."

"And you needed to be alone why?" Chavez raised his eyebrows so high Dena thought there might be a real danger of them flying off his face.

Dena became flustered. "I didn't *need* to be alone. I *wanted* to be alone."

"But Norbert was upstairs."

"I didn't know that." Dena squeezed her eyes shut and thought back through the events as they happened. "Let me clarify. I thought he *might* still be up there working, since he wasn't at his office. If he *was* still up there, I could make him talk to me about the problem with my lease. But if he wasn't, I could have some peace and quiet."

"How did you know he wasn't at his office?"

Dena had skipped over that whole part of her narrative, since it had nothing to do with Norbert's electrocution. But she suddenly realized it made her look suspicious. "I went over there."

Deputy Chavez made a big deal about flipping backward through his pages of notes. "Hm. I don't see anything about that."

Dena recognized that this might be the most excitement Deputy Chavez had ever encountered in his work as a Sugar Springs sheriff's deputy. But this was not a murder, despite what she'd said about Kober earlier. Even the paramedics said so. "Listen, Deputy Chavez, I understand you have an important job to do, but let's cut to the chase. I heard that paramedic tell you that Norbert had been electrocuted. None of us had anything to do with that, even though when you speak to us," Dena waved her arm around the room, "we'll all tell you we had a beef of some kind with Norbert. But what happened to Norbert was obviously an accident. I'm sure of it."

"Are you now." Deputy Chavez stared at her long enough to make her squirm. "If you had been eavesdropping properly—"

"I wasn't eaves—"

"If you had been meant to hear what that paramedic said to me, he would have spoken to you directly. As it was, he spoke to *me* directly and he did *not* say Norbert had been electrocuted."

Dena glared at him. She knew what she'd heard and she very clearly heard the word *electrocuted*. Unless she didn't. Did she simply expect to hear the paramedic pronounce Norbert had been electrocuted? Could she have misunderstood? Deputy Chavez was correct that she wasn't anywhere near them when they had been conversing. While Chavez scrolled through the pages of his notebook, Dena mentally listed words she could have heard instead of *electrocuted*. Substituted. Convoluted. Undisputed. Unpolluted. Parachuted. Executed.

Egad, that was even worse.

He finally dismissed a chastened Dena back to her seat.

Chavez continued to thumb through the pages of his notebook, reading and jotting more thoughts. Finally, he called Skyler to join him.

In her mind, Dena replayed the events of the day, her movements and conversations, as well as what she saw of everyone else's. It was true they all had issues with Norbert, and much of what happened today was weirdly suspicious, but did it only seem that way because a man died? If Norbert hadn't been found sprawled on the floor upstairs, would any of them have had another thought about what was said and done around the Marketplace today?

She suddenly remembered her intruder from earlier. The outside doors to the Marketplace had been unlocked when he came in. She'd locked them all after he drove away, but could someone have come in during the time they were unlocked and waited on the second floor until Norbert got there? She hadn't technically seen the man leave. She simply assumed he had driven away with his box of books. Maybe he hadn't.

Maybe Norbert wasn't even the intended victim. Maybe he was just the unlucky person who startled some other prowler or squatter, unseen by all of them. It wasn't out of the question, but certainly seemed improbable. None of this seemed random, however.

She mentally berated herself. Despite Deputy Chavez' equivocations, Dena reminded herself that Norbert was electrocuted, not murdered. She knew what she heard. But the image of Kober's face after Dena had found Norbert materialized in front of her. She couldn't fathom Kober doing something like that, but she also knew what she'd seen.

Dena's thoughts were broken by Skyler's voice, which had risen. "She grabbed my arm and wouldn't let me go upstairs where Norbert was."

"Who grabbed your arm?"

"Dena! She wouldn't let me go up." Skyler lowered her voice and leaned even closer to Deputy Chavez. "Maybe because she had just killed Norbert?"

Skyler didn't lower it enough because Dena heard. It seemed all the other tenants did too because there was a collective gasp usually reserved for horror movie audiences.

Dena jumped to her feet. "I grabbed your arm for balance!"

"Or to keep me from going up there!"

Hugo stood too. "Skyler wouldn't lie about that!"

Dena ignored him. "But you went up there anyway! You said you had something unpleasant to do." The importance of those words stopped Dena short. She cocked her head at Skyler and repeated slower, for emphasis. "You had something unpleasant to do."

Now Skyler jumped up. "I *said* a businesswoman has to do unpleasant things."

"What's the difference?" Dena asked.

"There's a big difference!" Skyler turned back to Deputy Chavez. "I did not go up there and I did not kill Norbert Wallace."

Dena's mind reeled. Kober out of breath at the bottom of the stairs. Skyler having to do unpleasant things. Skyler knew Norbert was up there. Was she lying? Did she go up to do her *unpleasant thing* after I came down? Dena glanced around the room. What about everyone else? She had already told Deputy Chavez all the Marketplace tenants had a grudge against Norbert, but until this minute that hadn't really sunk in. Balaam shot out of the second-floor room and he always stuck pretty close to Evelyn. Had Evelyn or Max—or both of them—been up there with Norbert? Hugo said he heard the couple arguing about something earlier. Did they do something upstairs? Is that why Evelyn was all chummy with Chavez earlier? Being all folksy, trying to subliminally remind him of their long relationships in Sugar Springs?

What about Hugo? He was being awfully quiet, except to call out Evelyn and Max's argument … and point a finger at Kober … and leap to Skyler's defense.

And why was Deputy Chavez still questioning all of them if the paramedic told him Norbert had been electrocuted?

"Everyone calm down and take your seats. I understand this is a volatile situ—" At their blank looks, Chavez started over more slowly.

Max interrupted Deputy Chavez. "Vince, you know as well as I do that nobody in this town likes—liked—Norbert Wallace. You better get reinforcements so you can start questioning everyone that horse's ass ever met. Starting with his kindergarten teacher."

Everyone had returned to their chairs.

Evelyn spoke. "Vince. Here's my statement. Get out your little notebook." After he did, pen poised, she continued. "We weren't going to be around the day our big backdrops for the studio were going to be delivered—"

"Why not?"

"Max had a doctor's appointment in Colorado Springs."

"Nothing serious, I hope."

"Nah," Max said. "Just another prostate exam."

Deputy Chavez winced. "Ew. Mine's coming up soon."

"Anyway," Evelyn continued, "I asked Norbert very nicely if he'd sign for the delivery or if one of his workmen could, but he refused. Something about liability, but I think he was just being ornery. Anyhowdy, we had to rent a truck and drive all the way to Denver to get them. Denver! Can you believe it? And you know how much Max hates to drive to Denver."

Dena wondered why Deputy Chavez would know such a thing.

"Does he hate it enough to want to kill Norbert?" Chavez asked Evelyn pointedly.

"Oh, definitely." She bobbed her curly white head with great emphasis. "But I doubt he would have had the time. I kept him pretty busy today. What with all the fussing and everything. Luckily, Skyler came in and interrupted us."

"How?"

"She brought us cheese samples." Evelyn glanced at Max, then back at Deputy Chavez.

"Max wasn't there," Skyler said quietly.

"What's that?" Deputy Chavez cupped his ear.

Skyler repeated herself a bit louder, casting a guilty look in Max's direction.

"Good thing too." Max patted his belly. "Cheese doesn't always agree with me."

"I love all kinds of cheese, except that Greek stuff, feta." Evelyn's eyes widened and she rushed to say, "But not Skyler's feta. Apparently, her goats aren't very goaty. Skyler's cheese is delicious. Every bit of it." She bobbed her head again. "You know who makes great cheese sauce?" Evelyn pointed a finger at Chavez. "Your mother. How's she doing, anyway?"

Deputy Chavez updated Evelyn on his mother in the nursing home. Then he said to her, "You don't seem too upset about Norbert's death."

"I will say I was a tad shocked, but then I thought, you live, you die. And it seems to me Norbert was always skating on thin ice."

"Why's that?"

Evelyn shrugged. "You knew him as well as I did. He ever strike you as a man who'd live to a ripe old age?"

"No, I guess not."

"And you know what Max calls him?"

"A horse's ass."

"Exactly."

"To be fair, though," Chavez said, "he calls everyone that."

Dena felt like she was in a play. What in the world was going on here? A man was dead upstairs—potentially murdered—and they're talking like they're at a Fourth of July picnic? Was Evelyn trying to get Max off the hook for this? Dena noticed how easily Evelyn sidestepped the part where Max had disappeared, going off on that tangent about Chavez's mother's cheese sauce. That's some sublime rhetorical skill there. And it seemed like Chavez fell for the entirety of Evelyn's silver-tongued sleight-of-hand.

"Um, Deputy Chavez?" Dena said. "You never followed up about where Max—"

Dena was interrupted when Sheriff Johnson returned to the Marketplace with Kober and another man. Kober went directly to her bakery, while the man headed for the stairs. As he passed the deputy, Chavez said, "Nice to see you, Cal. Hope your coroner duties didn't take you away from something else."

"Just learning how to vaccinate llamas, Vince. That new guy with all the exotics is keeping me busy."

"I'll let you get to it, then." Chavez turned to a blank page in his notebook then looked at Hugo across the room in his assigned folding chair. "Mr Dekker? Would you please join me up here?"

Dena sighed. She'd have to follow up on Max's whereabouts later if she wanted to get to the truth.

As Hugo walked to the twin pair of chairs, Chavez told the sheriff he was almost done with the statements.

"Thank you for your cooperation, everyone. The rest of you can go about your business now," Sheriff Johnson said.

Dena was relocating her folding chair to the table where it belonged.

"Ms Russo? Can I talk to you in here?" The sheriff indicated the bookstore.

Dena followed her inside. "Call me Dena."

The sheriff leaned nonchalantly against the counter with the cash register in the center of the shop. Dena felt anything but nonchalant, but leaned next to her anyway, matching her pose.

"I spoke with Audra, and I'm wondering why she found you riffling through Norbert's desk earlier today? You're lucky she found you instead of Royce, by the way. He can be a little high-strung."

Dena wondered if that meant he was under suspicion for killing Norbert too, but said, "I was looking for the lease that I needed Norbert to fix. I was hoping he had already made the changes and that it was just waiting on his desk until he could call me to come over and pick it up."

"And why weren't you forthcoming with this information when you and I spoke earlier?"

"Because things were a little chaotic?"

"Point taken." The sheriff offered a slight nod of acknowledgment.

"But I wouldn't have mentioned it regardless because I

didn't find my corrected lease and because I didn't kill anyone, if that's what you're implying." Dena knew that was exactly the implication, since Norbert was upstairs with the coroner. "I believe I did mention that I was angry with Norbert for not taking my concerns about the lease seriously. His mistake and continual delays could mean I lose a substantial amount of money, if he doesn't change it."

"And now he can't." Sheriff Johnson's words oozed out with gravity and significance.

Dena stared at the sheriff, squinching her eyes a bit as her mind whirled. "But I *wanted* him to change it. If he's dead, he can't."

"Exactly." She lowered her gaze at Dena. "Don't leave town."

Dena stared at her, cop wife to cop. "You and I know that's not a real thing, right? Besides, I have to go to Santa Fe to deal with some remodeling on the house I'm selling there and move out the rest of my stuff."

Sheriff Johnson smiled leisurely. "Just keeping you on your toes."

"I heard the paramedic say Norbert was electrocuted. Why are we going through all this?"

"Because an unwitnessed death occurred upstairs." She tipped her head toward the ceiling.

"I realize that. I don't mean to be insensitive, but accidents happen, don't they? And Norbert wasn't an electrician. If he made sloppy mistakes the same way he did with my lease, then ..."

Sheriff Johnson leveled her gaze directly at Dena. "I've investigated a lot of deaths over my career. And accidents aren't always accidents."

Kober

"THEY QUESTIONED ME LIKE A DIRTY, lowdown criminal! They threw me in the back of a squad car and drove me to the sheriff's office. The whole town saw." Kober paused, the full impact of being seen carted around in the back of a cruiser in a small town hitting her with its full force. "Son of a motherless goat! Everyone will think I did something." Kober knew her voice was too loud and screechy but she couldn't help it.

"Did you?" Max asked.

"No! Of course not," Kober bellowed.

"Indoor voice, dear," Evelyn reminded her.

"Then there's nothing to worry about, is there?" Max said.

"You're too old to be so naïve, Max. Think about my kids! Something like this never goes away. And what about you, Dena? And Skyler, and the rest of you? We were the last to interact with Norbert and we were all mad at him. We have *got* to get in front of this and do damage control. This stink will rain down upon our Grand Opening, mark my words!"

"Good grief, woman!" Max said. "You trying to peel the paint off my ears?"

Kober glanced around the vendor room. They didn't seem to be getting it. She needed to make them understand. A failed bakery would spell disaster. She might even lose the kids. She was just about to begin another line of reasoning—although she was sure someone would call it a tirade—when a young couple poked their heads into the vendor room through the photo studio's back door.

They stepped through. They couldn't have been long out of college. The man wore skinny black jeans with mismatched Keds without the laces—one shoe red, one purple—and an infinity scarf, perhaps two, over a vintage cartoon t-shirt. Kober squinted. It looked like the image of Fred Flintstone. The man's highly manicured hair swept up and over to the left, appearing to be a hirsute recreation of the perfect surfer's wave. His bushy beard and mustache looked like he ordered it from a catalog.

The woman wore an oversized chunky sweater, at least two sizes too big, over leggings and cut-off jean shorts. Her wispy hair stuck out randomly from the slouchy beanie pulled low over her forehead.

They both wore backpacks slung over one shoulder.

Ugh. Hipsters. Gentrification had officially reached Sugar Springs. A shame too, Kober thought, because a slouch hat would not work over this hair. She reached a protective hand up and patted the nest on top of her head.

"Excuse me," the man said. "I know the Marketplace isn't open yet, but the photographer's door was open, so we came through. I'm Cap Capitano and this is my wife, Aja. We're from the *Sugar Springs Courier*."

"Oh," Evelyn said with a wide grin. "You're Henry and Wynona's grandson. I heard you were coming to take over the paper for them."

"That's right." Cap nodded. "We've only been here since last week. Finally got all settled in."

"Fantastic," Kober bellowed gleefully. She immediately decided to overlook the superficial and concentrate on what mattered. At least until they were out of earshot. She wished Jain had been here to see them. They'd have great fun mocking these faux bohemians. Fauxhemians. But that could wait. "You're here to do a story about the Grand Opening." She swept an arm in a wide circle, taking them all in. "Everyone's here. You can interview all of us at once." Kober introduced the tenants. "And it seems like you already know Max and Evelyn. Who do you want to interview first?" Kober asked Cap.

Aja pulled a notebook from her backpack. "I'm actually the reporter. Cap will be handling the business side, mostly. I'll start with you, I guess." Aja pointed her pen at Kober. "What can you tell me about Norbert Wallace's murder?"

"Word travels fast," Hugo muttered.

"Murder? Who told you he was murdered?" Kober felt a flare of adrenaline fire up her brain cells. Had she been seen in the back of that squad car? Or worse, was the news of her riding around back there already spreading through town?

"You heard wrong," Max said.

"Norbert electrocuted himself," Dena said.

Cap shook his head. "Grandpa says Norbert was a general contractor for years and educated himself so he could hire good subcontractors and know they weren't cheating him. No way he electrocuted himself. You ask me, he was murdered, and that's what our story will say."

"Henry would know, I guess," Evelyn mused. "He and Norbert both belonged to the Elks Lodge."

"Henry's a horse's ass," Max grumbled. "No offense, kid."

"None taken? I guess?" Cap's professional demeanor seemed to slip a bit in the wake of Max's pronouncement. He recovered quickly, however, and made a power move that Kober recognized, since she used it herself all the time —using his triceps to propel himself up and backward to sit on the table. Kober envied his agility and wondered if her power move resembled that in any way, or if, now that she was older, she should alter her power move to crossing her arms over her ample cleavage and tapping her foot instead.

With all eyes on him, Cap's resolve reassembled itself.

Ah, the resiliency of the young.

"What can any of you tell us about the Sugar Mill Curse?" Cap glanced around the room.

"The what?" Skyler's eyebrows shot up.

"Aja and I have been looking into the dark history of the sugar mill. There have been all kinds of … unsavory and mysterious happenings around here. Norbert Walker's death is yet another example."

"Son of a printer cartridge," Kober muttered. Louder she said, "Are you sure the two of you don't work for The Twilight Zone instead of a small-town newspaper? There is no Sugar Mill Curse." She spat out the last three words as if they were week-old clams.

"What exactly is this curse you're talking about?" Dena asked.

"Let's just say there have been a bunch of mysterious deaths and leave it at that."Aja clearly enjoyed being cryptic.

"Regardless, the coroner will know more in a few days, showing Norbert's death was just an accident," Dena said. "We're pretty sure he electrocuted himself and that's what the report will say." She nodded confidently around the room until the rest of the tenants joined her.

Kober, in fact, nodded so aggressively she had to use both hands to push her hair back into place. "The fact the police talked to us and didn't arrest any of us should tell you something." In case they didn't already know, she didn't mention that she'd been hauled into the station and questioned like a common criminal and hoped nobody else would either.

"Not what my story will show," Aja said calmly. She had a smug, pretentious way of speaking that Kober found troubling. Her enormous fisherman's sweater made her look like a waif, but Kober had the feeling she was as tenacious as the dandelions she and the kids tried to pull from her yard. As soon as Kober was satisfied they'd pulled them all and released them from this mortal coil, two days later they were back, popping up in the grass like demons searching for more souls.

"You can't print a story yet! You don't have any facts." Skyler's neck turned red and blotchy.

Evelyn wagged a finger at Cap like she was scolding Balaam caught walking on the kitchen counter. "You wait one cotton-picking minute, young man. We are a week-and-a-half out from our Grand Opening. This Marketplace is good for the town and good for the newspaper, too. You don't want to jeopardize that. You'll ruin your grandparents' legacy. If you jump the gun to sensationalize this, nobody will ever trust you or the paper again. And every idiot knows, a free press is the cornerstone of democracy."

"Our new business model is to get some teaser content online to get eyeballs *and* advertisers." Aja answered for Cap. "Ultimately, we want both robust print and online editions. And this, my friends, is primo teaser content. The internet is where people get their news anyhow." She looked pleased as punch with herself.

Cap seemed a bit more reluctant.

"This is real life. Not the internet," Hugo said glumly.

"Listen," Cap said with what he probably thought was an urbane smile, obviously trying to soothe the tenants' ruffled feathers and perhaps mitigate his wife's blunt tone. "My grandparents made me promise to always have a print edition of the *Courier*. It'll still come out every Thursday, so I have to run a story in three days. And another one a week after that, and the week after that."

"We know how Thursdays work, dude." Kober rolled her eyes and crossed her arms over her ample cleavage. As a power move, it felt pretty solid. She might just keep it.

They all stared around the room at each other. Finally, Aja waggled her notebook in the air. "No takers?"

"Only if you want to talk about the Grand Opening," Kober said.

"No offense, but yawn."

"You will come to find," Max said, "that Sugar Springs runs on yawn."

"Okay, Boomer." Aja shrugged and dropped her notebook into her bag.

"I'll okay *your* boomer, if you're not careful!" Evelyn was so irritated she flounced over to a chair, pointedly turned it around, and sat with her back to the two reporters.

Kober hadn't seen her do that since Norbert told them he had refused to sign for the delivery of their studio backdrops. Kober cut her eyes at Evelyn's back, then at Max whose jowls seemed to vibrate with rage. The last time Kober saw Max do that was …. Oh no.

Cap had the decency to look a bit embarrassed by his

wife's demeanor. He handed his business card all around. "If you change your mind."

"We won't," Kober said defiantly over her shoulder. "But if *you* change your mind, you know where to find us."

Cap and Aja left. As they did so, Evelyn raised her voice so they'd hear. "I have half a mind to call Wynona and tell her what that boy's up to!"

"Threatening hipsters rarely works," Hugo told her. "Trust me, I know."

Kober tore Cap's business card in half and flung it across the room. It fluttered harmlessly at her feet. She kicked at the pieces and one stuck to her shoe. "Son of a hairless monkey," she muttered, scooping them up and shoving them in her apron pocket. "If that ... child ... writes an unflattering article, we're sunk. It'll be all over the internet. Nobody will come to the Grand Opening if they think we're a bunch of murderous ninnies. We will lose every last cent we put into this place. Bankruptcy, humiliation, destitution."

She let that sink in. She could tell they all understood the truth of her words.

"What if it really was that guy that came into Dena's store, that intruder?" Skyler finally asked.

Kober's head snapped around. "What intruder?"

Dena explained, but Kober didn't respond, simply nodded while staring at her.

Was that even true, she wondered. It was an excellent deflection on Dena's part. Kober was dismayed she hadn't thought of it herself.

Kober stared at Dena a bit longer then checked her watch. She walked to the white board, erased it with a paper towel, and rewrote in angry red strokes, "10 DAYS TO GRAND OPENING."

Skyler

SKYLER PUT AWAY the washed and dried cheese tray she'd taken over to Evelyn and Max earlier. She ran her hand along the edges of her charcuterie boards, nudging them across the shelf until they were lined up precisely, wooden soldiers in formation. She was still trying to wrap her brain around Norbert's death, but couldn't think about it or the sheriff for one more minute.

She decided to turn her attention to more practical matters, things she perhaps had more control over. Like dwelling on the fact that Evelyn had turned up her nose at feta cheese, making a snap decision about Skyler's choices on the tray.

Of course Skyler understood people had likes and dislikes; she had her fair share too.

She didn't like toenail polish because it always startled her in the shower when she saw her feet.

She didn't like gory movies, not because they made her squeamish or jumpy, but because they made her wonder how the props department made the fake blood, vomit, and splattered brains. She'd begin to concoct recipes in her head, always ending with her rushing to her refrigerator to dump ketchup, split pea soup, hamburger, and anything else her imagination had whipped up. Gory movies were simply too expensive and inconvenient to watch with any regularity. Especially if she'd just gone to the grocery store.

And there was that ski instructor she hadn't liked that one time and she never went up the mountain again. She really loathed him.

But none of that had anything to do with her cheese.

What if a customer did something similar? Had a small sample of cheese, didn't like it, then told everyone and nobody ever came in the shop again?

Skyler had an uncomfortable thought about that ski instructor, but reasoned it was entirely different because she hadn't told anyone about that. Ever. And, of course, now that she was thinking rationally and dispassionately about it, not one person had ever refused her cheese.

Evelyn and Max didn't count. They were more like family than customers. They would never say anything bad about her cheese or her shop, not in public anyway. There was too much at stake, and they wouldn't want to harm the Marketplace in any way.

The Marketplace was in harm's way though, wasn't it? If that newspaper article ran and people started thinking we were all crazy murderers over here, we wouldn't get any customers, not even terrifying ones who didn't like feta.

Skyler sat down on the stool she kept behind the refrigerated case, studying her stock of locally-sourced cheese. "It would be a shame if I failed before I even began," she said to a round of burrata. If she was being honest, she'd also admit it would be a shame never to have reason to see Jake, her favorite local cheese supplier, again.

Skyler thought about Hugo with a little twinge of guilt whenever she had twinges of the other kind about Jake.

She knew Hugo had a crush on her, made obvious by his gawking at her when he thought she couldn't see, and conveniently managing to be in the laundry room in the apartment building at the same time she was. Of course, she would tell him to knock it off immediately if she thought he was dangerous. But she and Hugo both needed friends in Sugar Springs so she hoped it wouldn't get weird.

She just didn't think of Hugo in that way. Not like how she thought about Jake. Jake had electrified her tingly bits the minute she laid eyes on him. When she met Hugo, on the other hand, she had decided that she'd be friendly to him, but not lead him on until he met someone else and got over his crush on her. She was sure it would happen. It happened to all the guys eventually.

Besides, the Marketplace was not the place for romance. It would be like an office romance which almost always went south after the initial stages were passed through. Denial, anger, bargaining, depression. Skyler giggled that she inadvertently thought of the stages of grief. Well, if the shoe fit, right?

Skyler told herself she was doing Hugo a favor. After all, they were both scrabbling, trying to get their businesses off the ground. Romance would be a permanent dagger in their success. If success was even on the table any longer.

She sighed. The only way they could save the Marketplace and all their shops was to figure out what really happened to Norbert. Those reporters seemed absolutely confident that he'd been murdered and not electrocuted. But if he really was murdered, who did it?

She thought about Dena gripping her arm on the stairs, and then explaining it was simply to help keep her balance. But was it? Now that she knew Dena was caught going through Norbert's desk, that threw a lot of shade over her words.

Skyler suddenly felt a pang of self-doubt. She wasn't always the best judge of character but had liked Dena right away. And now this? She might be forced to prove that Dena killed Norbert. If not to the police, at least to herself. She considered calling Royce over at Norbert's office to see what he knew about Dena snooping through his desk. Nobody ever said if Dena took anything, but would anyone know? Maybe Royce would.

She reached for the phone but had second thoughts because of what went down between her and Royce. But if she was wrong about Dena, maybe she was wrong about Royce too. Maybe there were things she didn't know, something she just wasn't understanding, some reasons that would explain everything. She reached for the phone.

"Hey, Royce, it's Skyler. Do you want to have lunch with me?"

"My calendar is wide open. When were you thinking?"

Hugo

HUGO WATCHED Skyler in her shop. If his back door was cracked to the correct angle, and hers was also, he had a clear view of her moving around the back of her shop. It comforted him, knowing she was just across the vendor room from him.

It was the only thing that comforted him these days, however.

This mess with Norbert was a real drag. It was hard enough opening his chocolate shop without all this drama. Norbert's death—unfortunate or not—probably had ruined everything for everyone here. If there was no Marketplace, there'd be no Skyler. And if there was no Skyler, what was the point of any of it?

He thought about last week when everyone screamed at him after they found out he wasn't planning on giving away free samples at the Grand Opening. They claimed they'd all agreed to do so—Hugo included—but he'd disagreed, having a completely different recollection of the conversation.

"Why would I give away something I want people to buy?" he'd asked, perplexed.

They all started talking at once, which made him explain his position more and more emphatically until nobody could hear anyone else.

Finally, Skyler put her arm on the sleeve of his white chef's coat and said quietly, "Hugo, this is my one and only chance at this. I need you to do this. We're all in this together. Please?"

He had immediately relented and promised he'd make special chocolates to give away on the day of the Grand Opening.

He leaned against his door, staring through the crack at Skyler, catching welcome and wonderful glimpses of her as she moved around her shop. Each time she came into view he relaxed. Each time she stepped out of sight he tensed.

A Gordian knot coiled and curled in his brain as he stared at her. This thing with Norbert seemed an intractable problem, but he knew he could untangle it if he picked at it steadily. He pictured very clearly what Dena had described of Skyler marching up the stairs to the second floor where Norbert had been found dead. If he could prove Skyler was innocent of any of these allegations and innuendos, maybe things would change between them. For the better. He could be her champion, sans white horse.

He did, however, have a bright white chef's jacket so he donned that and crossed through the vendor room to Skyler's cheese shop carrying a plate of toffees.

"Knock, knock."

Her smile dazzled him and made him bobble the plate.

"Hey, Hugo. What's up?"

"Nothing much. I just can't quit thinking about Norbert."

Skyler's eyes widened. "I know. Me neither."

"If this was a movie, we'd all have been hauled into the police station since we all had a motive."

"And opportunity."

"And opportunity," Hugo agreed.

"Sheriff Johnson would play Good Cop, and Chavez would be Bad Cop."

"I can totally see that. They'd shine a lamp right in our faces to torture us."

Skyler nodded. "They wouldn't let us sleep or use the bathroom."

"But they'd give us tons of water and coffee." At Skyler's blank look he added, "You know, for more torture."

She giggled. "But eventually the sheriff would go out to Corky's and bring us back a sandwich—"

"And Chavez would cut it in half for us and hand us a napkin."

"That's how the Sugar Springs Sheriff's Department really gets people to talk."

Hugo suddenly remembered he held the plate of toffees which he thrust toward Skyler. "I've been experimenting. Try one and see what you think."

Skyler bit into the crisp confection. "I like how it didn't fall apart when I bit it." She rolled it around in her mouth for a bit, then chewed and swallowed the rest. "Yum."

"What did you taste?" Hugo asked.

Skyler stared at the wall above his head. "Better have another one to be sure," she said with a grin, reaching toward the plate. She ate that one and began guessing. "Cinnamon? Allspice? Anise? Nutmeg?"

Hugo held the plate out once more. "Think floral, not kitchen."

She ate another one. "Oh my gosh, that's lavender! I

can smell it too. Hugo," she said, touching his arm, "you're a genius in that kitchen!"

Hugo's breath caught in his chest. "Genius? No way. You're the genius. Every time I come over here I love your shop that much more. You have such a way of decorating and making everyo—everything seem so comfortable. I predict Really Grate Cheese will have customers knocking down the doors to get in. And right on their heels will be people wanting to buy franchises from you. Don't doubt for one minute how successful you'll be."

Skyler shook her head. "I doubt that every minute of every day. I have absolutely no idea what I'm doing. I keep redecorating because I don't know what else to do."

"That's nuts. You've already done everything! You've made a lovely interior. You've found a niche with your local cheese suppliers." He waved a hand toward her cheese case. "You have a great selection—"

"I'm just making it up as I go along. That's why I wanted Norbert's validation. He's been around a long time and has seen lots of small businesses. I wanted to get his opinion about it all, but I couldn't get him to give me the time of day." Skyler's face clouded and her voice took on a hard edge. She crossed her arms and stared at the floor.

Hugo became alarmed at the sudden change in her demeanor.

When she raised her head and looked at Hugo, he saw tight lips that had lost their color and a bulging vein in her temple.

"And he wouldn't stop calling me *girlie*."

Hugo stepped so close to her he could smell her rose-scented shampoo. He whispered, "Skyler, did you kill Norbert?"

Dena

IT WAS late and she should go home. Dena left the vendor room through her back door and entered the bookstore. But instead of forgetting about this catastrophe-in-the-making and going home to leftover spaghetti and something binge-worthy on Netflix, or even doing something proactive like attacking the inventory that needed attention, she walked all the way through the bookstore and across the promenade to her favorite overstuffed armchair. It was one of three in a cozy configuration across from her store that invited conversation and coffee. Her grandiose fantasy of shoppers sitting here preparing for a visit to her bookstore grew dimmer every minute.

Kober was absolutely right. If those muckrakers masquerading as journalists write a story like that, we're sunk. There might be no clawing our way out of that kind of mud.

Who told them Norbert was murdered anyway? Was that the scuttlebutt around town or did Cap and Aja jump to that conclusion all on their own? Dena hadn't yet met Cap's grandparents, the previous journalists around town, but did they know something Dena didn't know about all this?

Dena idly picked at the nap on the arm of the chair with her fingernail. If the coroner's report came back quickly with the conclusion that Norbert really did electrocute himself, then the Grand Opening should be fine. She was sure that was what she heard the paramedic say, despite what Chavez would have her believe.

She wondered how long it would take for the sheriff to get the coroner's report in a situation like this. And would she pass along the information to the tenants of the Marketplace?

But what if the scuttlebutt was correct and Norbert couldn't possibly have electrocuted himself? Dena shifted uncomfortably in her seat. Then all those accusations flying around today—spoken and silent—would have to be dealt with quickly enough to do some damage control for the Grand Opening. It seemed that Sheriff Johnson and Deputy Chavez were on the ball, but again, how long did these things take? This was real life, not a sixty-minute crime drama solved in forty-seven minutes, less commercials.

She knew she didn't kill Norbert, and if she could prove quickly enough to Cap and Aja that it was someone else, then maybe they wouldn't write some sensationalized story—or worse, series of stories—about some nonexistent "sugar mill curse" and the Grand Opening could come off without a hitch. Maybe the bookstore wouldn't fail before it even opened. Maybe no bankruptcy, humiliation, and destitution like Kober predicted.

She thought about the other tenants. At some point over the last few weeks, everyone confessed to multiple fears about their business—financial, emotional, practical. All the Marketplace tenants had so much at stake.

The more Dena replayed the conversation she'd had with Sheriff Johnson earlier, the more freaked out she became. She felt like she was living in a pinball machine. When she first found Norbert's body, she was sure Kober killed him. THWACK. Then when the paramedics came, she was sure it was an accident. PLINK. Then when Sheriff Johnson told her that accidents weren't always accidents, she was back to thinking Norbert had been murdered, and her list of suspects had blossomed. CLUNK. Then these reporters waltz in to proclaim it was definitely murder and tried to somehow sweep them all up in some vague net of guilt. DING, DING, DING.

She suddenly empathized with Kober this morning when she'd accused her of killing Norbert.

Dena glanced at the dark bakery with its security gate pulled down and locked.

Dena felt sorry for Kober now, despite everything, as she thought about her children. Would a mother really kill someone like that, possibly with her kids in the same building? Had the kids left before or after Norbert was killed? Dena's stomach fluttered. Maybe Norbert had messed around with one of them. Surely if Kober found out something like that she would have made a thunderous vocal stink about it and the entire state of Colorado would have heard. Wouldn't she? Or would she have been so enraged she would have gone the other direction, silently plotting vicious revenge?

Dena stared out the dark window across the parking lot, just as she had earlier when she'd seen Kober's children crossing the parking lot toward home.

Wait. If Norbert's car was gone, but he had been dead upstairs, what did that mean? Was she mistaken and it hadn't been Norbert's car she'd seen at all? Dena shook her head to try and get everything to fall back into place.

It *was* Norbert's car, she was sure of it. She'd seen it many times when he pulled into that same parking space.

But where was the car?

She stared, unfocused, across the promenade into her bookstore. She couldn't fathom what had happened to Norbert's car, even though she kept looping through the vision of him parking this morning.

She tried to erase the image of Norbert getting out of his car, ignorant of what loomed in his future. Norbert sprawled across the floor upstairs. Dena closed her eyes tight. She needed to think about something else. Anything else.

Eventually, a new image emerged … the stacks of boxes full of used books she needed to catalogue and shelve. But first, she needed to figure out a pricing system. It was one of many things she hadn't thought through completely before rashly deciding it would be fun to own a bookstore. She remembered telling Charlee, "How hard could it be?"

Hard. Genuinely hard.

And now this.

She looked past the mess of her bookstore toward the back door leading to the vendor area. She could see movement and shadows. Dena had seen Evelyn and Max leave over an hour ago, and Kober's bakery was locked up tight. Skyler and Hugo must still be back there. No doubt they'd be talking about Norbert. But were they also talking about her? Everyone noticed when Sheriff Johnson asked to talk privately with her.

Until today Dena enjoyed the harried camaraderie of the other tenants complaining, bustling about, laughing, sharing business tactics. She wondered if that rapport had all ended with Norbert's death.

Surely not. Norbert's death was sad, of course, but it

had to have been an accident, it just had to be, despite the seriousness of the sheriff's investigation and Cap's baseless conclusion that he'd been murdered. He and Aja were simply covering their bases and something got misconstrued. Someone said something they shouldn't have to the reporters. Maybe the sheriff repeated her aphorism that accidents weren't always accidents. Maybe Sheriff Johnson said that to everyone to lend gravitas to herself or to a situation. Maybe it wasn't even true. Again, she thought that Norbert's death was probably the biggest thing that had happened in Sugar Springs in a long time. The cops were duty-bound to make sure to cross all those Ts properly.

But reporters? What were they duty-bound to accomplish? Get a story, however sensational, Dena acknowledged with dismay. Wasn't a journalist's motto *if it bleeds, it leads*? Dena hoped there wouldn't be any article published. At least not one without facts. At least not before the Grand Opening.

Dena remembered Charlee's fiasco with trolls on the internet. Was that going to be her fate too? Like mother, like daughter.

Two workmen walked past, toolbelts clanging. They were here late, she thought. One greeted her with a nod, but continued his conversation.

She wondered if the sheriff had spoken to all the craftsman putting finishing touches on the Marketplace. Dena never really paid attention to their comings and goings and probably couldn't pick any of them out of a line-up—no pun intended—but surely someone had a roster of all the people working for Norbert. Who would know, now that Norbert was dead? Maybe Norbert's employees, Audra or Royce.

Dena didn't know Royce very well, but the fact that Audra announced to Sheriff Johnson that Dena had been searching Norbert's desk certainly meant Dena couldn't ask her directly, as Audra obviously suspected that Dena was somehow involved. The idea made Dena sad. She'd finally made a friend in town and now—poof—fizzled.

How could Dena prove that, even though she had issues with Norbert, she didn't want him dead? But what about the other tenants? They all had issues with Norbert. Did they want him dead?

Again, she heard the sheriff's words in her head. *Accidents aren't always accidents.* Was the Sugar Mill Curse real? Was Sheriff Johnson trying to tell her something?

She sighed, rousting herself from the pinball game in her head. She was being silly. Norbert was being cheap and didn't want to spring for another bill from his electrical contractor. He thought he could fix the problem himself but didn't know what he was doing and electrocuted himself. That's all. An unfortunate accident. Surely that's what the coroner's report will say.

But what if it wasn't? Would the sheriff take so many statements—and Kober's *down at the station*, which had an ominous ring to it on TV and even more so in real life.

Who would hate Norbert enough to want to kill him?

Kober had heated words with him. She was also not burdened by a working relationship with the truth. But those kids of hers. Could a mother really kill someone? Of course a mother could kill someone, Dena thought. Especially if one of them were threatened in some way. It happened every day.

Hugo and Skyler walked through the cheese shop and waited as the security gate slowly lowered. They seemed surprised to see Dena in the armchair. "Is everything okay?" Skyler called.

Dena nodded and waved, staring at them as they headed along the promenade and toward the door.

"You're the last one here," Hugo called. "Don't forget to lock up before you go. I already checked both doors in the vendor room."

Dena assured them she would and watched them leave. What about the two of them?

Skyler had marched up those stairs earlier, all gung-ho to confront Norbert. But really? Was it even in the realm of possibility she'd kill him because he wouldn't validate her paint colors? That seemed pretty far-fetched. Dena felt a chuckle bubble up, but then it stopped in her throat. Maybe there was something she didn't know about Skyler's relationship with Norbert. Maybe what distressed Skyler went well beyond paint color and logo design.

Headlights swept the windows of the Marketplace. Dena wondered if Hugo and Skyler drove to work together every day. She knew they weren't dating, or even romantically involved, but wondered if that could be awkward. Working at the Marketplace, living in the same apartment building, and traveling to and fro was a lot of togetherness for two people who had only just recently met.

Dena checked the lock on the door Skyler and Hugo had exited, then walked the perimeter of the promenade checking the doors at the other three corners. Since Hugo was the only tenant on the west side of the building, they all typically used only the one door on the southeast corner, but with all the workmen trooping through, Dena felt better that they all agreed the last one to leave every night should check all the doors.

She wondered when the weather would be nice enough to walk to work. It felt indulgent to drive the short distance from her bungalow to the Marketplace, but not when the temperature dipped below zero like it had been lately. Then it was a necessity.

Sugar Springs wasn't a big town so commuting with

someone, even from the other side of town where Skyler and Hugo lived at the Village Apartments, wouldn't save but a few pennies in gas or wear-and-tear on a car.

Hugo hadn't mentioned he'd been having money troubles, but he had told them at the time, at some length, that Norbert cost him a ton of money when he wouldn't allow Hugo to use the sign he'd already bought and paid for above his shop. If Hugo was anything like the rest of the tenants, he was working on a thin profit margin where every penny counted.

Evelyn and Max, too. Norbert causing them all that effort because he was being a jerk and wouldn't sign for their backdrops? It had to be infuriating for them. It was clear there was no love lost between them and Norbert. And what was Balaam doing up there on the second floor? He usually stuck fairly close to Evelyn. Dena snorted in derision at herself. "I'm being ridiculous," she said with a firm shake of her head. How would people in their eighties get the drop on Norbert?

How would anyone get the drop on Norbert? And why? He wasn't the most popular guy, it was true, but killing him over any of these petty complaints seemed a bit extreme.

Dena simply couldn't come up with any logical answers. But maybe this wasn't logical at all.

She was alone in the promenade, but this was the first time she felt scared there.

Dena

WHEN DENA RETURNED HOME, she wasn't interested in leftover spaghetti or Netflix.

Ever since her jumbled thoughts about Kober and motherhood, Dena couldn't stop thinking about her own children, both fully-formed adults now.

But she still felt that protective mama bear angst when Charlee told her about those internet trolls, or that famous author who left her in the lurch, or those meanies who posted one-star reviews of her books. Dena felt her blood pressure rise like it did every time she heard Charlee laugh about silly reviews. Charlee may accept it as part of her job, but Charlee's *mother* certainly did not. She wanted to spank each and every one of them. Bringing down her daughter's rating simply because some dolt bought the wrong book, or decided they didn't like mysteries after all, or posted the inane "TLDR" absolutely infuriated Dena.

Or when Lance told her stories of the overlooked praise for an arrest he made, or how the public jumped to the wrong conclusions over body-cam footage, or when a girl he dated threw him over for a less taciturn man.

Dena wondered if her angst stemmed from guilt. She could have been a better mother. Should have been a better mother. She shouldn't have run away to Santa Fe after David's murder. She should have protected her kids from the fall-out of his undercover work, the lies, the innuendos, the veiled—and not-so veiled—accusations against him.

She had told herself at the time they were both old enough to move forward with their lives, Charlee finishing high school while living with her best friend's family, and Lance off to an early college admission. But the truth was, Dena had fallen completely apart and had lost all ability to take care of her children. She couldn't muster the strength or wherewithal to emerge from bed most days, much less make them a piece of toast for breakfast.

When she realized her kids were spending all their time taking care of her, she knew she had to go. She rallied the energy to make the calls that would propel Charlee and Lance into their bright futures without being dragged into Dena's dark abyss.

It shamed her now, but it was clearly for the best. She did what she had to do for her children who had, luckily, remarkably, thrived without her. They'd talked about it many times over the years, most recently when Charlee was in Santa Fe a few months ago for Thanksgiving. Neither Charlee nor Lance harbored any ill-will toward Dena and, in fact, mused that it truly was the best thing for everyone. They all came out the other side of that dark tunnel stronger and mostly unscathed.

Charlee had seemed to work through her issues after she'd been confronted with her agent's murder. The tremor she'd developed at her father's funeral disappeared when she learned the truth. And Lance was a good police officer, learning lessons from his father, some from beyond the grave.

Dena knew she had done what needed to be done at the time.

Was that what Kober had done too?

Her stomach gurgled and she knew she'd feel terrible tomorrow if she didn't eat at least a little something. Dena zapped the container of spaghetti in the microwave, then called Lance.

She wasn't sure what shift he was on these days, but the phone rang a few times before going to voice mail.

"Hey … just calling to say hey, so hey, and to make sure you know I love you more than monkeys." This was their private joke. When Lance was six or seven, he was obsessed with monkeys and apes of all kinds. That year for Mother's Day when he made her a card professing he loved her "more than monkeys," she was overwhelmed because it was, well, a lot of love.

Dena stirred the bowl of spaghetti and zapped it a bit longer. When it was the correct eatin' temperature, she sat down at the table with it and a fork and called Charlee.

"Hey, Bug. You busy?"

"Nope. What's up, Mom?"

"Nothing urgent. I was just thinking about you and Lance—"

"And how you want to give us a million dollars?"

"Hm. No."

"Okay, well, nice talking to you." Charlee laughed.

"Actually, I did want to talk to you about something. Since you have experience and all."

"Egads. Do I need to explain the birds and bees to you *again*?"

"Definitely not. I've sworn off dating. I thought you knew that."

"Then what? I can't think of anything I know that my mother wouldn't—oh! Books. Something about the bookstore?"

"Kinda. More about what happened at the bookstore."

"Sounds juicy."

"My landlord—remember Norbert Wallace?—well, he was … I think … maybe … murdered."

"In your bookstore? Mom, that's terrible!"

"Not actually in the store, but upstairs in that second-floor vendor room. Where all that storage stuff was?"

"I remember. What happened?"

Dena relayed the story to her daughter, not only what had happened, but her suspicions about all the other tenants, what the sheriff had said, and the potentially damaging newspaper article being written. "And now I find out there's a Sugar Mill Curse!"

Charlee let out a low whistle. "That's a lot. But what can I do?"

"Probably nothing. But you have some, uh, personal experience in this realm. I guess I was hoping for some words of wisdom. What should I do? I'm afraid if I do nothing, then perhaps we'll have a murderer as one of the tenants of the Marketplace, assuming the Marketplace could even survive that kind of bad press. But if I stick my nose in, what if I do something stupid and screw up the official investigation?"

Charlee was quiet for a moment. "When my agent was murdered, the police thought I did it. All I wanted to do was crawl under the covers. When Viv's daughter was kidnapped, I told her I wasn't going to get involved, but I'd take over her duties for the conference so she could deal with everything. But when Lapaglia threatened my career —such that it was at that point—something in me snapped. Of course, I stepped up in every one of those situations, but I finally realized I was so unlike the kickass female protagonists I wrote about in my books, and I started thinking about what they would do. Of course, I don't ride a Harley or wear leathers or carry all manner of weapons, but I can take the control I need to have agency over whatever situation I find myself in. It's not natural for me and it's never comfortable, but nobody is going to do it for me." She paused. "And nobody is going to do it for you."

Dena digested all of that. "So what do you think I should do?" she finally asked.

"I think you should go with your gut. Safely, of course," she added quickly. "What is your gut telling you to do?"

Dena pushed the bowl of spaghetti away. "First and foremost, it's telling me that eating leftover spaghetti at ten at night to somehow settle my stomach is a really bad idea. But I think it's also telling me that if I don't at least try to figure out what's going on around here, then I'll kick myself."

"Are the police doing their job?"

"I think so. Our sheriff is a slow-talking, methodical woman. This is the first time I've met her. She's not very old, but she clearly has something special to have risen through the ranks like she has. She's half the age of her deputy. He's the one who took all of our statements. But …" Dena trailed off without completing her thought.

"What?"

"I'm not sure they have the kind of experience they might need. I mean, this is Sugar Springs, for heaven's sake. Probably the first suspicious death they've had around here."

"But unless they've spent their entire careers here, maybe not the first suspicious death they've investigated."

"True." Dena thought about Deputy Chavez' relationship with Evelyn and Max. "Could be the deputy has always been here, but I don't think the sheriff has."

"Then she probably has some experience with possible murder investigations."

"Probably."

"Is it possible Norbert really did electrocute himself?"

Dena thought about this for so long that Charlee said, "Mom? You still there?"

"Yeah." Dena sighed. "I don't really know anymore. Everything is so twisted up in my brain. Of course, it could have been an accident, but with everyone around here acting so weird and with the scuttlebutt that Norbert was quite educated about electricity and wiring … well, it just really seems unlikely to me."

"That's your gut talking to you," Charlee said quietly. "It took me a long time to learn to listen to mine. Maybe you won't have such an internal battle with yours. You'll have to do whatever you can to get yourself and your friends off the hook—or on it, if that's how it will play out. And if your bookstore is on the line, you have to fight tooth and nail to keep it."

"If this was in one of your books, how would you write it?"

"First, I'd make you thirty years old, dress you in black leather and boots, then give you a frenemy who is a double agent in the CIA. Oh, and a sweet, self-reliant, and sassy kitty you come home to so I can show your humanity."

Dena thought about Balaam. "Ugh, a pet. No thanks. But I will take the time machine and the outfit."

Dena

AFTER NOT NEARLY ENOUGH SLEEP, Dena roused herself from bed the next morning. She ached all over for no discernible reason. She was almost positive she hadn't run a marathon, climbed a fourteener, or been hit by a city bus, but that's exactly how she felt.

She wondered if this was the aftereffect of a shock like they'd all had yesterday, the dissipation of the adrenaline that had coursed through her body. Hoping it could be remedied by a pot of coffee and some breakfast, she got busy in the kitchen.

Scrambled eggs, toast, and coffee seemed to do the trick and she felt almost human again.

While she cleaned up, she thought about what Charlee had said about trusting her gut and right then, between soaping and rinsing the skillet, she decided she would try to figure out what really happened to Norbert.

She'd start with the obvious and perhaps easiest—verifying whether or not he knew his way around electrical repairs.

After she showered and dressed, she went to the hardware store.

"Help you find something?"

Dena recognized him as the same person who had helped her when she needed brackets for her bookshelves. She'd never forget that majestic mustache.

"Actually, I'm looking for some information."

The man snapped his fingers. "You're the lady with the bookstore over at the Marketplace."

"That's right. Dena Russo."

"I'm Swede. This is my place."

He held out his hand and Dena took it. It was rough and meaty, the hand of someone who really worked for a living.

"Nice to officially meet you."

"Likewise." He cocked his head at her. "What kind of info are you searching for?"

"I'm wondering…" Suddenly Dena didn't know what to say.

Swede rested his backside against the front counter, crossing one cowboy boot over the other. "You're wondering how Norbert Wallace got himself electrocuted, I bet."

"Well, yes. How'd you know?"

"Because everyone and his great-aunt Penelope have been in here asking the same thing."

"And what have you been telling them?"

"I've been telling them they should mind their own beeswax, turn off the rumor mill, and let the police do their job."

Swede stared at Dena, but not in an unfriendly manner. She thought carefully about what she wanted to say next.

"Since I don't have a great-aunt Penelope, and it is kind of my beeswax, would you please indulge me?"

Swede let out a big guffaw. "I like you!" He glanced around his empty hardware store. "Not too busy. Care for a cup of coffee? Gotta warn you, though, I make it strong."

"Challenge accepted."

He led Dena to the back of the store where he unclasped a chain across the aisle. "Nobody's supposed to be back here but employees since this is where we cut lumber. But this is where the coffee pot is so ...."

"And this little chain keeps people out?" Dena refastened it across the aisle.

"Nah. But it makes my insurance company happy."

He pulled a ceramic mug with the John Deere logo from a shelf and blew sawdust out of it before filling it from a big forty-cup urn and handing it to Dena. He waved her to a rough-hewn table made from an old cable spool. A checkerboard had been painted on the top that had clearly seen thousands of games. She placed her mug on the table and sat on one of the folding chairs nearby.

Swede angled his chair so he could see the front of the store then sat across from her. He tipped his chin at her mug. "Not even gonna try it?"

"I am a little scared." Dena sniffed cautiously at the mug. When the aroma hit her, she wrinkled her nose.

Swede belly laughed. "I'll tell you what. If you drink that entire mug, I'll tell you whatever you want to know about Norbert."

"And if I don't?"

"Then I guess we'll both just have to go back to work."

"That doesn't sound like fun."

"No, ma'am, it doesn't."

Dena took a cautious sip. The coffee peeled a layer of

flesh from her tongue. And not because it was too hot. "Thaths thtrong coffee!" She took another tentative sip, losing another layer of her tongue. She looked Swede dead in his eye. "Delithouth. Never had better joe." Dena lifted her mug one more time, trying to keep her hand from shaking. Was the caffeine already coursing through her system?

Before she could sip, Swede took her cup from her. "You're killing me! You were really going to drink the whole thing?"

"Of courth. That wath our deal."

"The deal's off. You win. You've impressed me. Most people won't even try my coffee. And the regulars back here cut it in half with water. You'll have to come back on Saturday morning so I can show you off!" Swede dumped her coffee then filled her mug halfway with water from the tap and then topped it off with coffee from the urn.

She took a sip, then smiled. "Hey, thith ith really good."

"Let me get you something for that tongue." He came back with a frosted cinnamon roll as big as Dena's head and handed the plate to her.

"I don't know how thith will cure me, but I'm willing to give it a try." Dena took a big bite and swooned.

"Good, isn't it? That lady with the crazy hair came around giving away samples from her new bakery at the Marketplace."

Dena's mouth was full so she just nodded. She'd never had one of Kober's cinnamon rolls. And what a good marketing idea. When did she find the time?

Swede sipped his full-strength coffee.

Dena wondered how he wasn't bouncing off the walls.

"So," he finally said, handing Dena a paper towel.

"You want to know how in the world Norbert electrocuted himself."

She wiped her mouth. "There'th—" Dena tried again, concentrating on forming her words despite her tongue injury. "There … is … a lot of contradictory information floating around. It theemth … seems likely that Norbert was electrocuted. But people are saying he knew his way around electrical repairs. Of course, some of these people are looking to sell newspapers, so, you know, grain of salt."

Swede nodded. "That Capitano kid. Only met him once, but I know his grandparents, Henry and Wynona. They're good people."

"Why would they know anything about Norbert's skills?"

"Because Henry taught Norbert everything he knows."

———

Dena got directions to Henry and Wynona's house from Swede and parked in a circular driveway in front of a lovely old farmhouse with a wraparound porch. He'd phoned ahead so they were expecting her.

As they settled into chairs in the living room, Wynona offered Dena coffee.

Dena quickly waved her away, perhaps a bit hysterically, declining her offer.

"Did Swede force you to drink some of his sludge?" Henry asked with a laugh.

"He did. Said I got pretty far in, with three sips. I'm not sure when I'll grow back all those tastebuds, though."

"He tells me you want to know about Norbert. Shame what happened to him. What can I help you with?"

"Swede says you taught Norbert how to be an electrician."

"I did. I taught shop class at the high school for more than forty years."

"I thought you published the local paper?"

"Did both, with Wynona's help."

"I think half the construction workers between here and Grand Junction passed through Henry's classes," Wynona said.

Henry nodded. "Probably so. Taught all kinds of skills they don't teach anymore. And not just to kids. Taught farmers how to fix their machinery. Taught basic plumbing to homeowners so they could replace their own toilets and unclog their drains. Taught carpentry, electrical, car repair, and other skills to folks who lost their jobs and needed to train for a new one. They'd come for evening classes."

"Is that what Norbert did?"

"Norbert wanted to know everything about everything. Being in the construction business, he felt like he needed to know everything his sub-contractors knew to make sure—"

Dena said it with him. "They weren't cheating him."

"He couldn't stand the idea of being cheated."

"Tell her about the Elks convention, Henry," Wynona prompted.

Henry laughed. "Norbert and I were at an Elks convention in Denver once and were walking down this street they have there right downtown, where they block it off from cars."

"The Sixteenth Street Mall?" Dena guessed. She'd been there with Charlee and Lance before.

"That's the one. There were all these street performers and buskers and whatnot, and one of those find-the-ball-under-the-cup games where they move it around so fast and you're supposed to guess which cup has the ball. I told him it was a scam, but he insisted on figuring it out. Of course, he never did and was out twenty bucks in about half-a-flash. He stewed about that all weekend. And when we got back home, darned if he didn't teach himself how to perform that game. And I say perform because it was all sleight of hand." Henry smiled sadly at the memory. "He told me later he went back to Denver, found that guy, and turned the tables on him and got his money back, and more. That guy didn't know what hit him!"

"That's a side of Norbert I never would have imagined," Dena said.

"Oh, he was a character alright," Wynona said. "I didn't cotton to the way he spoke to women, though. He was what we used to call a male chauvinist pig. Never to me, though," she quickly added. "I don't want to speak ill of the dead." She made the sign of the cross.

Dena leaned toward Henry. "Do you think it's at all in the realm of possibility that Norbert Wallace did something wrong and got himself electrocuted?"

Henry took off his glasses and stared Dena dead in the eye. "I do not."

Dena

DENA PULLED around the circular driveway, thinking about Henry and that look on his face. She knew in the pit of her stomach—her gut, Charlee would say—that Norbert didn't have an accident up on the second floor of the Marketplace.

She didn't want to go to the Marketplace and she didn't want to go home. In either place her attention would be pulled in some other direction and she wanted to concentrate on this. She drove to River Park.

As she drove, she could only assume that Sheriff Johnson and Deputy Chavez were following the same train of thought, that Norbert didn't have an accident, having heard the same rumors from the same people that Dena had. She wanted to call and ask where their investigation was, but knew she couldn't. For one thing, they wouldn't tell her. For another, she herself was probably being investigated at this very moment.

A little shiver ran up her spine.

Knowing what she knew about police investigations from her husband and her son, Dena realized that a thorough murder investigation took time. Time she didn't really have if she wanted to solve this before the Grand Opening of the Marketplace, or before Cap and Aja could run a destructive article in the local paper.

Today was Tuesday. The *Sugar Springs Courier* came out on Thursday. Two days. What could she do in two days?

She pulled into a parking space at the edge of the park. In January on a frigid Tuesday she had the place to herself. She shut off her engine but didn't get out. She had a lovely view of the tumbling river and the pine and spruce forest on the other side. She knew there were aspen and cottonwood trees as well, but without their leaves, they were invisible to her this far away. She was looking forward to the spring and summer flowers that would bloom in the park, and knew the autumn view would be spectacular around Sugar Springs.

She took a deep breath. She could do plenty in two days if she went about it the right way.

First, she had to quit spinning her wheels and make a plan. Dena drummed her fingers on her steering wheel in an attempt to organize her brain. The sheriff's office would investigate all the tenants of the Marketplace, so she wouldn't duplicate that effort. Not right now, not unless she had to.

She'd concentrate on that guy, the intruder who came into her store. She kicked herself for not asking his name or getting any further information about him. Making a mental checklist, she focused on what she *did* know about him.

He had used Navy lingo—*shipshape, aye aye,* and *billet—* so maybe he'd been in the Navy. And he was old.

Perhaps he'd been to the VA Hospital recently.

She didn't really think they'd tell her anything, what with privacy laws and such, but you never knew who was going to answer the phone, right? She called the Denver VA Hospital and was not surprised at the brusque reception she received when she asked if they had any patients with a Sugar Springs address.

No harm, no foul. Nothing she didn't expect. She shook it off. Gotta play all the cards in your hand, right?

Dena did an internet search of veteran's organizations in the area of Sugar Springs and found a VFW post in Gunnison. She dialed the phone number listed but it rang and rang until the recorded message told her the hours when someone would probably be there. She checked her watch. At least a couple hours from now.

She dropped her phone to the center console of her car and returned to drumming her fingers on the steering wheel.

What else did she know about this man?

He had said something about schlepping the box of books "ten miles for nothing." Was that a figure of speech? After a bit, she started her ignition and headed back to the hardware store.

"You're back," Swede said. "Need some more coffee?"

Dena laughed. "No, I'm all set for caffeine. I need a good, fairly detailed map of this area."

Swede directed her to the maps he sold to tourists interested in camping, hiking, hunting, and fishing in the area. "It's not quite a town map and not quite a topographical map, but it shows all the trails and roads—private and forest service—as well as all the places for outdoor recreation of all kinds. I think they made it so tourists wouldn't accidentally end up recreating on private property."

She plucked one from the rack. It was titled "Outdoor Activities Map of the Greater Sugar Springs Area."

As she was walking to the cash register, another rack of maps caught her attention. "What are these?"

"Freebies from the real estate office in town. Doubt they're up to date since properties sell so fast around here."

Dena unfolded one and saw it included not just photos of properties, but a map with them all plotted on it. She paid for the outdoor activities map and took both out to her car, spreading them on her hood.

She studied them for a bit, shoved them up under her windshield wiper so they wouldn't blow away, then ran back into the hardware store.

"I need a ruler."

Swede pointed at a bucket of paint stirrers. They were all branded with the store info and along one side a ruler was printed. "Will that do the trick?" When Dena said yes he added, "Take as many as you need. Give them to your friends as gifts. You can see I have plenty. Don't know what I was thinking, ordering so many."

"You were thinking of ways to promote your business, something I should be doing more of. But just one of these will do. Thanks."

She checked the legend on the activities map and did some math. When she was reasonably happy with her calculations, she used the hardware store ruler to approximate a ten-mile radius from the edge of Sugar Springs. She hypothesized that if this mystery man really did schlep that box of books for ten miles, it would be on the Sugar Springs side of the river.

On her elbows, peering at the detail on the map, she could see both narrow hiking trails and what she assumed were paved roads, since they were wider. Perhaps they were gravel, but many were in the shape of suburban housing developments, although with much less density and spread out further. Some roads meandered in and around the topography.

Dena tried to match the area with the real estate map, but it wasn't an obvious fit. She opened a map program on her phone and tried to get the satellite view to match. That worked a bit better to give her a more detailed view, but she finally sighed and gave up.

Even if she had all the time in the world—which she didn't—there was no way she could cruise up and down all those roads, knocking on every cabin door. And for all she knew, this guy lived right in town.

She began to fold the maps, but got frustrated when they wouldn't return to their original creases and simply rolled them up and threw them on the back seat of her car.

Dena returned to the driver's seat and dialed the number for the VFW in Gunnison. Still no answer.

Some detective she was.

Kober

"SON OF A PURPLE PEARL!" Kober's eyes were crossing. If she had to proofread her menu one more time, she'd remove everything but brownies and cake. Why in the world did she think it was a good idea to include mille-feuille or anything with ganache?

She glanced at the time. The kids would be here any minute. Their first day back after winter break and it's cut short by a frozen water pipe. Why couldn't it have had the good sense to burst two weeks ago? Why would it wait until today when everyone was glad to have them back in school?

It wasn't that Kober didn't like having her kids around, quite the opposite, in fact. Everything she did, she did for them. Most of it she wanted to keep from them, however. They didn't need to be burdened with all the drama going on at home. She hoped they'd be burdened with math and grammar, not all the other stuff.

And now this.

She had managed to keep everything about Norbert quiet yesterday, but now with an early release, they'd be here at the Marketplace and would surely hear someone say something about it.

Kober groaned, suddenly missing the anonymity of living in Denver. Sugar Springs was a small town. There would have been chatter all over school today. She hoped her name hadn't come up. But who was she kidding? The odds were pretty high that some kid's Nosy Nellie mother would have seen her in the back of that squad car or doing the perp walk into or out of the sheriff's station.

She couldn't shelter her kids. Not from this. Not from any of it.

When Nic had moved them here from Denver almost three years ago now, it had been a bucolic, seamless transition. Nic kept his job in the city, but mostly worked at home. Kober had jumped at the chance to give up her job at the temp agency. While it had afforded her enough income to pay for extravagant long weekends for them in Telluride every so often, mostly it allowed her the luxury of a flexible schedule, so necessary when raising four kids.

But with the move to Sugar Springs, she was able to be a full-time, stay-at-home wife and mother, relishing both roles equally. She knew she projected an image of free-spirited, carefree worldliness, but deep down she was a homebody at heart. She loved nothing more than preparing full and hearty dinners—roast chicken, pot roast, lasagna—and greeting her children after school with mugs of cocoa and fresh-from-the-oven chocolate chip cookies.

That's actually where the idea for the bakery came from. Nic raved about the treats she created. Homemade bread dripping with honey butter. Flaky croissants. Crispy herb and cheese crackers. Lighter than air angel food cake. Braided babka. Sweet quick breads. Dense fruitcake. Bundt cakes with precise drizzles of glaze. Sheet cake frosted sky-high with buttercream. Every kind of cookie, pie, or tart you could think of, and some you couldn't. Nic and the kids loved them all. She baked whatever struck her fancy and indulged every one of her confectionary whims.

"You should open a bakery," he told her practically every day.

She'd brush off the suggestion, pooh-poohing the very idea. Until one day, after the kids were all tucked in, she and Nic shared a bottle of merlot. They were snuggled under an afghan in front of the fireplace. He looked directly into her eyes and said, "You should do it. I think you'd be really good at running a bakery. You've already mastered the art of wrangling me and the kids, maybe it's time for you to jump into a new challenge. The kids are getting older and don't need you as much and—"

"Don't say it."

"Don't say what?"

"Don't say I'm not getting any younger."

"I would never say such a thing." Nic sipped his wine. "But you're not."

Kober smacked him with a throw pillow from the couch.

He protected his head while she pummeled him with the pillow. When she finished, he said, "And neither am I. Neither one of us is getting any younger." He refilled her glass and handed it to her. "Is this really how you want to spend the rest of your life?"

"Drinking wine and beating you up? I could live with that."

"But do you *want* to?"

Kober had studied her husband's face for a long time, warm and rosy from the glow of the fire, and maybe a little bit from the wine. "You're really serious about this, aren't you?"

"I've been thinking about it for a long time. It would give you some financial security."

At the time it seemed an odd thing for him to say as he brought home a great salary, excellent health insurance, and they had a healthy investment portfolio.

At the time, she let it go.

At the time, she wasn't worried.

At the time, she'd been swept up into the thrill of a new adventure.

But now, she was up to her neck.

She didn't know everything, had proof of even less, but she did know one thing. She had to make sure nobody thought she was responsible for Norbert's death.

Kober went to the restroom. On her way back to the bakery, she tried the knob on Dena's back door, but it was locked. She wanted to feel out the situation with her, convince Dena that she had nothing to do with Norbert's death. Everything Kober had seen of Dena told her she was a reasonable woman. She'd listen to reason. That's what reasonable women did, right?

Kober simply had to show her she was a reasonable woman as well. How hard could that be?

Hugo walked into the vendor room to pick up something from the printer.

"You didn't hear what you think you heard, by the way," she said to him. If Dena wasn't around, maybe she could convince Hugo.

He didn't turn around, simply watched as papers slid out to the creaks and groans of the printer filling the tray. When the machine quieted, he jogged his stack of printouts and turned to Kober.

"I'm not deaf. I heard as plain as I heard you just now, even though for a change you aren't yelling at anyone. Among other things, you said clear as a bell, and I quote, *I will get out from under this lease if it's the last thing I do*, and *fix it before I fix you*, and *men are pigs*."

"They are … present company excluded, of course—"

"Of course."

"But I never said it."

Hugo stared at Kober. "You're trying to tell me you didn't say *any* of what I heard you say?"

"Oh, no. I said the other stuff. Just not men are pigs." Kober followed Hugo back into his chocolate shop.

Kober eyed the tray of truffles on the counter. Hugo nodded and she plucked one out. She chewed then licked her fingers. "You ever been married?"

"No. I'm not good with women."

"Geez, that's an understatement."

Hugo began to protest, then abandoned it with a forlorn little shrug.

They heard a commotion which startled Hugo. Kober took the opportunity to pluck out another truffle. "Just my kids."

"I'm not good with those either," he said as Kober hurried back to the bakery.

The twins burst from the back door of the bakery into the vendor room. Kober braced herself as they flung themselves into her arms.

"Mom!"

"Mom!"

"They cancelled school—"

"Because a pipe burst—"

"Totally flooded the cafeteria!"

"It was so cool. Like a lake in there!"

Kober bounced her attention from Leo to Lincoln as they reported the dramatic goings-on at school today. Having ten-year-old twins meant listening to stories in stereo. She hugged them tight, then took a knee in front of them. "That sounds super-duper boffo!"

The boys squirmed away.

"But they wouldn't let us go in."

"We were gonna help pick up all the floating lunch trays—"

"But they said we'd get hoof-and-mouth disease."

"Actually," Jain corrected from behind them, "they said nothing of the kind."

"But hoof-and-mouth disease sounds so cool! Leo, wanna play?" Lincoln pointed at the ping pong table and they jumped across everything in their path.

"Hey! I've told you a bajillion times," Kober shouted. "I don't give a fat Daffy Duck what kind of hurry you're in. No parkour in here!" She turned to Jain and Wyatt and hugged them both. "So, no hoof-and-mouth disease for the Bertoletti kids? What a flaming disappointment."

"Right?" Wyatt said. "It wasn't nearly as interesting as the kids made it sound."

Kober knew that because Wyatt was twelve, he wanted to distinguish himself from his younger brothers.

"No?"

"Nah. Just some squishy carpet. They say we can come back tomorrow."

"Thank goodness. I've had about all I can stand of you lot." Kober grinned.

"We know, Mom. You're a martyr. A tribute to humanity. A mothering fool." Jain said it with a practiced monotone.

"Smothering fool, you mean," Wyatt said, pretending to duck from an anticipated smack from his smother.

Kober laughed. "I baked brownies if you want some."

Jain grinned. "You got the oven to work?"

"Almost. It got halfway before fizzing out. Had to take the pan home and finish them there."

"Mom. You can't keep doing that," Jain said sternly. "Did you call the oven company?"

"Of course I did." Kober couldn't keep the indignation out of her voice.

Jain leveled a gaze at her. "Did you yell or did you talk?"

Kober's indignation melted away at her daughter's precise understanding of the situation.

Jain and Wyatt exchanged a look Kober had seen too many times lately. It was a look that said *sometimes it seems like we're the parents*.

Indicating Kober's phone, Jain held out her hand until her mother surrendered it.

Wyatt wandered over to watch the twins play ping pong. Kober wandered off to get the brownies.

Jain found the number she was looking for in Kober's call history and followed her mother into the bakery. "Yes, hello. I am representing the Sugar Springs Bakery in Sugar Springs, Colorado … That's right … She's standing right here. It seems she's having trouble making your company understand the seriousness of her predicament. In case you weren't aware, the problem with your oven may have been instrumental in getting a man killed … Yes, I will hold for the CEO's office."

Kober almost dropped the plate of brownies she held.

Jain mouthed, "I'm amazing."

Jain explained the pertinent details—as she knew them, the real ones and the ones she invented—to the nice lady in the CEO's office who promised to pick up the old oven and deliver a new one tomorrow. "That would be marvelous," Jain said. "And bring an electrician with you so that we're assured this time that everything works and is hooked up properly … Tomorrow afternoon would be perfect. Thank you so much. You've been quite helpful."

"And that," Jain handed the phone back to her mother, "is how it's done." She plucked a brownie from her mother's plate and took a big bite.

"You really are amazing. Hard to believe you're only fourteen."

Jain narrowed her eyes. "I'm actually sixteen." When her mother feigned surprise Jain knew she'd been teasing.

"Seriously, though. How'd you do that?" Kober asked.

"I didn't yell at the poor sad wretch who answered the phone." Jain finished her brownie and watched Kober mull over the concept.

"So simple, yet so hard," Kober said with a rueful shake of her head.

"You should try it sometime. You'll catch more flies with honey, or so I hear."

"I've never understood why anyone wants to catch flies. I use a swatter on them."

"You use a swatter on everyone," Jain said wryly. Her face turned serious. "Especially Dad."

If Kober hadn't been leaning against the table, she might have wobbled. Instead, she was able to continue keeping her cracks from showing. "Don't be silly. If I was mad at your dad, I'd use much more than a fly swatter." She screeched to the boys in the vendor room. "Brownies!" After they descended on the plate like a scourge of weevils in a cotton field and returned to their game, Kober turned back to Jain.

"What were they saying about Norbert Wallace at school today? Did you hear anything about … me?" Kober wasn't sure she truly wanted to know the answer.

Jain bit her lip and couldn't look Kober in the face.

"Just tell me."

"They said he died upstairs and you were in the back of the squad car." Jain looked up. "Is that true?"

Kober nodded. "Did the boys hear too?"

"Only Wyatt."

"Here's what happened. Norbert probably electrocuted himself upstairs, but because I was … yelling—" At the look on Jain's face, Kober said, "I know! But I was angry and upset, and everyone took it the wrong way. Besides, every single person here had an axe to grind with Norbert. I just happened to be the unlucky one they wanted to talk to at the station. Everyone else had their statement taken here."

"Who were you yelling at?"

"I'd rather not say." As an afterthought she added, "But it wasn't Norbert."

Jain didn't look convinced, but let it go.

Kober changed the subject. "Seriously, thank you for calling the oven place. I forget how awesome you are sometimes. I've been under so much pressure, trying to get this bakery going, I think I've been neglecting you."

"So what else is new?" Jain snagged the last brownie on the plate Kober had protected for her daughter and darted away as Kober pretended to swat her.

She tried not to, but Kober couldn't help but get misty watching her kids. What would happen to them? They were truly the loves of her life. They knew better than most that her bark was much worse than her bite. In fact, they might have been the only ones to know that little tidbit about her.

Certainly her husband hadn't realized. Perhaps because her bite was a tad more lethal around him. For good reason. Men are pigs.

Skyler

SKYLER WAS STILL REELING from Hugo's accusation that she had killed Norbert. Maybe not technically an accusation, but his question was darn close. Too close.

How dare he!

She balled her fists to try to get her hands to keep from trembling, but it didn't seem to help.

If Hugo thought she had something to do with Norbert's death, then what must the other tenants think?

Skyler pressed one of her balled fists to her lips. What if he talked to Sheriff Johnson about her? What if he talked to those reporters? One would be just as troublesome as the other.

If only she hadn't seen Norbert go upstairs.

If only she hadn't followed him.

If only she hadn't talked to Dena.

If only Norbert had returned her calls.

Evelyn walked into the cheese shop and interrupted her conversation with Hugo. It was just as well, it seemed he'd already made up his mind about her. Skyler stepped away from Hugo. "Of course I can help you, Evelyn. I'd be happy to."

Evelyn

THINGS WITH MAX had been tense ever since she told him his photographs were subpar. He was angry and, for the first time in their life together, she was scared, not conducive to household harmony. When she got out of the shower, he was already gone. Neither had said good morning.

Evelyn was surprised when she didn't see him at the Marketplace. She figured he had walked over to avoid uncomfortable small talk instead of spending time dancing around their quarrel. After all these years of harmony, they never really figured out how to argue very well.

She had hoped she'd find him here practicing with the equipment. No such luck. She opened up the studio and turned on the lights without him.

With only ten days to go before their Grand Opening, Evelyn knew what she needed to do. She was scared but also a bit curious and exhilarated about what it all might mean.

She walked into the vendor room. Kober's three boys were playing a rousing game of ping pong and she admired their exuberance. Jain slouched against the wall, absorbed in a book.

"Kids, I need you," she said. When they didn't respond she raised her voice a bit and repeated herself.

The boys immediately set down their paddles, Lincoln —or was it Leo?—trapping the ball underneath his.

"Yes, Mrs Milligan?"

"Would you dress up in some of the clothes in my shop so I can practice taking pictures of you?"

"Oh boy!" one of the twins said.

The other said, "I want to be a pirate!"

"I want to be a cowboy!"

"Tell you what," Evelyn said. "We'll do both. I need practice with the props too."

The twins and Wyatt ran through the back door into the photography studio.

"Do you want me too?" Jain asked shyly from where she sat on the floor.

"You're the linchpin to the entire operation, my dear!"

Jain smiled and followed her brothers into the studio.

Kober hurried into the vendor room, wiping her hands on a towel that she then slapped over one shoulder. "Are they bothering you, Evelyn?" Before Evelyn could answer, Kober raised her voice to a shout. "I told you kids not to bother everyo—" She glanced around. "Where are they?"

Evelyn twitched her head toward her own door. "In there. They're going to help me practice. Are you busy? The more, the merrier, you know."

"With my kids, it's really just the more, the more."

Evelyn laughed. "Your kids are wonderful. You've done a good job with them."

Kober's face softened. "Thank you for saying that. I know it seems like I bust their chops a lot, but it's all just a game. They are a constant delight. My pride and joy."

"Constant delight?" Evelyn clarified with a wink.

"Oh, that's right. You have kids. You know it's constant, but not always a delight, no matter how much parents lie."

"Kid. Max and I just had the one. I don't know how you do it with four."

"I don't either," Kober said with a melodramatic hand over her brow. "Let me figure out the problem with my snickerdoodle recipe and I'll be right over. I love playing dress-up. The kids and I used to do it all the time." She scurried back to the bakery.

Evelyn stuck her head in the back door of the bookstore. "Dena? You here?"

A muffled voice called out, but Evelyn couldn't make out the words and it worried her, especially after what Dena had told them about the intruder who showed up miffed that she wouldn't buy his box of books from him.

She stepped through. "Dena? Dena, are you okay?" She heard a loud thud near the corner of the store and then more muffled noise. Evelyn glanced behind her, conscious she might be heading into trouble, but didn't want to alarm Kober or the children. Evelyn hurried alone toward the sound.

She reached the corner and saw books strewn across the aisle. Evelyn stopped, then cautiously crept forward. She searched for a weapon she could use, but only saw books. She armed herself with the biggest one within reach, an illustrated hardcover copy of Charles Dickens' *Bleak House*.

Evelyn tried to peek through the shelves, but the books were packed tight. It was obvious there was a scuffle going on back there, just out of sight. She glanced at the book in her hand and wondered if she should run back to the bakery and fetch Kober. But if Dena was in trouble, by the time they returned, whoever it was could be long gone out the front door of the bookshop. Evelyn gripped the book tighter. Maybe Norbert's killer had returned. Evelyn's sensible shoes propelled her forward and she knew the element of surprise was on her side.

When she reached the corner, she let out a loud war cry, raising the book above her head and rushing forward.

Dena sprawled on the floor, books strewn about. "Evelyn, geez! You scared me to death!"

"What happened? Who did this to you?" Evelyn dropped *Bleak House* and reached for Dena to help her up.

"My worst enemy."

Evelyn glanced around, alarmed.

"Me," Dena explained. "I'm my worst enemy." Evelyn's pale face and shaky hands made Dena realize Evelyn was truly frightened. "My gosh, Evelyn, what did you think was going on?" Dena struggled to her feet, kicking away the books in her way.

Evelyn slumped against the shelf to catch her breath. "I don't know what I thought, but with Norbert and that man ..." She trailed off and Dena pulled her into a quick hug.

"Everything's fine. I was just putting these books away when the bottom dropped out of the box. I lost my balance, grabbed for the shelf and knocked off more books. I'm okay, just frazzled."

"Oh, thank goodness." Evelyn picked up *Bleak House* and brushed it off. The book she'd chosen finally registered with her and she gave a little shiver. "Isn't this the book they think began the detective fiction genre? How appropriate. How Dickensian."

"How expensive." Dena took it from her. "Wait. You thought Norbert's killer was back here attacking me?"

"That's just where my brain went."

"So, you must not think I killed Norbert." Using her foot, Dena pushed books out of Evelyn's way and guided her back to the center of the shop.

"I have no idea what happened to Norbert. I don't wish anyone ill will, but I'm pretty sure the world is better off without him in it."

Dena nodded. "He wasn't a likable guy, was he?"

"No, but I'm not here to talk about Norbert."

"What can I do for you?"

"Come play dress up with us."

"Dress up?"

Evelyn explained the plan to Dena who readily accepted. "Anything is more fun than getting clobbered by unruly boxes of gothic mysteries."

Dena led the way to Evelyn's studio. Evelyn, however, detoured into Really Grate Cheese.

She walked in and saw Skyler and Hugo standing very close together. They quit whispering as soon as they saw her, and Skyler took one giant step away from Hugo. "You two look as thick as thieves," Evelyn said. "What are you conspiring about?"

"Nothing," they both said, much too quickly.

Their discombobulation tickled Evelyn. Young love was adorable. "You're not fooling me, but if you're not too busy plotting some secret tryst or … whatever, I'd appreciate your help in the studio."

Balaam appeared at Evelyn's feet which he'd been doing whenever Evelyn went near Skyler or the cheese shop. He really loved that feta, thank goodness. She picked him up, but Balaam looked longingly over his shoulder at Skyler's cheese case. "Cool it," Evelyn whispered.

When everyone had gathered in her studio, Evelyn said, "I need practice taking pictures and knowing where to put the props for each scenario and which backdrop goes with which setting. Everyone who comes in here will want different costumes and will have different numbers of people in their group. With the eight of you, I should be able to get a zillion different contingencies to figure out how to get customers in and out quickly."

Dena said, "Maybe you can use them as examples, or promotional pieces."

"That's an excellent idea! If I get any good ones, that is."

The boys had decided on the Old West scene first and were already in the cowboy outfits.

Evelyn patted herself on the back once again at how clever she and Max were in their hunt for period clothing and costumes that could be arranged over tourists' regular clothes. The chaps, the Velcro, the spats. The bonnets and cowboy hats that could camouflage a wide variety of hairstyles. Except maybe Kober's.

Evelyn peeked at each hanging backdrop until she found the Old West parlor scene. Waving away any offered help, she pushed easily rolled props into place while everyone giggled their way through costuming. As they were ready, they all migrated toward the props and chose spots. Evelyn placed the women in the chairs and settees and had Hugo and the boys stand nearby.

Hugo was already wearing jeans under his chaps and boots so she had him place one foot on a bale of hay with his long gun prominently displayed. The boys were so cute in their hats and dusters she wanted them prominently displayed as well. She steered the twins in front of Hugo, Wyatt on the other side of the women. They all had rifles, as if Black Bart was in town and they had to protect the womenfolk.

When Evelyn mentioned this, Jain said, "That's so old school, Evelyn. I can protect myself." She jumped up and grabbed a rifle before returning to her velvet settee. She smoothed her skirt and placed the gun across her lap.

"But Jain, dear, that didn't happen back then."

"It must have," Jain said. "Men weren't always around to protect their families."

"She's got a point, Evelyn," Dena said.

Skyler and Kober both nodded.

"You win!" Evelyn said. "And thank you, Jain, for pointing this out to me. I guess it's not my job to tell anyone what character they should be. If a woman wants to be a gun-totin' varmint or a man wants to be a conscientious objector, then they should."

"And there's a boy in my class who got his parts all switched around before he was born so he came out as a girl, but he's really a boy. There's no way he'd want to wear a dress." Wyatt glanced around at the adults staring at him. "What?"

"You have given me much to think about, children. Now let's take some pictures!"

Everyone settled into their poses, the boys trying extra hard not to smile because they were supposed to be tough hombres. Evelyn took tons of photos with all of them in all different configurations, moving props around as she envisioned the shot.

She ended with a photo of just Skyler and Hugo on the velvet settee together. "That's going to be a keeper!"

They both blushed and hurried to opposite sides of the room. Evelyn found that adorable but refrained from telling them so.

Everyone recast themselves from the Old West scene to a pirate ship, but this time all the women dressed as pirates, and Hugo and the boys dressed as wenches. After much laughter and a hundred more photos, Evelyn shut down the photo shoot so she could next practice editing and printing the photos. "I feel like I have to do this step fairly quickly because people wouldn't want to wait too long."

"But if they have to hang out for a while, that would be great for the rest of us," Dena pointed out. "They could browse the bookstore, or get cheese, chocolate, or cupcakes."

"Or all of the above," Hugo said.

"That's a great idea," Skyler said. "Maybe I could design some coupons just for your customers so while they wait, they have incentive to visit our shops."

"No matter how little time it takes you, Evelyn, make sure to tell them it takes you an hour, sometimes more, if there are lots of them," Kober said. When she saw everyone looking at her, she added, "Oh, relax. It's just a white lie."

"Speaking of white lies…"

Everyone turned toward Max who had come in the front of the studio.

Evelyn held her breath, wondering how he'd react to her moving forward without him.

He eyeballed the gender-swapping pirates and wenches. "What's going on in here?" he grumbled.

Evelyn couldn't tell if that was his normal grumble or not. She hated that she couldn't tell.

The boys tripped over their words, each trying to explain. Lincoln, or Leo, asked Max, "Do you want to dress up too?"

"Leave me out of it." Max waved away the pirate hat the boy offered.

When the boys realized dress-up time was over, they handed their costumes to Evelyn then ran out of the studio.

"What white lies were you talking about when you came in?" Dena asked after they had gone.

"They were talking at the barbershop about Norbert. Apparently, Norbert's car was found across town with the keys still in it," Max said.

"What's the big deal about that?" Skyler asked.

Dena caught Kober's eye and made a small gesture toward Jain.

"It's okay." Kober placed an arm around Jain's shoulder. "She knows about Norbert."

"The big deal is that I think Norbert was still upstairs after his car was already gone," Dena said with a frown.

"Why do you think that?" Skyler said suspiciously.

Dena explained again about seeing Norbert drive up the morning he was killed, then his car being gone, but he wasn't at his office.

"He obviously had another appointment somewhere else," Max said. "No mystery there. But a lie nonetheless, whether intentional or not."

"I know what I know," Dena insisted.

"Why would he be over walking at the park, though?" Jain asked. "It's freezing out and he's old—"

"Ahem," Evelyn warned.

"He was … way older than me, and I wouldn't want to go for a walk in the park," Jain said.

"What makes you think he was walking in the park?" Kober asked her daughter.

Jain held up her phone. "That's what this online article says."

"Oh no!" Dena said.

"Son of a sticky bun!"

Skyler grabbed for Hugo's arm to steady herself. "This is exactly what we didn't want to happen! This will be terrible for the Grand Opening."

Evelyn began to hang up the boys' costumes, thankful

she could turn her back on her fellow tenants. She tried to keep her hands from shaking. "Read it to us, dear."

———

ANOTHER SUGAR MILL CURSE?
By Aja Capitano

Sugar Springs, Colorado is widely known for its historical and deadly curse. Numerous people have succumbed to the eerie and often unexplained mysteries surrounding the sugar mill throughout its years in operation, and now, at the inception of its transformation into the shops and restaurants of the Sugar Mill Marketplace.

Reports of bodies found in vats of pulp, horses gone mad, mill employees gone missing, disappearing from thin air. All of these, and presumably more, a small part of the Sugar Mill Curse.

And now, Norbert Wallace, esteemed local property developer, found dead in the unused second floor of the Marketplace, under unusual and cryptic circumstances. His car, a 2019 Infiniti Q50 in factory color Graphite Shadow, however, was found parked, with the keys still in the ignition, in front of River Park.

When asked for a statement, Sheriff Keisha Johnson would only verify that they were "investigating the sudden death of Norbert Wallace" and that Wallace's car had been towed from the park in the dead of night.

Deputy Vincent Chavez would only give a terse, "No comment," and referred us back to the sheriff.

This reporter wants to know why this murder investigation is so hush-hush. Why is there no transparency from the sheriff's office? Why do they refuse to acknowledge the Sugar Mill Curse? Why was Wallace's vehicle located at River Park instead of the Sugar Mill Marketplace where his crushed and broken body gasped its final breath?

None of the tenants of the soon-to-be-opened Sugar Mill

Marketplace offered any insights on the record, preferring to keep the facts out of public view.

The staff of the Sugar Springs Courier, however, will continue to dig for the facts of this case, to bring them to you, the readers, who deserve to know if the Sugar Mill Curse has reared its ugly head again.

Kober

AFTER JAIN FINISHED READING the article from her phone, it seemed as if the air had been sucked from the Marketplace. All the fun and frivolity of the last couple of hours disappeared in an instant. Like it never happened.

The article was so full of inaccuracies and innuendo, nobody knew where to begin to pick it apart for comment. Almost everyone began to speak, then simply shook their head, at a loss for what to say about it.

They all agreed, however, that it was catastrophic for the Marketplace and by extension, for all of them.

Kober bit her tongue. An *I told you so* would not be welcome at this moment. Nor would it be helpful.

As everyone drifted from the photography studio, Kober corralled Dena, gripping her bicep. "Listen. I feel like I should clear things up with you."

Dena took a step backward and Kober realized she was being a bit aggressive. She let go of Dena's arm. That wasn't the way she wanted to project herself right now. She had told all the tenants that if an article was published it would be awful for them, their businesses, and the Grand

Opening. She knew it immediately after Norbert's body was discovered. The others might not have believed her at the time, but they certainly believed it now. But they had to keep up. Kober was three steps ahead of them.

Kober spoke softer and made sure to give Dena her space. "Now that the article has been published—and it's worse than I expected—I think we all need to buckle down and get to the bottom of all this. I feel like I should tell you that Hugo didn't know what he was talking about when he said those things about me. And I think you might have jumped to the wrong conclusion too. I didn't have anything to do with Norbert's death."

Dena let out a breath she'd been holding. "I saw you at the bottom of the stairs all out of breath just before I found Norbert up there."

"Yes, you did."

"What was I supposed to think?"

"That I just finished a cardio workout?"

Dena's face registered she didn't appreciate the levity.

"Can't you just believe me when I say I didn't do anything and leave it at that?"

"Kober, you tell lies the way fish swim. I don't even think you realize it."

"I don't *tell lies*," Kober said firmly. "I say what needs to be said based on the situation."

"I fail to see the difference."

"Clearly," Kober said miserably. "Will you at least think about it? You have to know that I couldn't possibly have done anything to Norbert."

Dena stared at her for a long time. "I'll think about it."

"That's all I can ask."

Kober watched her disappear into the bookstore.

Now to convince the rest of them.

Balaam

BALAAM USED his front paw to rub the pirate's eye patch off his face. He hopped down from the gangplank he'd been posing on and ambled through the studio listening as the girl recited from that black thing always in her hand. It must be important. They're all staring at her like it's an open can of tuna.

He took the opportunity to hiss at everyone individually and then collectively before leaving.

Balaam had a moment of alarm when one of the little boys acted like he might pet him, or worse, pick him up. Balaam explained to him precisely why that wouldn't be happening, and the boy stepped away, finally seeing it his way. An intelligent lad, it seemed.

Balaam padded silently away from them, since the girl apparently did not have an open can of tuna in her hand, making his way into the cheese shop next door. He'd never do anything as crass as jump on a table or countertop like some barbarian, but cheese had been known to fall on the floor and it would be rude of him not to help clean it up.

Balaam sniffed and prowled all around but found nothing. That woman was as neat as she was neurotic. He remembered sneaking in the cheese shop one day while she kept repeating, "You have to try a new food seven times before you like it." He had walked around, trying to ascertain to whom she might be talking, but there was no one there with her.

It seemed bizarre to Balaam because, even though he only truly enjoyed his own company—and on rare occasions, that of Evelyn—he rarely talked to himself.

Balaam remembered that was also the day Evelyn slipped him those bites of cheese, *feta* they had called them. It made an impression in his memory not only because of the delectable taste, but because it would be an excellent name for a cat. Rolled right off the tongue. Perhaps one day I will sire offspring and could christen one of them Feta.

Balaam made another search of the cheese shop, slower and more thoroughly this time, but remained disappointed. His swished his tail in resignation before heading to the bakery, which he knew would be a treasure trove of treats.

Again, never on counters or tables, as if he had no manners, but today was his lucky day. Crumbs everywhere, and even half an eggshell he happily slurped clean, never breaking the shell. The loud woman must have dropped it and couldn't find it, so he left it in the center of the floor where she'd find it when she came to tidy up. Assuming she came to tidy up.

He found a splotch of thick whipped cream traveling down the cabinet and was relieved it wasn't up higher. He didn't want to have to solve some philosophical conundrum about whether standing up against a cabinet was venturing too near barbarian territory or not. It was bad enough he had never figured out that theory Schrödinger and his cat had devised, he didn't need to add a definition of "climbing on the counters" to his lengthy list of what thinking folk considered poor behavior.

A chocolate chip caught his eye, but he knew enough to let it be. Humans always say curiosity killed the cat, but Balaam knew it was chocolate.

Balaam heard noise in the vendor room and realized everyone was on the move. He didn't want to be cornered by those kids when he was in the bakery, so he slipped back to the cheese shop.

The neurotic woman wasn't likely to drop any cheese any time soon because she was just sitting on her stool staring into space.

Balaam tried his luck at the chocolate shop because sometimes there was pumpkin or blueberries within reach. He stared for long hours at the man in the white jacket while he in turn stared for long hours at the neurotic woman. Balaam couldn't understand why he was the only one who noticed.

Come to think of it, he was also the only one who noticed wayward pumpkin, blueberries, and eggshells. Maybe it wasn't such a mystery.

He slipped into the photography studio knowing there would be a scoop of kibble, but only at the proper time. He nosed the empty bowl. Nope, not the proper time. Although, with the charged atmosphere between Evelyn and Max, perhaps they forgot about his kibble and would find him collapsed in a heap, dead of starvation.

Balaam's ears pressed back against his head when he remembered how he'd been locked upstairs during the Ugliness, as he'd come to think of it.

The vitriolic voices. The fury crackling in the air. The crash. The sparks. The whiff of smoke.

All he'd wanted was a snack from a friendly face.

Dena

DENA LEFT KOBER, promising to think about what she'd said, which was easy because her head was spinning. It was all she could think about. Kober's claims of innocence muddled up with that absurd article Aja had written. Aja's journalism mentors would be appalled if they read that jumble of nonsense and Dena had half a mind to track them down and show them exactly what Aja had done to their profession.

But first, she had to figure out exactly what this article had done to *her* profession.

Sadly, Dena glanced around her bookstore. It was finally shaping up into something everyone could recognize as a bookstore, but it seemed nobody would even get the chance to see it.

Dena plopped on the tall stool she kept behind the front counter. She stared across the room with unfocused eyes. Did she really think Kober—or any Marketplace tenant—was guilty? She unspooled the entirety of the last couple days, from seeing Norbert's car pull into a parking place all the way to Kober getting in her face to profess her innocence.

She'd forgotten something, though. She should have spooled back to when that man came into the bookstore.

Dena picked up her phone and called the VFW in Gunnison again. Someone answered on the second ring.

"Oh, thank goodness!"

A man chuckled on the other end of the line. "I don't usually elicit such a reaction from the ladies."

"I'm sorry, it's just that I've been calling and never seem to catch anyone there."

"Don't take it personally. We come, we go, we don't always care about phone calls. Especially if we're eating or have a speaker or something. Not that you've caught me, what can I do for you?"

Dena didn't quite know where to begin, so she started with the obvious. "I'm looking for someone."

"I'm someone."

"I think the someone I'm looking for was in the Navy, probably quite a long time ago, since he seems pretty old. Loud voice, doesn't seem to shave very often. Not a very big guy, despite his voice. Perhaps a book collector or just an avid reader."

"Sounds like O'Dell."

"Seriously?" Dena was gobsmacked that her vague description might actually elicit results.

"Comes in here every so often. Haven't seen him in a while. Thought he moved on. I heard he had some trouble."

Before Dena could ask what kind of trouble, the man had shouted to others at the VFW hall. "Hey, any of you heard from O'Dell recently?"

She heard muffled voices then the man came back on the phone. "Nobody has seen him for at least a few months. He was here for the parade in July. That's the last anyone remembers."

"What's his first name?"

Again the man shouted to his cronies. "Nobody knows. Around here we use last names mostly." Dena could picture his shrug through the phone.

"What about an address? Does anyone know where he lives?"

After further muffled conversation at the VFW, he told her, "Nope. Doesn't seem so."

Dena sighed.

"O'Dell in some kind of trouble? Why are you looking for him?"

"I own a bookstore in Sugar Springs and he came in to sell me some books. I'm having second thoughts about not talking to him more."

"Strike while the iron is hot, I always say. Good luck in your search. If he shows up, I'll tell him you're looking for him."

"Thanks."

Dena disconnected and immediately typed "o'dell navy colorado" in her internet search bar. She scrolled through pages and pages of results, most related to the Odell Brewery in Fort Collins, but an equal share of obituaries and active-duty sailors winning awards or performing other newsworthy events.

She jumped at the sound of Evelyn's voice. "You look like you just lost your winning lottery ticket."

"Kinda. Remember that guy I told you about in my store yesterday morning?"

"That intruder who scared you?"

Dena nodded. "I thought I found him. Tracked him to the VFW in Gunnison, but that's a dead end. I think it's the same guy. They called him O'Dell and said he was in the Navy, but they didn't know his first name or where he lives or anything so I'm back at square one."

"That must be frustrating, dear. But maybe it's for the better if you don't find him. He sounds like trouble."

"Maybe, but he also sounds like someone Sheriff Johnson should talk to. I thought if I could do some of the leg work, they could do the important stuff and figure out if he has any involvement in Norbert's death."

Evelyn's hand waved up to her throat. "Do you think he really does?"

"Honestly? I have no idea. He may just be some guy trying to sell some old books. I don't really want to sic the police on him for something he may have nothing to do with. I mean, he's pretty old, seemed kind of frail to me."

Evelyn nodded. "I'll ask around if you want."

"Yeah, that would be great."

"But you be careful."

"I will." Dena smiled. It was nice to have someone worry about her, even just a little. "But that's probably not why you came in here. What can I help you with?"

"I was wondering if you had any books about photography around here."

Dena slid off her stool. "You're in luck. I just unloaded half a box a couple days ago." She led Evelyn to the section where she'd shelved them and waved her arm. "Go nuts."

Evelyn started investigating the books and Dena went back to her internet search for O'Dell the Navy man. Her screen had gone dark. When she woke it up again, her business page for the bookstore showed a bunch of Face-Plant notifications. "This is why I didn't want to mess with social media," she grumbled.

She jabbed at the app and immediately wished she hadn't. A flood of comments screamed at her from the

Thrice Sold Tales page. When she clicked to see what they were commenting on, she saw Aja's article with her name and the name of her bookstore tagged, along with all the other tenants of the Marketplace.

She groaned.

Evelyn called, "What's that, dear? Did you say something?"

Dena went to show her.

Evelyn let out a groan that matched Dena's.

Dena started to read the comments but quickly realized that would only cause misery and frustration. She turned off her phone.

"Evelyn, what's all this about the Sugar Mill Curse? Have you heard of it?"

She wrinkled her nose in distaste. "It's a bunch of hooey. I used to work there, you know, when the sugar mill was in operation."

"Oh, that's right. You told me that. What's it all about then?"

"Just small-town stuff. Since nothing ever happens here, people have always felt the need to make Sugar Springs more interesting. That's what those so-called reporters are doing too." Evelyn pulled a tissue from her sleeve and dabbed at her nose. "I still need to give Henry and Wynona a piece of my mind, letting those kids ruin our newspaper like that. The *Courier* is their legacy!"

"What about the curse?" Dena asked gently.

"Hooey, like I said."

Dena woke her phone and clicked on the article to refresh her memory. "Aja said something about a vat of pulp, horses gone mad, and employees who mysteriously disappeared. What's that about?"

"The body found in the vat was a guy who had too much hooch and fell in. They didn't find him until the next day. No mystery there. Whole town knew he was a drunk. He almost drowned in a stock tank the week before that. And his own bathtub the week before *that*."

"And the horses?"

"Just a runaway team. Spooked by a rattlesnake nest."

"And the disappearing employees?"

"They just went home. Processing sugar beets is hard work. Some couldn't cut it and just moved along, looking for easier work. We got plenty of itinerant workers and freight-hoppers through here back in the day, looking for honest work. Like I said, most of them just took off if they couldn't take it, but there were a thousand ways migrant could die. Men got crushed by shifting loads, or crushed between cars, or fell off the rails underneath. Maybe they worked for a day or two, so they were classified as employees of the mill, but many just stayed long enough to earn enough for a hot meal or a new pair of shoes and then they were on their way again. It was sad, but not supernatural like some *curse* makes it sound."

Evelyn went back to the photography section and Dena went back to her stool.

Evelyn's explanation sounded reasonable and plausible, but Dena couldn't help but wonder if that completely ruled out a curse.

Dena

LATER THAT AFTERNOON Max came into Dena's bookstore. She was in the stacks and jumped when he called out, "You in here?"

She met him in the center of the store. "I am. What can I do for you?"

"It's what I can do for you." He handed her a piece of paper with the name Quint O'Dell and an address scribbled on it.

"What's this?"

"Evelyn told me about your *intruder*." Max used air quotes. "I think this might be him."

"You know him?"

Max nodded.

"How?"

"Long story. But Evelyn told me you were scared. I don't think you need to be. Pretty sure he's harmless."

"Pretty sure?"

"Pretty sure." With that Max strode out of the bookstore.

Dena stared at the paper in her hand, not entirely

certain she wanted to find this guy after all. If Max knew him, or at least knew of him, and said he was harmless—pretty sure—maybe that was good enough. She dropped the paper on the front counter and went back to shelving books.

Two minutes later, curiosity overwhelmed her and she plugged Quint O'Dell's address into her map app. She pulled up directions to it from the bookstore and had to laugh when she saw it was nine-point-eight miles away. He'd been off by two-tenths of a mile when he said he schlepped those books ten miles.

She considered her actions for a few minutes before going into the photo studio. "Is Max here?" she asked Evelyn.

"Nope, he's out gallivanting somewhere. Why?"

"I wanted him to go with me someplace."

"Where?"

"To see that intruder guy with me. Apparently his name is Quint O'Dell and this is his address." Dena waved the paper Max had scribbled on. "I wanted to go out there and thought it might be easier if Max joined me."

Evelyn picked up her phone. "I'll text him."

"Instead of calling? I thought only kids did that," Dena teased.

"Us vintage folk text when we don't want to talk to each other."

"You don't want to talk to Max?" Dena pursed her lips.

"I do, but we're in the middle of a … tiff."

Dena knew it was none of her business and let the topic drop.

Evelyn texted Max and Dena was encouraged when he texted right back. That was probably a good sign their tiff wasn't serious.

Evelyn read it. "He says he's busy all day. It'll be dark

before he gets home. He's in Colorado Springs trying to get a dry cleaner to give us a bulk discount if we used them exclusively for the costumes."

"That's a good idea. I guess I'm going to go talk to Mr O'Dell alone then. It sounds like he's harmless. I just want to talk to him to see …" Dena decided not to concern Evelyn with all the details as to whether Quint O'Dell was truly just a harmless book seller, or if he might know something about Norbert. "… if I should buy books from him. But it seemed like a good idea to let someone know where I was, so tag, you're it."

"Shouldn't you let Keisha or Vince take care of this? That's why we pay taxes, after all."

Dena had wondered the same thing herself, but explained her reasoning to Evelyn. "First, I don't think he's dangerous."

"You said he was when you told us about him."

"No, I didn't. I told you he scared me. There's a difference. He surprised me by coming in here when I wasn't expecting anyone. If he'd done the exact same thing when I was open for business, I probably wouldn't have given him another thought. And second, I really think he just wanted to sell me used books and if I don't find out for myself, it'll drive me nuts. Third, Max told me he's probably harmless."

Evelyn narrowed her eyes. "Max *knows* this guy?"

"He's the one who gave me his address."

"Max did." Evelyn sounded skeptical.

Evelyn's brow furrowed and Dena didn't want her to worry about her, so she quickly added, "And fourth, he's a frail old man and I think I could take him if he started anything. Plus, I have bear spray."

"Let me call Vince to go with you. There's no reason not to take a policeman."

"Evelyn, how would you like it if a cop showed up on your front porch like that? I'm just going to see if he really has a bunch of old books to sell."

Evelyn looked dubious. "You have your bear spray in your purse?"

Dena nodded.

"You'll call me when you get there?"

Dena nodded.

"And if you don't answer your phone when I call fifteen minutes later, you won't get mad if I send Vincent over there with his lights and siren?"

"All of that sounds perfectly reasonable." Dena made sure her phone number was programmed into Evelyn's phone. "I'll call you when I get there." Dena grabbed her purse, making sure her phone and her bear spray were both inside, and left the Marketplace.

————

Dena rode a rollercoaster of regret and bravery the entire nine-point-eight miles to Quint O'Dell's house. By the time she got there, her emotional roulette wheel had landed squarely on *brave*. She simply couldn't believe this elderly navy veteran was anything other than a harmless book lover.

She wasn't stupid, though, and made sure to text Evelyn as promised, waiting until Evelyn gave her the thumbs-up emoji before walking up the path. Then she set her phone alarm for fourteen minutes so she could thwart any lights-and-siren action Evelyn might put into motion.

She'd been rehearsing what she wanted to say, having sketched out their entire encounter in her head.

When he eventually opened the cabin door to her

knock, all of her preconceived notions flew out of her head.

After several episodes of knocking, louder and louder in case his hearing was shot, Quint O'Dell inched the door open. Dena could only see one eye and half his nose.

"Mr O'Dell? I don't know if you remem—"

"I remember," he said gruffly. "You're that dame from the bookstore."

Dena took a breath so she wouldn't say the words that sprang to her lips. "Well, I'm Dena Russo, the owner of Thrice Sold Tales. You came to see me and brought a box of books?"

"What of it?"

Dena's plan was simply to see if Quint O'Dell was a harmless seller of used books, and if he had any kind of relationship to Norbert Wallace. The sooner she could cross him off her list of suspects or, if she suspected something was fishy, pass along his information to the sheriff, the better for everyone. But where was the booming-voiced, pushy man who came into the bookstore?

"Could I come in? I'd like to talk more about those books you showed me. The Colorado history ones?"

Quint O'Dell's single eye narrowed and stared at her for a moment longer. Then he blinked and fully opened the door, stepping aside so she could enter.

The front door opened directly into the main room of the cabin and Dena stood, gaping.

The cabin was well-kept and clean but decorated in a manner completely at odds with what Dena knew—and expected—of this man. She'd expected threadbare carpet and rickety furniture, old-fashioned ice box, maybe a pot-bellied stove in the center of the room.

Instead, the entire cabin was decorated in a bright, colorful Southwest style. Baskets of all shapes and sizes dotted corners in groupings of three. At least fifteen flat baskets hung on one wall in a large, tasteful display. Comfortable-looking rope chairs offered stylish seating, with a plethora of pillows in Native American themes dotting the furniture. Several fanciful saguaro cactus sculptures, clearly a series created by the same artist, stood sentinel around the room.

Quint O'Dell never projected the image of a married man, but clearly, his wife decorated this place.

"This is lovely," Dena said.

O'Dell grunted and pointed to one of the chairs.

Dena sat. "The reason I'm here—"

"I know why you're here."

Dena nervously tucked a strand of hair behind her ear. Had she made a mistake coming here? She scooted to the edge of her seat in case she needed to bolt. "I simply wanted—"

"To apologize for throwing me out of your bookstore and to reconsider my offer." O'Dell leaned back in his chair, fully manspreading, like an overly confident peacock.

Dena resisted the urge to roll her eyes, deciding instead to play to his macho attitude. "Perhaps I was a bit hasty. Tell me again about those books."

He launched into a long diatribe about his collection of Colorado history books. Dena listened carefully for a while, until he veered into lecturing and over-explaining minutiae that was simply too much information for her purposes at that moment.

She peeked at the timer on her phone counting down the minutes until Evelyn would summon the Sugar Springs Sheriff's Department to ride to her rescue. It was close, so she surreptitiously texted Evelyn her own thumbs-up emoji to let her know everything was fine. She needn't have worried about being rude, because Quint O'Dell had that glazed look on his face that everyone got when they drifted down the rabbit hole of sermonizing on their topic of expertise. She could have magicked an old-style British phone booth directly into the room, entered and closed the door behind her, dropped in her twenty pence coins, and asked Mary Poppins to connect her with Evelyn, and Quint O'Dell wouldn't even have noticed.

But when he paused to retrieve the book that was part of the Ted Talk he was delivering to her, Dena took the opportunity to steer the conversation in a different direction.

"You seem to know a lot about the used book business, Mr O'Dell. What do you think of my new bookstore?"

He handed her the book and again gave a throaty grunt. "I think you might be in over your head." He dropped back into the chair opposite from her.

Dena tried not to show it, but she felt as if he'd just slapped her. It certainly didn't help matters that she felt like this herself seven thousand times every day. She swallowed and stared down at the book on her lap, rubbing her thumb over the embossed title. Instead of responding, she adopted a tone lighter than she felt and asked, "What do you think of the Marketplace?" Clearly, he knew about old Colorado history books. It was time to find out if he knew anything about Norbert Wallace.

O'Dell's entire body tightened. Dena saw it in his face and the way his limbs flexed. Again, she scooted to the edge of her seat. She thought about Evelyn holding tight to *Bleak House*, and gripped the book on her lap with both hands, just in case.

"What do I think of the Marketplace? I think what every person should think—that's it's a blight on this town. It'll be the ruination of Sugar Springs. Too many tourists, too much crime, gentrification. What's next? A Blockbuster on every corner? I want to know who that thug Norbert Wallace drove out of business to build that monstrosity."

Dena was shocked by his outburst, but quietly responded, trying to elicit more information, perhaps a true motive for murder. "Norbert didn't build it. He refurbished the sugar mill that went out of business years ago."

O'Dell grunted again.

"So, you think Norbert Wallace shouldn't have developed that property?"

O'Dell stared at her, but Dena didn't think he was mulling over her question.

Suddenly he stood and pointed a bony finger in her face. "You a friend of his?"

Dena leaped to her feet too and hurried toward the door, still gripping the book. "He's my landlord—*was* my landlord. He's been murdered."

"Why are you really here?" Without waiting for her to answer, he added, "Give me three hundred dollars for those books or get out!"

Dena fled out the front door, dropping the book on a side table as she passed it. She ran to her car, made sure the doors were locked and started her engine. She expected O'Dell to be chasing her, but he stood in the open doorway, holding the book she'd dropped.

She peeled out to the road, pulling over about a quarter mile away when she realized she hadn't been followed. She dialed her phone.

"Sheriff Johnson? I have some information for you."

Dena

WHEN DENA GOT BACK to the Marketplace, Evelyn was in her face before she even got her coat off.

"So what happened?" Evelyn was twisting a tissue she'd pulled from her sleeve.

Dena told her all about her time with Quint O'Dell and subsequent conversation with Sheriff Johnson.

Evelyn's eyes bugged out. "She said she'd look into it? That's all?"

Dena shrugged. "Isn't that enough? She'll go talk to him and then deal with him appropriately. I'm just glad to have figured out that O'Dell hated Norbert Wallace and that there's a very good probability he killed him that morning."

Evelyn threw her shredded tissue away, then plucked another from the box underneath Dena's front counter. She began to worry it as well. "And you say Max knows this guy?"

Dena nodded. "I really think he has something to do with Norbert's death."

Evelyn's eyes widened. "Max?"

"No! O'Dell."

She shook her head. "It seems a little too … I don't know, convenient. And if he's a friend of Max's …"

"He must not be a friend if Max never spoke to you about him. He's just an acquaintance, or someone he runs into at the barbershop or something." Dena tried to make sense of it too. She always assumed couples who were together as long as Max and Evelyn have been wouldn't have secrets from one another. But maybe they did. And they were fighting about something. Did it involve any of this?

Evelyn pressed her lips together. "This O'Dell's motive —if that's what it really is—isn't any stronger or more obvious than any of ours. I mean, nobody liked Norbert, but we all couldn't have killed him, right?"

Dena's confidence slipped. "Regardless. It's in the sheriff's hands now." She stowed her coat and purse and picked up the To Do list she'd made herself. "I'm sure Sheriff Johnson will call when she knows anything, but I have other stuff to do now." She glanced at the list and groaned. "So much stuff."

"I'll leave you to it, then. I have a list that's at least that long."

After Evelyn left the bookstore, Dena studied her list, reordering it by importance, which seemed to change every day. Today the number one item was to get her lease fixed, once and for all.

———

She sat in her car, idling at the curb in front of Norbert Wallace's office, trying to work up the courage to go in. It was obvious that Audra thought she'd had something to do with Norbert's death, based on the fact she told the sheriff about her searching through Norbert's desk that day.

If there was anything more awkward than asking for help from someone who thinks you're a murderer, Dena didn't know what it was.

It had to be done, though, so Dena plodded into the office. She let out a deep breath when she saw Audra wasn't at her desk. But neither was Royce. Dena called out a tentative, "Hello," but nobody answered. She peeked into the break room, again seeing the light on the coffee pot, but the carafe empty. Just like before, she clicked it off then tiptoed down the hallway to Norbert's office.

This time, however, all the lights were blazing and Royce stood over Norbert's desk. He had a slightly crazed look on his face, eyes darting around, hair disheveled.

Dena looked at the scene with alarm. When he was alive, Dena knew Norbert's desk was pristine. That very first day when she and Charlee had stopped in over Thanksgiving weekend, she'd noticed and remarked on the fact he'd only had one thin manila folder in the tray serving as his in-box. When she was here the day he died, his desk had papers piled on it. But today Norbert's office looked positively ransacked. Papers and folders were strewn all over Norbert's desk. There were no piles to speak of, just one big mess.

Dena backed away from the doorway. Her purse thumped the doorjamb and Royce spun toward her.

"What are you doing here?"

"I still need my lease fixed," she stammered. "But I can come back when Audra is here."

Royce seemed to calm a bit. He took a deep breath and leaning against Norbert's desk, smoothed his hair. "Audra took a personal day." He gestured around the room. "And I can't find anything I need. She's the one who knows his filing system and, of course, isn't here when I need her."

"She must have been upset."

"I don't know. She said she needed to see some old friends." Royce wrinkled his forehead, then relaxed it. "Oh, you mean because of …" Royce trailed off, waving his hand around vaguely.

They both paused for a respectful moment.

"What about your lease?" Royce finally asked.

Dena thrust her copy into his hands. "Norbert made a math mistake and wrote that my space at the Marketplace was more than two times its real size. When I went to town hall to finalize my paperwork, they calculated my taxes based on the higher number. They gave me until the Grand Opening to resubmit. Otherwise, I have to pay them a fortune."

Royce glanced at the paperwork, then walked to Norbert's computer and tapped a few keys. When papers sputtered out of the printer, Royce stapled and signed one set of printouts, then stapled and signed the second set. He handed both to Dena, pointing. "Sign both copies there and there."

Dena cleared space on Norbert's messy desk and signed, handing one copy back to Royce. "That's all? If it was that easy to fix, why didn't Norbert just do it?"

"Because he was a jerk?" Royce walked to the front and dropped his copy of Dena's lease on his own desk.

"What's going to happen to this place now?" Dena asked him.

"Unclear. I was trying to find his will or business agreements or anything." He tipped his head toward the hallway. "That's what I was doing in there. Can't find anything about it. I don't even know who his attorney is. And Audra isn't answering her phone. Completely useless today."

"He doesn't use attorney Finster next door?"

"That's what I thought, but Finster says no. Seems Norbert kept his business dealings close to the vest."

Dena

"I'LL BE BACK in a couple of days. Stop worrying," Dena said to her fellow tenants the next day. She had some loose ends to tie up with the house she was getting ready to put on the market in Santa Fe, and she was going on one last winter hike with her friend Georgia. Dena knew it was a bad idea to stop into the Marketplace before she left for Santa Fe, but there was a book she had unboxed recently that she wanted to give to Georgia, who had finally, grudgingly, forgiven her for the misunderstanding of the gift-wrapped rat over Thanksgiving. Dena hoped Georgia would laugh at—and be enamored with—an illustrated copy of Beatrix Potter's *The Tale of Samuel Whiskers.*

"But it's only eight days until the Grand Opening!" Kober wailed, pointing at the white board.

"I'm aware," Dena said dryly. She did a doubletake at the white board. Someone had written, "3 Days Without a Murder!"

"And by the time you get back, even less than that!"

Dena ignored the obviousness of Kober's statement and place the final piece of tape on the wrapping paper covering Georgia's gift. Kober's wailing had brought the others at a run. How she longed for the good old days two weeks ago when she was the only one who came to work early.

"You really shouldn't go at this crucial time," Skyler said with solemn eyes.

Dena almost laughed because her face was so serious and her words so overwrought and dramatic, like she was reciting lines from a Chekov play.

"Guys, it's fine. I'll be back in a few days. You don't need me here. I've given out flyers everywhere I could think of. I've introduced myself to everyone in town and invited them to the Grand Opening. What more can I do?"

Everyone grumbled but Dena placated them as best she could. "Tell you what. Print me off some more flyers and I'll stop at places between Sugar Springs and Santa Fe. Maybe we can grab some tourists passing by." That seemed to satisfy them, so Dena left for Santa Fe with a pile of flyers on her front passenger seat.

On the road, she glanced at them guiltily as she sped down the highway, hoping she wouldn't forget, but knowing the probability was higher than average. She had Santa Fe on her mind. There was so much to do about the house, and she was more than a little nervous about spending time with Georgia, after what had happened between them. She was second guessing her decision about how funny Georgia would find her Beatrix Potter gift. Dena had been so shocked when Georgia actually offered her guest room to Dena for the time she was going to be in Santa Fe. She didn't want to screw up their tentative détente.

Dena dutifully stopped at all the corner stores, gas stations, and cafes in all the small towns along the highway between Sugar Springs and the interstate. At her first stop, she plucked the wrapped book from the passenger seat and slid it under the seat. On the drive, she'd mull over the wisdom of handing it to Georgia. She had five hours to decide.

At each stop, Dena was relieved when people accepted flyers and seemed truly interested in hearing about the Marketplace. They obviously hadn't read Aja's article in the online edition of the *Sugar Springs Courier*. Dena knew it was only a matter of time, though. At least now her guilt was ebbing the teensiest bit. She could honestly declare to the other tenants that she'd posted more flyers just like she'd promised.

She reached the turnoff where the highway met the interstate and had just hit her cruising speed of seventy-five miles per hour when BAM. Struggling to control her car at that speed, she fought with it until she got it to roll to a stop on the shoulder, thumping and bumping the entire way. She illuminated her flashing hazard lights and hoped for the best. Unfortunately, she got out and saw her initial reaction had been correct … blowout.

Cars and trucks whizzed past her while she scanned the interstate ahead. She couldn't see anything, but perhaps that was because of the hill she'd been climbing. She turned to look behind her and saw the back of a road sign fifty or so paces away. She trudged back to read it, hugging her arms to stave off the chill.

She was amazed how gigantic the sign was when standing right in front of it. Hurtling past on the interstate didn't do it justice. It reminded her of the first time she came face-to-face with a white-tailed deer on a hike. From a distance, they seemed a manageable size, for wildlife at least. Up close they were terrifying. Especially the one who thought Dena was crowding her fawns. She'd given a snort and took three quick steps toward

Dena who had turned and fled back the direction she'd come.

At least the sign didn't scare Dena. It didn't appease her much, either. The sign told her there was fast food and gas at a big truck stop at the next exit a mile away. Could be worse, she thought. But it definitely could be better.

Dena walked back to her car and stared with hands on her hips at the shredded tire. She hadn't changed a tire in years. She couldn't even remember the last time.

She opened the passenger door and threw the remaining flyers on the back seat before sitting down. She pulled her owner's manual from the glove box and flipped through the fat book until she found the instructions she'd been searching for. She scanned the diagrams. Ah yes, it was all coming back … jack, lug nuts, weird-looking wrench.

She repositioned the car so it was further off the shoulder and more on flat ground.

Zipping up her coat, she popped the trunk. She dug through the beat-up plastic container of emergency supplies she'd carried in every trunk of every car she'd ever owned until she found an old pair of work gloves and a knit cap. She pulled them on. She relocated everything— the plastic container, a filthy green tarp, some jumper cables, a big bag of kitty litter she never remembered she had when there was ice on her sidewalk, a collapsible shovel, and a box of old clothes she never got around to dropping off at the thrift store—out of the trunk and far off the roadway so she could haul out the spare tire.

She took a moment to admire her clean trunk before tugging open the hidden compartment underneath. She stared inside, uncomprehending. No spare tire. Not even a place for one. The compartment wasn't even tire-shaped.

"What the—?" She rooted around in a half-hearted

attempt to find the tire, knowing there was nowhere else for it to be. She did find a tire sealant kit, however, completely useless on her shredded tire. "Well. That changes things." She gave a rueful laugh at her unintentional pun.

After reading the owner's manual more thoroughly, and seeing the tiny asterisk alerting her to the absence of a spare tire, she decided to risk it and drive to the truck stop at the next exit.

She returned everything to the trunk, then sat in the car for a bit. She took a deep breath, made sure her hazard lights were still on, and crept along the shoulder at a pace she hoped wouldn't ruin anything permanently. She breathed a sigh of relief when she reached the exit. As she crept forward to merge on to it, a tow truck slowed and drove next to her.

The driver was saying something to her so Dena rolled down the window.

"Need any help?" he asked.

Where was he forty-five minutes ago? "I had a blowout but don't have a spare. I'm heading to this truck stop to see if they'll change it for me." Before she could ask him to follow her down in case they couldn't, he raised a hand, waved, and roared off.

On the exit ramp Dena had no shoulder to drive along. Traffic bottlenecked almost to a stop behind her, frustrating everyone anxious to get to a toilet or find coffee or a burger. "Just hold your horses and count your blessings you aren't me right now," she muttered.

Everyone zipped past her when she pulled into the parking lot to see where the mechanics might be. She spied a sign for the garage on the other side of the building and limped toward it.

Now she sat at a table in the food court of the truck

stop with coffee and a well-deserved chocolate doughnut, waiting for the mechanic to text her when a new tire had been attached. She'd had to restrain herself from kissing him full on the lips when he told her not only did he have a tire for her—and a spare she could throw in her trunk— but he could have the job finished in an hour. He explained that car manufacturers these days had to do everything possible to reduce the weight of their vehicles so they could comply with gas mileage standards, and one of the ways they did that was to remove spare tires from trunks. Lighter cars got better mileage. Unfortunately, they rarely advertised the lack of a spare to their buyers. She debated whether to buy the one he offered, because what were the chances this would ever happen again? Not appreciating the lure of Las Vegas high-stakes gambling or even elementary school fundraising raffles, however, she didn't debate for long. Odds were odds, and she was a chicken.

While she waited, she'd picked up a regional newspaper, the *Arkansas River Valley Gazette*, near the doughnut kiosk and was idly flipping pages. She almost choked on her coffee when she saw Aja's online article had been reprinted.

Dena groaned loud enough that a trucker sitting nearby glanced over at her.

Double whammy. Today was Thursday when the *Sugar Springs Courier* print edition came out too.

Ugh.

Dena read the article. It was the same online one Jain had read to them. Light on facts, heavy on innuendo. No real information, just that Norbert had been found dead at the Marketplace "under mysterious circumstances" and that his car was found with the keys in it near the park. None of the tenants or their businesses were named, but all of that nonsense about the Sugar Mill Curse still took up a couple of inches.

She sipped her coffee and glanced closer at the page.

Aja's article was a smaller article, more like a sidebar, to a lengthy, more in-depth article about the increase in crime in the region. In addition to Norbert's death in Sugar Springs, there was also a woman who'd been run off the road, a park ranger involved in a shooting, a home invasion, and a hiker who'd had a suspected run-in with an illegal marijuana grow operation. All of these incidents ended in a death. The article admitted in none of the cases had the authorities concluded whether the deaths were suicides, accidents, or homicides. More jumping the journalistic gun.

Dena searched for the *Sugar Springs Courier* online article. It was exactly the same as she'd just read, no additions or deletions, except for the tags of all the Marketplace businesses linking the article to each of them and their social media presences.

She scanned the online comments. There were only a few, but aside from one that offered opportunities for investments in cryptocurrency, they all covered the same territory: the readers of the *Courier* did not appreciate Aja writing the story before having any substantive information. One said, "Only fact in this article is that Norbert Wallace died." Another said, "Where's the beef?" Another pointed out, "None of this is news. You didn't have to tell us Norbert died, the whole town knew about that the same day it happened. Report the details of his death when you have them."

Dena felt a bit of hope bubbling up. Maybe their Grand Opening would be okay.

THE REST of Dena's trip was blissfully uneventful. She checked a few items of business from her to-do list over at her house, then crossed Santa Fe to Georgia's house. After some initial awkwardness, Dena suggested treating Georgia to dinner at her favorite restaurant.

The meal was pleasant enough, but Georgia seemed a bit preoccupied with whomever kept texting her. When Dena asked who it was, Georgia immediately changed the subject. Dena took the hint and Georgia stowed her phone for the duration of the evening.

After dinner, things seemed mostly back to normal to Dena, but she sure wasn't going to bring up Thanksgiving or the rat incident if she could help it. And she hoped Georgia wouldn't either.

The Beatrix Potter book remained hidden under the passenger seat of her car. Too soon for that little joke.

The next day dawned perfect for a winter hike—crisp and cold, no wind, with a bright azure sky—and they packed supplies for a day trip to their favorite trail.

Normally they took turns leading, but today Dena

found herself in front of Georgia most of the way. She hoped Georgia didn't find that too obnoxious, but Dena had a lot to do and couldn't really afford one of their typically leisurely hikes. She was hoping to have time after their hike to get back to her house to repair the wire shelves in the laundry room and make sure the dead and dormant stalks had been removed from the garden. Anything she could do herself would save money. Her subconscious seemed to be controlling her feet. Regardless, even though Dena was twenty years younger and a foot taller, Georgia wasn't lagging too much. For that Dena was glad.

They didn't talk much when they hiked, sometimes pointing out an unusual wildflower, or calling for a break, or offering a warning of loose gravel. They both preferred listening to the sounds of nature, which is why they liked hiking in the first place. The constant chatter of squirrels. The songs of birds hidden high up in the canopy. The crunch of their boots over gravel, leaves, and sticks. The occasional thud of a pinecone dropping from a fifty-foot-tall blue spruce. A stream flowing in the distance.

They were often startled by some noise in the underbrush just off the trail. When they first began hiking together, these noises had the power to frighten them, requiring constant vigilance, and often ruining their hike. When they realized they'd probably been scared by a bunny or ground squirrel, they began to ignore all those minor rustles and clatters. They accepted that just because they were humans it didn't mean they owned these trails, acknowledging that every time they went on a hike, there were many eyeballs on them, from high in trees, and low under bushes.

At one point on the trail Dena glanced around at the

familiar landmarks. "Starting now there's no cell service, remember? So be careful. No jazz moves."

Georgia performed a little soft shoe dance in the wide section of trail, which was also one of their traditions.

They hiked further along the trail, lost in their own thoughts, until Dena realized she was a bit too far ahead of Georgia. She turned and waited for her.

"I'm coming, I'm coming." Georgia huffed and wheezed.

Dena vowed to slow down but knew enough not to say that out loud to Georgia. She'd learned that lesson on a previous hike years ago when Georgia had taken keen exception to Dena's offer of slowing down the pace for her, with a joking apology for her long legs and overly caffeinated energy.

They took a short break, swigging from their water bottles. They both perspired, despite the air temperature, and took the opportunity to shed some layers. Dena removed her knit cap, fluffing her hair afterward.

"How do you manage to have hair that just goes right back into place like that?" Georgia used a hand to flick Dena's hair, brushing her shoulder. "You're so pretty. I hate you." Then Georgia removed her own hat and scowled as she felt her hair going every-which-way.

"Remember, pretty is as pretty does, and climbing a mountain when you're in your seventies is pretty pretty." Dena grinned at her friend. "Besides, your hair is in a class unto itself. Everyone should be so lucky."

They stowed their water and continued along the trail. Dena knew the trickiest part was coming up. The trail narrowed and had roots and rocks just waiting to jump out and trip you. She called back, "Be careful!"

Georgia didn't answer, but Dena knew she wouldn't. They had this conversation all the time. Dena habitually said generic things like "be careful" when pointing out an icy sidewalk, or when someone climbed into their car to drive home, or like today, when hiking.

Georgia was of the mind that saying such a thing was a complete waste of energy and perhaps even rude. She'd said on numerous occasions, "Do you really think anyone is just going to march right out on an icy sidewalk without being careful? Do you believe me to be so daft that I won't pay attention to the trail when I hike? I'm still kickin', baby. And I've never needed your reminder to be careful."

Dena couldn't help herself, though. She'd been saying it ever since her kids were born. That's why they called it a habit.

Dena smiled to herself and was almost going to say it again, as a joke, when she heard Georgia yell. Dena slid to a stop on the gravel and turned but didn't see her. Using a tree for support on the narrow trail, she reversed course and hurried toward Georgia.

She wasn't in sight, not on the trail anywhere.

Dena frantically searched for her, finally hearing a faint sound. She peered over the edge. A bit of blue caught her eye. Georgia's coat. She leaned as far as she dared. Her foot slipped in the loose dirt. Dena dropped to her belly. Pulled herself further over the edge.

"Georgia! Are you okay?" Another stupid question. "Are you hurt?"

Dena only received a moan in response.

She made a quick mental assessment of her backpack. Nothing in there for a rescue. Georgia presumably still wore hers, unless it had slipped off her shoulders when she fell. Dena frantically glanced around the area, as if a rope and pitons would magically appear.

"Georgia, talk to me! Is anything broken? Can you climb back up?"

No answer.

Dena wormed and wiggled herself as far out as she dared. She couldn't see much, but it seemed to her that Georgia must be on some sort of ledge down below. She hadn't fallen too far, so maybe she was just shaken up rather than injured. She didn't appear to be dangling like in some cartoon.

But Georgia also wasn't responding. Not a good sign.

"Georgia, I'm going for help," Dena shouted. "If you understand, say something."

Nothing.

Dena thought her heart would pound out of her chest while she broke branches to mark the trail so she could find it again. She used a stick to write HIKER FELL with an arrow on either side of the impasse she'd created. Surely nobody could miss that.

She called to Georgia one more time. No response.

She jammed her arms through the straps of her backpack and flung it on. Dena knew they were closer to the west trailhead, since they hadn't come to the switchback that led them back to their car parked at the east trailhead. The west trail was a shorter, easier hike, and she could get to the trailhead—and hopefully help—much faster.

She wasn't sure when she'd be back in cell range, so as she hurried along the trail, she stopped every so often to try a call.

She was beginning to think she'd never get a signal when suddenly, one wavering bar popped up. She dialed 911 and quickly explained the situation. The dispatcher understood that the signal could be lost at any time, so she told Dena she'd be sending a ranger up the west trail, but if they didn't meet on the way, Dena was to call again from the trailhead.

Dena hurried as fast as she dared, willing the ranger to

move quickly, but she was almost to the trailhead by the time she saw him.

She led him back, relieved when she saw the pile of branches and the message in the dirt. Dena pointed and the ranger got to work. They both called to Georgia but there was only silence on the trail. A knot formed in Dena's stomach. She had been so confident that as soon as she got help up here, everything would be okay.

The ranger stood and used his walkie talkie. Dena couldn't make out the actual words, but relief flooded her when he smiled and gave her the thumbs up.

He signed off, then said, "A group of hikers came up behind you on the east trail and took your friend back down that way. An ambulance met her and took her to Santa Fe General."

"Thank God. Is she okay?"

"That's all they knew."

The ranger prepared for his return down the west trail. "Be careful," he said.

Dena hurried the opposite direction down the east trail, back to where her car was parked. Thank goodness for small mercies that Georgia hadn't driven, or Dena would have been stranded.

She ran the trail wherever she could until she reached her car. She threw her backpack in the trunk and raced to the hospital.

When Dena got there and finally found someone who could tell her about Georgia's condition, they wouldn't tell her anything because she wasn't family. Dena tried to tell them she was as close to family as Georgia had and that she had been with her on the trail and she needed to know something—anything—about what was going on.

Finally, a nurse pulled her aside. "I don't know much about your friend's specifics, but it's not looking good for her. She's in surgery now for a broken arm and they're talking about a medically-induced coma. That's all I know."

"A coma!"

The nurse said, "They must be worried about swelling in her brain. They give her deep sedation so her brain can heal. The anesthesiologist will monitor her."

"How long will they keep her under sedation?"

"It depends. Might just be today, might be longer. I'll show you where the waiting room is and I'll add to the chart that you're her … um … cousin. They'll page you when she's out of surgery."

Dena convinced the nurse to add Dena's cell number to the chart so they could call if she didn't hear the page or something. Dena followed her back to the surgical waiting room, but there was a large family taking up most of the seats, and many of them were weeping loudly.

Dena made her way to the cafeteria to wait. It was large and open. She took a table near the window. The peaceful azure sky above belied the trauma down below. She stared outside, willing Georgia to be okay.

After an hour, her stomach rumbled, and she realized she hadn't eaten since their early breakfast of a hard-boiled egg and a piece of toast that morning. They normally stopped for lunch when they got to the switchback.

Dena glanced up at the menu board, but her stomach was churning with hunger and too much adrenaline. She finally settled on what she hoped would be a tummy-friendly bowl of oatmeal with berries, carrying the tray back to her table.

While she picked at her food, Dena idly listened to the conversation of the two nurses at the table next to her.

The first one said, "My friend is a nurse in Colorado Springs and took care of him."

"How does someone get run over by a bulldozer?" the second one asked, shaking her head.

"Just a freak accident. The same way someone drowns or burns down a house—"

Or falls off a trail, Dena silently added.

"—inattention."

"Or foul play," the second nurse said.

"You watch too much TV."

"Speaking of which …" The second nurse began talking about a series she'd been watching on television and Dena lost interest.

Dena had finished her oatmeal, bussed her tray, checked her email, called Charlee and told her what happened, and they still hadn't paged her about Georgia. She decided to go upstairs to pester someone for news. On the way up, she heard her name over the intercom. She took the remaining stairs two at a time and screeched to a stop in front of the nurses' station.

"I'm Dena Russo. I just got paged about my friend, er, cousin, Georgia Pisch?"

The nurse's face softened. Dena braced herself. "Ms Pisch is in a medically-induced coma. She's out of surgery and stable, but there's nothing more they can do right now. Your info is in her chart. I suggest you go home. They'll call you when they have any news."

Dena had a million questions but knew this nurse couldn't answer them. Maybe no one could. The nurse moved on to other business and Dena headed back toward the stairs. She got halfway down and realized she didn't have a way to get into Georgia's house. She retraced her steps back to the nurse's station, but a different nurse was there, sitting in front of a computer.

"What room is Georgia Pisch in?"

The nurse didn't even look up. "Two-oh-three."

Dena took tentative steps down the hall, sure she didn't want to see Georgia in a coma, but equally sure she needed the keys to her house.

She opened the door to the atonal beeps and clangs and whooshes from various machines, all hooked up to Georgia. The antiseptic smell of the hospital became concentrated the further Dena walked into the room. As the door closed behind her, the harsh fluorescent light from the hallway disappeared, leaving the warm soft glow of ambient lighting in the room.

Dena stared for a long time at Georgia in that hospital bed, ventilator covering her face, arm in a cast hanging from a traction device, curly hair splayed every which way across her pillow.

Dena's eyes swam when she thought about Georgia complaining about her unruly "hat hair" this morning. If Dena had only known what was in store for Georgia, she could have done something. Had her hike in front. Insisted she use her hiking poles. Suggested an easier trail. Tears fell freely from Dena's eyes. In her head she knew this wasn't her fault, but seeing Georgia completely helpless and motionless in that hospital bed while she was upright and healthy sure made it seem like it.

Dena pulled a chair next to the bed and held Georgia's limp hand. She squeezed it like they do in movies, hoping Georgia would squeeze back. But she didn't.

She sat there until the light outside grew dim, then she forced herself up, away from Georgia who hadn't even twitched the entire time Dena sat next to her.

Dena stood, surveying the room. It hadn't occurred to her until that minute to wonder if Georgia's backpack had been rescued with her. She didn't see it anywhere. The neon orange backpack would surely stand out against the muted beige colors of the hospital room. Cupboards lined one wall and Dena began opening them one by one. She found extra pillows, blankets, and boxes of tissues, but no backpack.

She smacked her forehead. It was probably locked up somewhere. How would she be able to retrieve her belongings from Georgia's house now? She plopped into the beige-on-beige patterned easy chair across the room to think when she spied a tall cabinet next to the bathroom. She hadn't seen it because the open bathroom door hid it.

She yanked the handles, expecting it to be empty like most of the others, but practically swooned when she saw a plastic bag labeled PERSONAL EFFECTS shoved in the bottom. Dena picked it up and peered through the clear plastic. Score! Georgia's backpack.

She plopped it on the seat of the easy chair and began rooting through it. Unlike Dena, it appeared Georgia did not empty her backpack after every hike. There were scads of empty granola bar wrappers, three empty water bottles, a fold-out topographical map of New Mexico, a windbreaker, a pair of bedazzled sneakers, a half-empty roll of toilet paper, four bottles of sunscreen, aspirin, a pedometer, a pair of plastic children's binoculars, three bandanas, and a moldy sandwich in a plastic bag. She wrinkled her nose and carried the last item by two fingers to the trashcan in the bathroom.

Dena piled up the rest of the trash on the chair but still hadn't located Georgia's housekeys. She was about to give up when she spied a hidden interior pocket. She let out a huge breath when she pulled out a set of keys which she shoved in her pocket. Rummaging a bit more in the hidden pocket, she found Georgia's wallet too.

She checked to see if security or someone had emptied it of the important stuff, but Georgia's driver's license and credit cards were still there.

As she fanned the cash to count it, so she could make note of the amount, a nurse walked in.

"What do you think you're doing?" she demanded loudly.

Startled, Dena dropped the wallet and spilled the contents on the floor. The nurse dropped to one knee to collect the money before Dena could, giving her a body block in the process.

Dena was knocked to her backside. "I'm just … I was …" Dena took a moment to collect her thoughts. "I'm staying with Georgia so I needed her house keys."

The nurse scrutinized Dena's face. It was obvious that she was highly dubious of Dena's explanation. With a withering glare, the nurse scooped everything back into the backpack, even the pile of trash on the chair.

Dena started to protest, then decided against it.

"This should have been locked up, to avoid this very thing," the nurse muttered.

"I wasn't stealing anything. I was the one hiking with Georgia this morning. I'm from Colorado and I'm staying with her. All my stuff is there at her house and I didn't want to have to break in or anything."

The nurse continued to give Dena the stink eye. "Likely story. Show me some ID."

Dena pulled out her driver's license and handed it over.

"This is a New Mexico license. You said you were from Colorado." The nurse took a picture of it with her phone, then sidled toward the call button.

Dena felt her palms get sweaty. In her nervousness, she spoke too fast. "I just moved to Colorado and haven't had a chance to change my license. That's why I came back, I'm selling my house here. And that's why I'm staying at Georgia's." Frantically, Dena pulled up the listing for her house on her realtor's website. "See?"

The nurse studied the listing. "This says it's not available yet."

"That's right. I'm here to finish getting it ready to sell." Dena nodded and knew she smiled too big in a creepy effort to be non-threatening. She hoped she didn't look like The Joker, but realized she probably did.

The nurse kept scrolling through the listing for what seemed like forever before returning Dena's phone to her. "Seems overpriced."

Dena bit her tongue as the nurse swept across Georgia's room, carrying Georgia's personal effects. She paused at the door and gave Dena another dose of stink eye.

Thirty seconds after the nurse walked out of the room Dena thought of the perfect thing to say. "Don't blame me if your hospital can't follow protocol!" Well, maybe not perfect, but at least it was something.

She was so thankful she had already pocketed Georgia's housekeys.

Dena gathered up her own things, then stood next to Georgia's hospital bed. She listened to the pneumatic noises playing their mechanical symphony. She watched Georgia's chest rise and lower as it kept time. She took her hand. "Rest well, my friend. I'll be back later."

She pulled open the door to a clutter of women just outside. She recognized them from the Arts Committee she had been a member of until the fateful rat incident over Thanksgiving.

"What are you doing here?" Beige Ann said.

"You have some kind of nerve!" Sue said.

Cassandra got right up in Dena's face. "You really have it in for Georgia, don't you? Why don't you just leave her alone? What did she ever do to you?"

Dena was flabbergasted. "You think I had something to

do with this? Georgia and I were hiking and she lost her balance."

"Do you really think anyone will believe that after what you did to Georgia over Thanksgiving?"

Dena clenched her fists so tight she felt her nails dig into her palms. "I don't know what you think happened," she said in a low, precise voice, "but whatever it is, you're completely wrong. Now, if you'll step out of the way, I was just leaving."

After some posturing and very little stepping out of the way, Dena got out of there.

"And don't come back!" she heard Cassandra calling after her.

Dena didn't give her the satisfaction of turning around, just kept hurrying down the hallway. Geez, she thought. First the nurse and now these kooks? How suspicious do I look, anyway?

Dena got to Georgia's house long past dark. She rooted through the refrigerator until she found a take-out container with a piece of lasagna in it. She zapped it in the microwave, then gobbled it down. She ate an apple too, then fell into bed, exhausted.

The minute she woke she called the hospital for an update about Georgia. The nurse told her they'd been no change.

"When will she wake up?" Dena asked.

"Absolutely no telling. She's in good hands, though. Being monitored constantly."

Dena thanked her and hung up.

She showered, then scrambled some eggs and buttered a bagel for breakfast. By the time she'd finished cleaning up, she knew she had to go back to Sugar Springs. The Grand Opening was barreling toward her and there wasn't one thing she could do for Georgia. She knew that Georgia's friends, especially the ones from the Arts Committee, were devoted to her and would be by her side throughout this entire ordeal. And they made it abundantly clear they didn't want Dena around anyway.

Dena packed her suitcase and loaded it in the trunk of her car. She'd stop by the hospital on her way out of town and give the nurse Georgia's housekeys and a few items she might need when she woke up—toothbrush, prescriptions, pajamas, her favorite kaftan, and a couple of magazines that had been on her nightstand. On her way out of Georgia's bedroom she spied an oil diffuser. She held it to her nose and inhaled a calming scent of lilacs. She took that too.

When she got to the hospital, the nurse she'd had the run-in with yesterday was blessedly nowhere to be found, but that also meant nobody could tell her where she might find Georgia's bag of personal effects.

Dena went into Georgia's room and found a place near the head of the bed for the diffuser then sat with her again. Nothing had changed. The machines continued with their rhythmic noises and Georgia's chest raised and lowered in time.

She sat there for a long time, finally offering up a prayer, before she was ready to get back on the road to Colorado. She remembered about the other personal items she'd brought for Georgia, but decided against trying to track down that nurse to add them to the backpack. Besides, it was nothing too valuable. Except the keys. She jammed them deep into the pocket of the kaftan so they'd be hidden until Georgia donned it. Since it was her favorite, Dena had no doubt that as soon as she was able, she'd put it on.

Kneeling in front of the open closet door where she was stashing Georgia's belongings, she banged her head when a sharp voice said, "What's going on here? There are no visitors signed in for this room."

Dena rubbed her head and hastily pushed the items into the closet. As she stood, the nurse stared at her, eyes widening. "I heard about you. You were trying to steal Ms Pisch's wallet!"

"I was doing nothing of the kind." Dena knew that by hurrying out of Georgia's room, which is what she wanted to do, would make her look like a criminal scurrying away from the scene of a crime so she walked slowly, trying to pace herself. Now she looked like a criminal sauntering away from the scene of a crime.

The nurse, hands on her hips, scorched Dena with a scowl.

As Dena pulled the door open, she said to the nurse, "To reiterate, I wasn't stealing anything. And now I'm leaving so you and that other nurse can stand down now." Dena paused. "But thank you for your due diligence with my friend. She's lucky to have you both looking after her."

Dena stopped at her own house before she left Santa Fe. When she got to town the day before yesterday she'd met for a walk-through with her realtor and contractor. They discussed everything that needed to be done and in what order, then settled on a time frame everyone could live with.

She didn't have time now to do the little chores she'd wanted to, but Dena was dismayed to see there was nobody at work on any of the chores on the contractor's list either and the house was in disarray. Tools scattered around. Scraps of lumber and drywall littered the floor. Paint trays, wooden stirrers, and brushes strewn about.

"This doesn't bode well for our schedule," she said loudly. Her words echoed in the empty room. She took the opportunity to mosey around the house. She hadn't said a proper goodbye to the old place, since she'd been in a hurry to get to Sugar Springs before dark on move-out day.

She wandered around nostalgically, remembering fun parties, late nights with Georgia watching old movies, times when Lance and Charlee had come to visit.

When she was ready to leave, she stood in the front yard and surveyed her curb appeal. The nurse's words echoed in her ears. Overpriced? No way. Some family was going to love this place.

Dena

THE NEXT AFTERNOON Dena was back at the Marketplace. The first thing she noticed was the whiteboard in the vendor area. "7 Days Until Grand Opening— 4 Days Without a Murder." But in addition to the countdown, someone had written a haiku. She tried to identify who wrote it by their handwriting, but couldn't.

> Grand Opening is
> Just around the corner and
> I want to vomit

Dena stuck her head into the photography studio. "Hey, Evelyn, who wrote the haiku?"

"No idea."

"What about Max?"

"What about him?"

It was clear by Evelyn's tone that she and Max were still tiffing, so Dena tried the cheese shop. "Skyler, do you know who wrote that haiku?"

"Not a clue."

Dena asked Kober and Hugo who both denied it. She smiled to herself. A much better mystery to be solved than Norbert's death, she thought.

And definitely more fun—at least right now—than opening a new business.

With a sigh, she got busy shelving more books. It occurred to her she may never finish organizing books on shelves, like a Möbius strip of bookstore work. She reminded herself once again how much she loved books. In general, though, not at this very moment. It would have helped if the inventory of books she received had been boxed in some kind of order, but she had found mysteries in the same box with romances, westerns, children's books, and cookbooks. She thought she'd cracked the code when she pulled out a bunch of books with authors that all began with the letter T. But when she dug further, she found mysteries written by Libby Klein, Shari Randall, Edith Maxwell, and Catriona McPherson, so that theory was debunked.

About every eight minutes Dena second-guessed her strategy about her shelf tags. Should she have it by section like a traditional bookstore? Or just alphabetize everything? Last week she'd called Charlee in a panic to ask her that very question. Charlee had laughed at her.

"Mom, you can't alphabetize all those books. For one thing, it's too big a job and you'd have to rearrange it every time you got a new shipment. You obviously need sections like in a bookstore or library," she'd said, sounding perfectly logical. "All I ask is that you make the mystery section right in the center of the store. With my books prominently displayed."

"Of course," Dena had replied. "I'm just losing my mind. But I already decided, your books get a table all their own. They'll be the only new books in the store."

Dena glanced over at "Charlemagne Russo's table" and smiled. That was the only thing she felt completely confident about in the entire store. Her daughter's autographed books would fly out the door. And that meant she'd see Charlee more often because she'd have to come and sign the replenished stock.

Dena sighed. There'd be no stock to replenish if she didn't get her in-store signage finalized. To save money on printing, because she had no idea what permanent signs should say, she bought some small chalkboards she could easily move around the store to highlight different sections or explain the table she planned for rotating themed books. If there came a time when she wasn't erasing and moving chalkboards, then she might consider permanent signage.

She was excited about her rotating themes. Holidays, Banned Books, and classics, of course, but also unusual themes like Books With Red Covers, or Music-Themed Novels, or Books With The Word "Calliope" In The Title. She'd already found three of these, which is what inspired the rotating themes. Dena was looking forward to the fun she and her customers could have with that.

Customers. That might be the missing piece to her plan, she worried. How was she going to attract customers to a used bookstore?

After she finished shelving three more boxes of books, she relocated herself to a table in the vendor area to brainstorm yet another list, this one about marketing and promotion. She'd made multiple iterations of this list ever since she bought the store but hadn't crossed off many of the items. Coming up with ideas was the easy part. Implementation, on the other hand … She needed something small enough that she could actually complete quickly that didn't cost much money and that would get customers in the door.

"And when I find it, I'll bottle it," she muttered.

Newspaper ads. Radio spots. Social media. Dena wrote these three ideas fast, thinking she might be on a roll, but then her short-lived streak ended, and she sat tapping her pen on the pad. She didn't want to do any of these.

What she really wanted was for people to hear about the Marketplace and rush to visit. When they saw how delightful it all was, they'd come every day and bring their friends and families, who would in turn do the same, until everyone on the planet had visited and bought a minimum of ten books per person per visit.

Was that so impossible?

She returned to her skimpy list. She had to start thinking outside the box, like corporate bigwigs said. Create some paradigm shift. Bring the new normal to the table. Pivot. Move the needle. Refrain from boiling the ocean. Scale up.

The personal pep talk she only half understood did indeed pep her up a bit and she began scribbling all the ideas that began to bubble up.

Dress up in a book costume and twirl a sign on the corner.

Tell people there's a hundred-dollar bill hidden in one of the books and if they happened to buy that book, they could keep the money. Dena immediately crossed that one out, envisioning her store with books strewn everywhere as people swarmed the shop, opening every page of every book without buying anything.

Have a "Sip & Shop" night with free-flowing wine. She crossed that out too, since she'd probably need a liquor license. But she'd stick a pin in that one and circle back later.

Punch cards. Buy ten books, get one free.

Coupons for people when they sign up for her newsletter.

Make a newsletter.

Book signings with Charlee. And other Colorado authors.

Dena began to feel better about her list. If she could implement a few of these, maybe customers would show up. It dawned on her that perhaps she *was* trying to boil the ocean and make everything harder than it really was. She didn't need to do everything; she just needed to do something.

Sheriff Johnson walked through her bookstore and into the vendor room, interrupting her. "You can't just leave your store open like that, you know. Anyone could walk through."

Dena felt a pang of guilt. "I know. When the Marketplace is finally open to the public, we've already decided these back doors will remain closed." Dena doodled in the margin of the notepaper. "I just find it stressful right now to see a bookstore with no browsers." She glanced up. "How'd you get in, anyway? We're being careful to keep the outside doors locked."

"I have keys to most of the buildings in town." Sheriff Johnson jingled them in the air. "Don't worry. You'll have scads of customers in no time. This town will wonder how they lived without a used bookstore for so long." The sheriff glanced around the vendor room, her eyes landing on the white board. A smiled formed at the edges of her mouth as she read the haiku. "You write that?" she asked Dena.

"Nope. It's pretty good, though, huh?"

"I've seen worse poetry. Heck, I've written worse." Sheriff Johnson walked to all the doors to the shops and gathered the tenants in the vendor room. When she came back with Skyler, the last to be herded, the sheriff walked to the whiteboard and made a big X over the four in "4 Days Without a Murder."

Everyone gasped and began murmuring.

Sheriff Johnson narrowed her eyes, then it dawned on her. "No! There hasn't been another murder. In fact, that's what I came here to tell you all. There was never a murder. The coroner's report says that Norbert's death was an accident. Seems he left the panel cover off the breaker box and forgot to turn the power off. He electrocuted himself." She looked around the room. "That's why you don't dismantle the safety features on anything."

Dena flashed to her house in Santa Fe and the disarray it was left in. She hoped the people working on her house were following safety protocols.

"Everyone is off the hook," the sheriff said.

The tenants remained quiet.

Sheriff Johnson cocked her head. "I thought you'd be happy."

"Doesn't change the fact there was a dead man just above our heads," Max grumbled.

"Well, no—"

"And it doesn't explain why his car was way over by the school," Evelyn said.

"It wasn't by the school, it was by the park," Sheriff Johnson said. "Norbert liked to walk over there, along the river."

"When it's so cold out?" Dena asked.

The sheriff laughed. "Sugar Springs doesn't roll up the sidewalks from October through April. People still like to walk in parks."

"If he parked over there, he'd have to carry his tools all that way to the Marketplace. Why would he do that in the middle of January?" Skyler asked.

The sheriff didn't have an answer for that.

Dena was going to remind them that she saw Norbert park his car outside the Marketplace the day he died, but Hugo spoke first.

"Who cares where his car was?" Hugo said. "Aja and Cap said in the paper what people around town have since verified, that Norbert knew his way about building construction, educating himself about everything so nobody could take advantage of him."

"If by *verified* you mean gossiped," Sheriff Johnson said, glancing around the room. "Listen. Regardless of what the *Sugar Springs Courier* prints, we are convinced Norbert's death was an unfortunate accident."

"Is there any other kind of accident?" Max asked.

Sheriff Johnson ignored him. "Our findings will be in the news too. People will see that previous article was just a new reporter trying to make a name for herself or gin up sales with intrigue rather than facts."

"Plenty of people in town have said that Norbert wouldn't have been so stupid as to get himself electrocuted," Hugo argued.

"Plenty of people also say Mrs Calloway's tractor is haunted and a Black woman shouldn't be sheriff," the sheriff said calmly.

Dena knew both those things were true. She could tell by the uncomfortable shuffling of feet that everyone else had heard similar rumors. Dena also knew they should all be ecstatic about the fact Norbert hadn't been murdered. They were off the hook. All the tenants who had been under suspicion should be jumping for joy right now.

Maybe the curse had been lifted from the Marketplace and the Grand Opening would go off without a hitch.

But from the conversation, it seemed the same thoughts continued to nibble at many of them.

Why was Norbert's car way across town? How would he do something so dumb and dangerous to get himself electrocuted? Had the sheriff spoken to Henry Capitano like she had and found out about Norbert's skills? Dena also wanted to ask the sheriff what she found out about Quint O'Dell.

Dena shook her head. "You know we should all be glad that—"

Suddenly Sheriff Johnson's radio blared full blast. Deputy Chavez said, clipped and fast, "Sheriff, Royce Reynolds is dead. Single car accident on Monarch Pass. His brakes failed. Looks suspicious."

Skyler

THE WORDS that crackled out of Deputy Chavez's radio thrummed in Skyler's brain.

Should she tell them?

The tsunami of memories of the times she spent with Royce flooded back.

Their first date. All that wine and flirting. She'd had so much fun that night.

But then their second date. Also plenty of wine and flirting, and even a trip back to Royce's place. As he was opening more wine, he told her to choose a movie from the cabinet. When she opened the doors to the cabinet, however, instead of movies, she'd seen a dozen framed photos of a striking woman. On a beach. Head thrown back, laughing at a party. Holding a surfboard. Playing with a dog. Waiting in line wearing Minnie Mouse ears at Disneyland. In front of the Eiffel Tower. On a gondola in Venice. In ski clothes.

But the photo Skyler lifted from the shelf in the cabinet was the woman in a wedding dress. Standing next to Royce in a tuxedo.

She stared at it, then tried to make sense of why these photos were shuttered behind closed doors.

Royce had appeared at her side. He gestured with a glass of wine. "The DVDs are actually in that one."

"Is this your … sister?" Skyler showed him the photo she held.

Royce traded Skyler a glass of wine for the photo and returned it to the cabinet. "That's my wife."

It had all suddenly made sense to Skyler. "Oh my gosh, she's dead?"

Royce had laughed. "Dead? What makes you think that?"

"Because you had them all hidden away. You couldn't bear to see them, but couldn't bring yourself to throw them away. It's tragic, but understandable."

"My wife isn't dead. She lives in Colorado Springs."

"You didn't tell me you were divorced." Skyler sipped her wine.

"I'm not."

Skyler's glass stopped halfway to her mouth. "Your wife is alive and living in the Springs but you're not divorced and you keep a zillion pictures of her in a cabinet." Skyler's mind raced and she began to feel overheated. "What am I missing?" She pointed at the cabinet. "Why are those photos in there?"

Royce had taken Skyler by the hand and gently led her to the couch. After they were seated, he said, "Those photos are in the cabinet because it's awkward when I have girls over for them to see pictures of my wife." He sipped his wine, searching her face for comprehension Skyler knew wasn't there.

Until it was. "Wait. You're married but you still date other women?"

He shrugged. "Why shouldn't I? After my dad died, I

had to stay here to be close to my mom and my wife didn't want to leave her job. It works out okay. At least until someone can't figure out where the DVDs are." He grinned at her.

Skyler jumped up, splashing wine on the couch. "That's the most disgusting thing I've ever heard!" She placed the glass on a nearby table and grabbed her coat.

Royce stopped her before she got her arms in the sleeves. "I don't know why you're making such a big deal out of this."

"Because married men aren't supposed to date! It's just not … done!"

"It's a new world, Sky. Relationships are messier every day."

"Then thank goodness we're not in a relationship!"

She had hurried out of there and returned home, disgust morphing into anger with every step. When she opened the door of her apartment building, Hugo had blocked her way to ask what happened. She remembered telling him that Royce was not the nice guy he pretended to be, but refused to tell him the details. It was too humiliating, too gross. And none of Hugo's beeswax.

But when Royce had asked her to meet him at Corky's, saying he wanted to explain everything, she agreed to meet him. He hadn't explained anything, she realized later, but somehow he managed to smooth things over with her nonetheless. He had apologized, and what he said made sense. They had to work together since his boss was the landlord of her cheese shop. Sugar Springs was a small town. It didn't make sense for them not to be friends.

"But we're never going on a date again," she'd insisted.

He'd laughed and agreed, then gave her a beautiful silk scarf of a Monet art print, and everything was fine until she had called to ask him if they could have lunch. She wanted to find out what Dena had found on Norbert's desk and if he thought she was the one who killed Norbert, but instead he had the nerve to ask her to spend the weekend with him in Gunnison.

And now Royce was dead.

Dena

THE SHERIFF SCRAMBLED to silence the radio and hurried from the vendor room.

Dena chased after her and caught up to her in the promenade.

"Not now, Dena."

"You should know, Royce came in one day when I was organizing my shelves. He asked if I had a section about electricity or wiring."

Sheriff Johnson stopped short and stared at Dena. "You're just now telling me this?"

"I just remembered."

"Isn't that a bit too convenient?"

First the nurses at the hospital in Santa Fe and now Sheriff Johnson didn't believe her? Dena felt her face grow hot. "You told us to tell you anything new we think of, so I'm telling you. I'm sorry about the timing. I've had a lot of things on my mind."

Sheriff Johnson kept staring at her. "So, you think Royce electrocuted Norbert and has now cut his own brake line?"

Flustered, Dena ran a hand through her hair. "I don't know what to think. But that's one scenario, right? People commit suicide for lots of reasons. Probably killing their boss ranks right up there."

Sheriff Johnson's face softened. "I'm sorry, Dena. I didn't mean to snap at you. That was unprofessional."

"That's okay. You've had a lot on your mind too. But I guess you're right. Cutting your own brake line would be a stupid way to kill yourself."

Sheriff Johnson nodded and hurried away, saying into her radio. "On my way, Chavez."

Dena returned to the vendor room. Cutting brake lines was indeed a stupid way to kill yourself, but not a bad way to kill someone else.

"Does anyone else think this has something to do with Norbert's death?" Dena asked.

"It's too coincidental not to be related," Evelyn said. "But how?"

Nobody had an answer.

"I just had lunch with Royce." Skyler turned her head and covered her mouth. "He invited me to go on that trip to Gunnison with him."

"What trip to Gunnison?" Hugo asked quickly.

"That's where he was heading over Monarch Pass. He said he had something to do there and asked if I wanted to spend a long weekend there with him." She spoke quietly, almost to herself. "I could have been in that car with him."

Hugo stared at her.

"We've known Royce since he was stealing hubcaps and smashing mailboxes," Max said in a flat voice.

"He seemed to have turned a corner, too," Evelyn said, slipping her hand into Max's.

Dena noticed Kober hadn't said anything, which was entirely out of character for her. But Kober had known

Royce for some time now, and had worked closely with him getting her bakery open. She must be in shock.

Dena felt a little twinge of guilt that she didn't feel worse about Royce and her first thought hadn't been about his accident, but rather her suspicion about him. Royce was essentially a stranger to her, however. Other than that brief time in the bookstore, and the other day when he fixed her lease, she'd never really had a conversation with him. Now she wished it had been a longer one. If so, maybe she wouldn't be so suspicious.

Or, she reasoned, maybe she'd be more suspicious.

Did Royce's murder have anything to do with the papers scattered all over Norbert's desk and his disheveled appearance that day?

She'd probably never know.

Before she left the Marketplace that evening, she went into the vendor room to turn off the printer.

She noticed Sheriff Johnson's big X on the whiteboard. Dena picked up the eraser and wrote "0 Days Without a Murder."

Hugo

ALL WEEKEND HUGO tried to understand Skyler agreeing to go out with Royce again, especially after what had happened on their previous date. He didn't know the specifics, but was smart enough to put two and two together and figure out that Royce had done something terrible to her, perhaps even violent.

He couldn't concentrate on anything, just kept shuffling around his apartment in his robe and fuzzy socks. He hadn't bathed, he barely ate, and when he did, it was whatever he could shove into his mouth from a bag or box without having to think too hard about it.

The same thoughts kept rolling through his head.

Who else knew what Royce had done to Skyler? Who else had seen that smug look on his face? Who else needed to protect Skyler?

Skyler

SKYLER HAD a million things to do at the shop, but couldn't bring herself to do any of them that weekend. Wrapped in a soft afghan, she hadn't moved from her couch most of the day. Deep down she knew all of it could wait until Monday, and realistically, some things on her To Do list probably didn't even need to be done at all.

She just couldn't stop thinking about Royce. Sheriff Johnson hadn't told them any details, but Skyler's imagination had Royce careening around a hairpin turn and sailing off the mountain. Or maybe he just lost control on a hill. Or maybe it wasn't dramatic like that. Maybe he just tapped his brakes, overreacted, and crashed into a tree or the guardrail.

She didn't know what it really meant to have your brakes cut. That was the only suspicious thing she could think of that might be considered brake failure. And that's what Deputy Chavez had said, wasn't it? But didn't that only happen in movies? Did someone really tamper with Royce's brakes? How could they even determine that?

Ultimately, she realized it didn't matter. Royce was dead, regardless of how it happened.

All weekend Skyler started and stopped herself from going to Hugo's apartment to talk to him.

But what Skyler really wanted to know was, did Hugo have anything to do with it? Did Hugo do something stupid? Skyler wasn't an idiot; she knew Hugo had a crush on her. But was it more than that? She never felt concerned or threatened when she was alone with Hugo, but could he have a screw loose?

She should have confronted him when she saw him spying on her first date with Royce. But she reasoned he hadn't done anything, and she'd look like a fool if he just happened to be at the same restaurant when she and Royce were. She groaned, thinking there'd be nothing more egomaniacal than accusing Hugo of stalking her when all he wanted was to treat himself to a nice steak dinner.

Skyler pulled her afghan tighter around her. Had Hugo watched for them the other day too? Was this more than him having a little crush on me? Hugo was right there that night when she came home mad from Royce's house, and he was again conveniently there right after Royce gave her the scarf.

Since she met him, she thought Hugo was simply socially awkward. But would that escalate to him trying to hurt Royce in some ill-conceived plan to salvage her honor or something?

Skyler hadn't told Sheriff Johnson anything about Royce yet. She needed to sort it out for herself first.

Images of Royce, Hugo, and the woman in Royce's photos all danced through her mind.

Was that really Royce's wife? Could he have made up that story about her? Definitely, but why would he do something like that?

A crystal-clear memory of Jimmy Throckmorten, a boy she knew in elementary school, jumped into Skyler's mind. One day he had brought a picture of a gorgeous black stallion to Show and Tell, bragging about his new horse. The horse was much too big to bring to school, he'd explained, so he brought the photo instead. He talked for weeks about his horse. He named him Debutante because he heard that word on the radio and he liked it. Skyler didn't have the heart to tell him that a debutante was for a girl horse, since he was so proud.

But one day the truth came out. He never had a big black horse. In fact, he didn't have any horse at all. He made the entire thing up in some ill-conceived plan to win friends or something. Skyler and her friends talked about it at the time trying to make sense of his motives. She never understood how he thought his scheme was going to work. If he used a non-existent horse to gain friends, wouldn't those same friends want to see the horse, give it an apple, or even ride it? It made no sense to anyone.

Except maybe to Jimmy Throckmorten.

Was Hugo doing something similar, but on a bigger, more dangerous scale?

Skyler's phone rang, interrupting her eddy of thoughts.

"Hi, Evelyn. What's up?"

"I'm here at the Marketplace, and there's a weird beeping in your shop. The door's locked so I can't get in."

"I'll be right there."

Skyler threw on some clothes and raced to the Marketplace. Evelyn greeted her at the door and they both hurried to unlock the cheese shop door. They searched for the source of the beeping, but couldn't find it. Skyler had assumed it was the smoke alarm running out of battery power, but that wasn't it. She finally found the culprit—the pedometer she'd grown disgusted with and threw in a box.

She turned it off, then held it up to show Evelyn. "It's this stupid thing. I thought I would track my steps since I thought I was walking so much. I barely cracked two thousand steps most days! So annoying."

"I'm glad it wasn't anything serious. I'm sorry to drag you out here just for that."

"No, I'm glad you did. I was going crazy in my apartment by myself. All this stuff about Royce."

"Shall we make a pot of coffee and talk about it?" Evelyn asked.

When they had settled in the vendor room with their mugs, Evelyn said, "Now, tell me why you look like you haven't slept in a month."

Skyler took a deep breath, then told Evelyn everything about Royce and Hugo.

When she finished, Evelyn said. "You have to call the sheriff." When Skyler didn't move, she said more emphatically, "Right now."

Skyler nodded.

Evelyn dialed the phone.

When Sheriff Johnson arrived, and Skyler had repeated everything to her, the sheriff had reached over and patted her hand. "I'm sorry you put yourself through all this turmoil. We already knew about Royce's wife and spoke to her right away after the accident. She was very shaken up. Her arrangement with Royce was … unconventional, it's true, but their relationship was amicable."

"You're saying she didn't have one darn thing to do

with messing with Royce's brake line?" Evelyn asked sharply. "And you're sure about that?"

"Yes. There's no motive—"

"That you know of," Evelyn interrupted. "What about insurance? That's always a good motive."

The sheriff continued, emphasizing with her eyebrows what she'd already said. "There's no motive and no possible way she would have had the opportunity to tamper with Royce's car."

The three of them stared at each other for a moment.

"What about Hugo?" Skyler asked quietly.

The sheriff chose her words carefully. "We'll look into everything you just told me, but I don't want either one of you jumping to any conclusions or doing or saying something rash or inflammatory. Let us do our job."

They both promised, but Skyler had her fingers crossed.

Evelyn

EVELYN SPENT the rest of the day fiddling with the photography equipment, making sure she understood how it all worked and what capabilities it had, which ones she could figure out, and which ones completely eluded her.

She was also glad to be away from Max. Things had thawed a bit between them, but probably due more to habit than anything else. He had been showing up at the Marketplace, but not coming with her and not staying all day like he had been. They still hadn't talked about what had happened the other day. Evelyn hadn't told him she'd been practicing with the equipment, but he came in that day when everyone had all been in costume. He wasn't dumb, he must have known what was going on.

But it was the elephant in the room unless one of them made an excuse not to be in the room.

Everything about their plans had changed the minute she realized Max was not up to the role as photographer and studio chief. Evelyn understood after more than sixty years together that he had to work through things himself. He had been head honcho for so long it was a habit for him, as much as how he brushed his teeth or shaved that grizzled old face. So, whether he accepted their new direction or not, he moved like refrigerated molasses to officially reach where Evelyn already stood at their starting line.

Perhaps all she'd have to do was point out that the money part of the business was really much more important than the photography part. She didn't believe that for one minute, of course, because any ninny could see that if the photos were subpar, there'd be no money.

Everything had gone on too long, though. Every hour they hadn't talked about it seemed like a year to Evelyn. She was waiting for Max to bring it up, and he was waiting for her. They'd never been this out of sync before, not even about their son. They discussed those dark times until everything had been said, and never technically got on the same page, despite all the words and tears. But at least they spoke, and didn't simply tiptoe around each other. Why did this feel so much harder?

With the weight of everything pressing down upon her, Evelyn rummaged through the desk where she knew Max kept his little flask. Who did he think he was fooling anyway? How dumb did he think she was? It was practically in plain sight. She shook her head and gave some little *tsk-tsks*. Evelyn had been figuring out so many of Max's secrets over all these years.

She pulled out the flask, leather-covered and almost as old as Max was. She settled in the desk chair, leaning back with her feet on the desk. Evelyn put the flask to her lips, waiting for the burning sensation down her throat.

She closed her eyes and took a deep swig. She swallowed. Eyes wide. Feet thumped back to the floor. Roared with laughter.

"Lemonade. That old coot!"

She closed up the studio and returned home with a semblance of what she wanted to tell him.

She opened the door to the aroma of roast chicken. "You made dinner?" Surprised, she hung up her coat.

Max remained in his chair reading one of his ever-present books about some period in history he found fascinating. *History du jour*, she thought of it. It was one of the things she admired about him, his ability to read and synthesize any era and succinctly explain what was important at the time and why, ranging from the Peloponnesian War or the Vietnam War and anything in between. Unfortunately, all that information seemed to push out the useful and everyday knowledge he needed, like the location of the laundry hamper where she would prefer his dirty socks to land, how to fold a towel, or where the spatula lived.

"I figured if you were trying to keep me barefoot and pregnant, I'd better make sure I could find my way around the kitchen at least," he rasped, without taking his eyes from the book.

"What do you mean?" she asked warily.

"I mean," he said, closing his book, "that we've been going about this all wrong. You need to take the photos."

Despite all the work she'd been doing recently, Evelyn felt her mouth go dry. The comforting aroma of roasting chicken suddenly made her stomach lurch. "Max, I … I don't think I can."

"Of course you can."

Evelyn shook her head slowly. "I don't think so."

Max rubbed his jaw, then ran his hand to the back of his neck and massaged it while staring at his wife. "Well, why the heck not?"

"I can't do everything. I'm already doing the appointments and the books." She looked at him with watery eyes.

Max barked out a guffaw. "You nut! I'll do the appointments and the books, and you do the studio work. We'll trade jobs."

Evelyn suddenly felt giddy, relief coursing through her. "Max, are you sure?"

He made a noise in his throat. "Don't go all anti-feminist on me now, woman. You're better at that than I am, so you should do it. I saw the work you did the other day." Max pulled a large envelope from the end table next to him and handed it to her.

"What's this?" Evelyn opened it and slid out a dozen eleven-by-fourteen full-color glossy photographs from the session she took for practice the other day when they'd all played dress up. She shuffled through them. Cowboys and schoolmarms. The gender-swapping pirates and wenches. Flappers and dandies. Hugo and Skyler on the settee. The boys as cavemen. She looked over at Max.

"They're great photos, Ev. And I thought they'd make good advertisements to hang on the walls so people could get an idea of what they could do at Step Into History. I'll get them framed and hung tomorrow."

"Max …" Evelyn was at a loss for words. Just two hours ago she was crawling through a desert, searching for information about what Max was thinking and how their business was going to survive, and now she felt like an oasis appeared right in front of her.

"We never really talked about it. You just assumed— and maybe I did too—that I'd be good at taking the pictures. But just because I had a successful career don't mean squat as to whether I can point a camera at someone." He stood and pulled her into a hug, his voice soft. "Besides, this is your time. I had mine. It's your time to fly. I'm sorry I've been such a horse's ass."

"Oh, Max." Evelyn buried her face in his shoulder, tears that had been threatening all day finally spilling over.

"There's one thing, though." Her voice was muffled. She looked up into his eyes, very serious.

"Anything."

"You have to launder the costumes too."

Max faked some bluster. "You're telling me after an entire career of having secretaries and assistants, now *I'm* the assistant? They don't get treated nice, yanno."

Evelyn pinched his butt. "I'll treat you nice, old man."

He feigned indignation and plopped back into his chair. She stood behind him and gave him a kiss on the wisps of hair fighting a valiant battle to cling to the top of his mostly bald head. "Just be sure to cook the chicken long enough so we don't die of ptomaine."

"Honestly, woman. Do I have to have the babies *and* keep you from dying?"

"If it's not too much trouble." Evelyn sat on the couch near him. "Oh, by the way, I found your flask today."

Max snorted. "Took you long enough. How'd you like it?"

"Little too sweet for my taste, you old coot."

———

The next day they had leftover chicken dinner for Sunday lunch. As they ate, they talked about Royce and his wild ways for the last ten years.

"Janet and Bernard were at their wits' end with him," Evelyn said. "Remember?"

Max nodded. "That *youthful exuberance* they were always bragging about almost got him arrested many times."

"Almost? He *always* got arrested. Any time there was trouble in town, Janet said the police were knocking on the door. It was only because of Bernard that the charges against him mysteriously went away."

"Bernard was a good man."

"But he sure didn't know how to raise that boy." Evelyn saw Max flinch. "What? You know he didn't." She was quiet for a moment. "You could have taught him some things," she said softly.

"Yeah, right."

After another pause, Evelyn said, "Royce wouldn't have fared so well any other place but Sugar Springs. It's such a small town and Bernard and Janet were so well respected here."

"I think it was hard on Royce when Bernard died."

"Janet too." Evelyn looked across at Max. "And now Royce is gone too."

They ate their food.

"Thanks for making broccoli. I was having a craving, but I still haven't figured out what this mystery seasoning is on the chicken," Evelyn said, licking her fingers.

Max looked over the top of his glasses at her. "It's love."

"Love? Oh yeah, I picked up a new jar last week." She grinned at him. "I bought a big one so we'll never run out."

"It's been sixty years. We haven't yet. Doubt we will any time soon." Max stabbed two broccoli florets and placed them on Evelyn's plate.

Evelyn added a smear of soft butter on top of her mashed potatoes then scooped them on to Max's plate.

He winked at her.

Evelyn finished the broccoli Max had given her then crossed her fork over her knife in the center of her plate. "I think I'll go over to Janet's this afternoon, see if she needs anything."

"You're a good egg, woman."

"So are you, you old coot."

———

Evelyn rummaged through the freezer until she found something suitable to take to Janet.

When Janet opened the door, Evelyn took one look at her and knew she was still dazed and shocked by her son's sudden death. She seemed translucent to Evelyn, as if she could see right through her. A shell of herself, grief swallowing her whole, making her disappear.

Evelyn bustled past her to set the tuna-noodle casserole on the kitchen counter. She settled Janet into a kitchen chair then made them both tea.

"When did you eat last, dear?" Evelyn asked, gently.

Janet stared at her like she didn't understand the question, or maybe worse, like she didn't much care.

Evelyn popped two pieces of bread in the toaster. While Evelyn worked, she tried chatting with Janet, but she would not engage.

She placed a cup of tea with milk next to a plate with the toast, one buttered and one with jelly, in front of Janet. "Eat," she commanded.

Mechanically, Janet chewed toast and sipped tea, but Evelyn knew she wasn't tasting any of it.

Every so often Janet would look plaintively into Evelyn's face and ask, "Who will take care of the fans now?"

Evelyn didn't know what she was talking about and even less sure how to respond. Until, that is, Janet jumped up from the table and hurried from the room. Evelyn followed close behind.

"Can Max put up my fans?" Janet pointed to two boxes stacked in the corner.

Evelyn studied the boxes. "Oh. Ceiling fans." Evelyn took Janet's hand and led her back to the kitchen. "No, dear, Max has no business climbing ladders. We'll get your fans sorted later. It doesn't need to happen right away, does it? It's still the middle of January."

Janet stared at her for the longest time. "It doesn't ever have to happen."

———

When Evelyn got home, she told Max about her visit, tearing up as she spoke. "Janet was so out of it, I called Laura from next door to come sit with her. She said she'd move Janet into their house until she's stronger. This has hit Janet harder than I even imagined. And I knew it was going to be bad."

Max pulled Evelyn into a hug. "It's never easy losing a child. No matter what age, no matter under what circumstances."

Evelyn pulled away, wiping her eyes. "Don't you start with me."

"I'm not starting anything, love," Max said softly. "Truth is, Royce's death has hit me kind of hard too. You know how I always plan for the future?" Evelyn nodded. "Well, this is a shining example of how you can plan everything but it can all go away like that." Max snapped his fingers. "I was a horse's ass complaining about the studio and mucking about over there. I should have recognized immediately I was no good and given you your turn to shine. I was watching what you did over there, and you're a natural. You've waited long enough for me to get out of your way. I will support you in every way I can, and we will make this work. You're the boss and I'll do exactly as you say."

Evelyn snorted. "Does that include using the hamper?"

"Let me rephrase. You're the boss and I'll do exactly as

you say … at the studio." At Evelyn's cocked eyebrow he added, "You know how it is. Old dog, new tricks. That hamper is invisible to me. Always will be."

Later Evelyn listened to Max snoring in bed next to her. She believed him when he said he was ready for her to take over the reins at the studio. Even though she knew he wouldn't manage to get his socks in the hamper, he would learn new tricks there, as many as they'd need.

But now, laying there in the dark, she wondered what Royce's death had churned up inside of him.

Would all this lead right back to those times with Oscar? Would they both be sucked back down into that quagmire?

Balaam

COPPER-COLORED eyes slicing through the dark bedroom, Balaam sat listening to the odd noises Max was making. Humans were so disgusting. But at least they roasted chicken and shared their largesse. A few noises could be forgiven.

Balaam could tell by her breathing that Evelyn remained awake. He'd sit sentinel until he knew she was safely asleep. There were too many strange happenings lately, and he'd been jumpy ever since getting locked on the second floor that day.

Knowing what he knew, seeing what he saw … well, it made him feel fretful and restless, like his collar was too tight, or a hairball was imminent, or there was the hint of a visit to the veterinarian in his future.

Or maybe this is what it felt like when his people were in trouble.

Kober

KOBER WAS hand beating a stainless-steel bowl of cake batter and had worked up quite a sweat.

"Getting some frustrations out?"

Kober jumped and shrieked when Sheriff Johnson spoke. After a string of colorful invective, she reassembled herself and calmly said, "I didn't hear you come in."

"I'm sorry. Didn't mean to startle you." Sheriff Johnson gestured toward the bowl. "You were really going to town on that dough."

"Batter."

The sheriff peered into it. "Ah, batter. I stand corrected. You were really going to town on that batter." She now peered at Kober.

Kober realized the sheriff hadn't come out to the Marketplace to see what she was baking today. She stalled a bit by addressing her hairdo, pushing it back into place, using her forearm to move curly tendrils from her face. "Can I help you with something?"

Sheriff Johnson leaned casually against the prep table.

"Saw your name in Royce's appointment book the day he died."

Kober picked up the bowl of batter and busied herself by stirring it, turning her back on Sheriff Johnson. "I wanted advice about renegotiating my lease, maybe just taking half this space." Kober waved her whisk around the area, splattering batter in an arc across the floor. Dropping to one knee, she wiped it with a paper towel she snatched on the way down.

"And?"

"And he couldn't help." The batter had been cleaned up, but Kober kept scrubbing the floor.

"Couldn't or wouldn't?" Sheriff Johnson asked.

Kober scrubbed the same clean spot for a long time, agonizing over her answer. "Wouldn't," she finally said. "I made that appointment with him before Norbert died. I wanted him to convince Norbert to change the terms of my lease. He refused, said he didn't want to get on Norbert's bad side."

"Then why were you meeting with him on Friday?"

After a pause, Kober said, "I thought I could convince him to do it after Norbert … was gone, bribe him with chocolate cake. He ate my cake and still refused."

"I understand you had words."

"Who told you that?" Kober said sharply.

The sheriff didn't respond, just kept staring at her.

"Fine, yes, we had words. But that doesn't prove anything. I have words with most people."

"Not ones that end up dead a few hours later."

"True." She quit scrubbing at invisible spills on her floor and sat back on her heels. "I didn't kill Royce. I brought him lunch and tried to get him to do the same thing I tried to get Norbert to do, let me just rent half this space. They both refused."

Kober expected the sheriff to say, "And now they're both dead," but she didn't.

Sheriff Johnson just nodded the slightest bit, watching Kober's face. "Thanks for your time." She glanced around the bakery. "Good luck with this place, by the way. And for what it's worth, it doesn't seem too big to me."

Kober stared after her as she left. She carried the stainless-steel bowl to the front of the bakery, then stared out to the window across the promenade, watching the sheriff get into her car. "She only came here to talk to me," Kober said quietly, realization dawning. She let out a breath. She'd expected to be hauled down to the station again.

She thought back to her encounter with Royce and regretted ever confiding in him about her financial problems. He had acted like what she told him wasn't even important, when in reality, her finances were the only thing that were important. Why couldn't he have seen that? Why did he refuse to help?

"Kober?" Dena touched her elbow. "I don't mean to pry, but you've been beating up that batter for half an hour out here. Do you want to talk about anything?"

Kober looked at Dena, then at the bowl wedged against her sternum. She dropped the whisk into the batter and shook out her arm and hand that had begun to cramp. "Half an hour? Really?" She used the back of her hand to wipe tears threatening to fall.

Dena shrugged. "At least." She asked again, "Do you want to talk?"

She waved Dena toward the bakery and followed her inside. Kober set the mixing bowl on the counter then filled two mugs of coffee from the hot pot behind the counter. She placed them on one of the bistro tables near the front counter and they sat.

She knew Dena was waiting for her to speak but she simply didn't know where to start.

After several moments of awkward silence and sipping of lukewarm coffee, Kober cut to the chase. "I'm in deep doo-doo here."

Dena raised her eyebrows. "Has the sheriff found more evidence against you?"

"Geez, Dena! Do you really still think I killed Norbert?"

"I don't know. I saw the sheriff." Dena's eyes widened. "Was she here about Royce?"

Kober sputtered, unintelligible words tumbled out before she could stop them. She clamped a hand over her mouth and took a deep breath. "Yes, she was here about Royce, but I didn't kill him either." At Dena's perplexed expression, she added, "She saw my name in his appointment book."

Dena relaxed. "Oh, I can't believe that's a big deal. Half the town was probably in there."

"The day he died?"

"Well, no," Dena conceded. "But surely that was just a coincidence?"

"Yes, but do you really think that's how it looks?"

"Again, probably not. But—"

"I wanted to see if he could help me get out of my lease, or at least cut my space in half or something. And I guess, technically … I was going to bribe him."

Dena's eyes widened. "How much?"

"Chicken and artichoke quiche. And a chocolate cake."

"I don't think that's technically a bribe. Or against the law. But why would you—"

"Because I'm broke." Kober's face turned stony. "I'm broke and I'm an idiot." She held up one hand to stop

Dena from speaking. "I *am* an idiot. I trusted that man and he screwed me over but good."

"Royce?" Dena asked.

Kober had started crying again and just shook her head.

"Norbert?"

Kober blew her nose loudly then stared directly at Dena. "No. My no-good, dirty-rotten, cheating-on-me husband."

Dena's hand fluttered to her face drained of all blood. "Oh, Kober. You killed him too?"

Kober's stony face softened and she began laughing. And laughing and laughing. Louder and harder. She knew she'd begun to sound hysterical, but couldn't rein it in. Besides, she'd felt hysterical for quite some time and it felt good to finally let some of it out. She felt tears once again streaming down her face and honestly didn't know if she was laughing or crying. Perhaps it was both.

She finally began to wrest control over herself again, and just in time it seemed, as Dena practically levitated above her chair, whether ready to flee or call for help or something else entirely Kober wasn't sure. She gulped some air and waved Dena back down.

"I'm sorry," she said, wiping her face with both hands. "I've been under some, um, stress lately."

"That's evident." Dena gripped her coffee mug so tightly her knuckles turned white.

After several more deep breaths, Kober had calmed sufficiently.

Enough for Dena to ask in a whisper, "Is your husband … still with us?"

"Unfortunately." She gestured to Dena's coffee. "Want some more?" Dena shook her head, but Kober walked over to the hot pot with her own cup.

"Maybe you've had enough?" Dena said tentatively.

"Nah, I'm fine." Kober filled her cup and smiled. "Actually, I feel pretty good right now. I guess it's true what they say about laughter."

"That it makes you forget about murder?"

"Temporarily, I guess." Kober slid back into her chair. "But thanks for reminding me."

"I didn't mean to—"

"It's fine. It's not like I wouldn't have come back to reality eventually."

They both fiddled with their mugs.

They both spoke at the same time.

"You go," Dena said.

"My husband moved us out here to Sugar Springs a couple of years ago from Denver. He said it would be better for the kids—and it has been, I think. But almost immediately he began spending more time in Denver than with us, even though he could do most everything remotely. Work was getting crazy, he said, and he needed to be there. I believed him at first, but then it seemed like he parked us here to get us out of his way. Nic told me I was crazy, and then when this Marketplace started shaping up, he thought it would be the perfect thing for us, starting a bakery together. I've always dabbled in the kitchen, but when he began getting excited about it, so did I. I thought this would be the thing to keep him in Sugar Springs. He could quit his job in Denver, and we'd be small business owners. Entrepreneurs. Sugar Springs elite."

"And now you are," Dena said.

Kober shook her head. "We're broke."

"Oh no!"

"Nic talked me into taking this big space, saying we'd grow into it as the Marketplace grew. He convinced me to buy an oven bigger than I actually needed, top-of-the-line, and you know how that turned out."

Dena nodded.

"I think he's trying to get me all set up so he can leave and set up house with some bimbo without a guilty conscience."

"Ugh. Kober, I'm so sorry. What a rat."

"That's putting it nicely."

"You said you *think* he's doing that. You don't know for sure?"

Kober shook her head.

"Maybe that's not his intention at all."

"But maybe it is," Kober said glumly.

That sat in silence for a few minutes, sipping their coffee.

Dena said, "So you were trying to get Royce and Norbert to cut you some slack with your lease to try and save money."

"Exactly." Kober slumped in her seat. "I'm so glad someone understands. It sure doesn't seem like Sheriff Johnson does."

"Did she accuse you of anything?" Dena asked warily.

"She didn't have to. I know what she's thinking." Kober gazed unfocused into the space over Dena's head and said quietly, "And Royce didn't even care. Not about any of it."

Dena

AFTER A BIT, both Kober and Dena had work to attend to, but as Dena went back to the bookstore, she wondered if Kober meant to say that last bit out loud. After all, it was so quiet Dena barely heard her.

While Dena shelved books, her mind kept turning toward Kober. She was deeply sympathetic to everything Kober had just told her. Dena knew first-hand how terrifying it was to suddenly lose a spouse and be tasked with raising children alone. It was overwhelmingly difficult for Dena even though her kids were both teenagers at the time. Kober's twins were only ten, with Jain and Wyatt just a few years older. Plus, there were four of them.

But all of that notwithstanding, Kober's story still sounded very peculiar to her. While Kober told it, Dena was all in, believing absolutely that Kober's husband Nic was a huge philandering jerk. But now, in the quiet of her bookstore, with a bit of space, was this another of Kober's tall tales?

Dena had never met Nic, so she had no personal firsthand knowledge of the man. But she was well-versed in KoberLand and Dena knew it wasn't always as it seemed.

Dena sorted through the facts, as she knew them.

Kober claimed to be in financial free-fall and went to Royce for help. Royce wanted to learn about electric wiring which killed Norbert, the person who could help Kober the most. Actually, the *only* person who could help Kober. But now Royce was dead too? Did Kober enlist Royce to get Norbert out of the picture and then when he did, Kober got him out of the picture too?

Dena still didn't believe that Norbert's death was an accident, despite Sheriff Johnson's official report. There were too many people talking about how much he knew about electricity and construction for Dena to accept that he did something to electrocute himself.

But what would Royce get out of that? Something about Norbert's business? Would he benefit somehow from Norbert's death? She remembered how disheveled he looked when he told her he was looking for Norbert's will or any estate information. But would someone up to no good confide that to a relative stranger?

And what about Kober? If Norbert was gone, maybe she'd get out from under her expensive lease, but maybe not. Could killing Royce have ensured that? Was her husband truly leaving her and, presumably, taking half their money, or more? Leaving her with even less income and all the debt?

Whichever way Dena spun these scenarios, it didn't look good for Kober. Was she lying about all of it?

Dena

THE NEXT MORNING dawned exactly how every day of the past week had—cold and with never-ending piles of books for Dena to shelve.

As Dena waited for her security gate to rise up into the housing, she stared in dismay at the boxes scattered around her store. "I swear there are more this morning than when I left yesterday," she muttered. "They're multiplying like rabbits."

She couldn't face any of it without more coffee and hoped there was a fresh pot brewed in the vendor room. She dropped her coat and purse and tried to overlook all the boxes until she was properly caffeinated.

Dena did a double-take and a backward step when she saw Quint O'Dell sitting at a table, facing her with a glower. Her heart beat faster and she wondered how he kept getting into the Marketplace when it was closed. Her phone was in her purse in the bookstore. She tiptoed backward toward it, eyes locked on him. She hoped Sheriff Johnson was already on duty this early.

Just as she got to the threshold of her shop—neither

one of them speaking—Max came out of the photo studio carrying a small box in one hand and its lid in the other. "Here's what I was telling you—" When Max saw Dena, he snapped the lid on the box and held it close to his chest, like he was protecting a baby in a Snugli. "Good morning, Dena. Didn't hear you come in."

"Hi," she finally said.

"I think you two know each other," Max said.

"We do. Hello, Mr O'Dell." She knew she sounded formal and unnatural, so she tried to lighten up. "What brings you here so early?"

Max quickly answered for him. "We're on our way out to breakfast. C'mon, Quint."

Making no move to leave his chair, Quint O'Dell gave a small shake of his head. "I don't care if she knows."

Max's eyes widened. "Quint, you—"

"Max and I belong to a support group."

"Quint, don't."

"I'm not ashamed."

One look at Max's ashen face and Dena knew that regardless of how Quint felt, Max didn't share his opinion. Dena waved a hand around the room. It was absolutely none of her business what support group they belonged to. "Just let me get some coffee and I'll leave you to it, then." She walked toward the pot, thankful it was almost full.

As she poured herself a cup, Quint said, "I used to own a bookstore. Not as nice as yours, of course."

Dena realized he was speaking to her. "Is that so?"

Quint nodded and tipped his chin toward the pot. "Any of that mud left?"

Dena got a mug out for him and raised her eyebrows at Max, silently asking if he wanted some too. He nodded.

"Yep, my son and me, we owned a dusty little bookstore in Colorado Springs. It was our pride and joy."

Dena delivered the coffee and stood sipping hers. "What happened to it?"

"Buncha crooks got the entire neighborhood blighted, knocked down the entire block, and put up luxury condos." Quint sighed into his cup before sipping. "We lost everything."

"That's terrible. I'm so sorry that happened to you. What kind of person would do such a thing?"

Dena meant it as a rhetorical question, but Quint answered. "Norbert Wallace."

She almost choked on her coffee. "Our Norbert Wallace?"

"One in the same," Max said softly.

"My son quit talking to me. Going on six years now. Blamed me for not fighting hard enough. Thought I just rolled over. But I knew there was no winning that battle." Quint sipped his coffee. "That's how this old codger and I met." At Dena's confusion he added, "Men's group to talk about problems with our adult kids."

"For the love of—" Max sighed from the bottom of his lungs. "Quint O'Dell, your head is emptier than a church on Monday morning. Ever think maybe I didn't want that to be public knowledge?"

"I assumed you were alcoholics or gamblers or something." Dena offered a bewildered shrug.

Max continued to stare at Quint who looked confused by his outburst. Dena didn't know where to look or what to say. She was just about to make a break for her bookstore when Quint finally said, "Max, I'm sorry. I didn't know it was such a big secret."

"Well, it is." He glanced at Dena. "Well, it was."

"Don't worry. I won't say anything." Dena made the *cross my heart* sign on her chest. When Max continued to stare at her, she added the *zipping her lip and throwing away the key* motion.

He gave her a slight nod. "That's why Quint is squatting in that nice lady's cabin."

"Hey!" Quint protested.

"Turnabout is fair play," Max said.

"The cabin where I visited you? That's not yours?" Dena asked.

Quint rolled his eyes. "Did it look like mine?"

She thought back to the décor. "Not really. But seriously? You're squatting there?" Dena thought he could be many things, but didn't peg him for a squatter.

Max chuckled. "He's so broke he can't even afford to pay attention."

Quint laughed with him. "Broke as a sailor on his second day of shore leave." He glanced at Dena. "Thought you came that day to throw me out."

"No, I was there to—" Dena remembered she went to visit him to see about his relationship with Norbert. And now she had a terrible motive for him to harm Norbert. She stared at the two elderly men sipping coffee, then maneuvered herself closer to the back door of her shop. If she needed to grab her phone, she was confident she could outrun Quint. "Can you account for your whereabouts last Monday?"

"Why?" Quint asked suspiciously.

"The day Norbert was murdered?" Realization dawned on Max. His gaze bounced from Dena to Quint.

Quint squinted up at Dena. "You think I killed Norbert Wallace?" When she didn't answer he said, "I've thought about it a hundred times."

"But you didn't—"

"Of course I didn't."

"You were here at the Marketplace the morning he

died," Dena pointed out. "It was the day you came here with that box of books."

"What of it?"

"You could have killed Norbert." Dena thought for a minute. "Did you drive away in his car?"

"What are you talking about? I called Mel."

"Who's Mel?" she asked.

"Mel is Sugar Springs' taxi service. He's like an Uber, Lyft, airport shuttle, cab, and limo driver all rolled into one. He'll dogsit too, if you need him," Max explained.

"Give me his number," Dena said.

"I didn't know you had a dog." Max read it to her and she entered it into her phone and dialed. "Is this Mel? … Hi, my name is Dena Russo … No, I don't need a ride, but I'm interested to know if you picked anyone up last Monday and brought them to the Sugar Mill Marketplace … Did you say Quint O'Dell? What time was that? … And did you pick him up too? … What time was that? … Are you sure? … Thank you, Mel … No, I don't have a dog … You'll be the first one I call."

"He says he picked you up before ten o'clock that morning, so you were long gone before Norbert even got here." Dena stared at Quint for a moment. "Do you have a phone?"

"Of course I do."

"I just wondered, since you said you lost everything."

"Everything important." He pulled his phone from his pocket and held it out to her.

Dena reddened, but checked his call history anyway. "Exactly what Mel told me." She handed it back.

Max looked relieved and Quint crossed his arms smugly. "Told ya."

She and Quint stared at each other for a moment. "So, you know about bookstores?"

He nodded.

"And you think those Colorado history books will sell?"

He nodded again.

"How about I drive you back to your, er … that house, and you can show them to me again, maybe help me set up a display?"

"Three hundred bucks."

"Deal breaker. I've got no cash to spare. But whatever sells I'll split with you fifty-fifty."

Quint made a dismissive grunt.

"Don't be a horse's ass, man," Max said with irritation. "You got nothing to lose. If they're as good as you say, they'll sell like hotcakes and you'll get the money after the Grand Opening."

Quint tried for a show of great annoyance, but Dena saw him grin into his coffee cup.

Hugo

HUGO SAT in the vendor room facing the whiteboard that now proclaimed, "3 Days Until Grand Opening … 4 Days Without a Murder." He was reading the most recent *Sugar Springs Courier* article. It was yet another unflattering article about the Marketplace, this time highlighting the deaths of both Norbert *and* Royce.

Today was Tuesday. The printed version of this article would come out on Thursday, the day before the Grand Opening. Hugo knew the article—enhanced and longer— would fill most of the front page.

The Marketplace was doomed. He rolled the words around in his mouth a little. He said it under his breath, elongating the syllables. "The Marketplace is doomed."

Evelyn sat at one of the other tables, stitching the Velcro tighter to one of the pirate shirts. Even though she was concentrating and her head was bent close to the costume, she heard him. "You're such a pessimist! Nobody has actually *said* they won't come to the Grand Opening. I haven't heard any scuttlebutt about a boycott or anything. Remember when they were trying to open that ugly gas station and fast-food complex out by the highway?" She gestured at Max and Kober. "You guys were here. Remember? Practically the whole town was out there waving signs, showing up at council meetings, giving their opinions about everything."

"They're all horse's asses," Max said.

"The protesters?" Dena looked up from her laptop, confused.

"Town council," Max said. "All of 'em."

"No, they're not, dear. Just because they make decisions you don't like doesn't make them horse's asses. And I've told you before, you should run for council if you don't like what they're doing."

"And turn into a horse's ass myself? Perish the thought."

"Then pipe down, you old coot." Evelyn wagged a finger at him. "My point is that when the good people of Sugar Springs don't like something, everybody knows it."

"But there's nothing to protest here," Hugo said. "The Marketplace is already built and we've all moved in. The only thing left for the good people of Sugar Springs to do is ignore us completely." Hugo looked up from his phone and scanned the faces of his fellow tenants. "We should cancel the Grand Opening. Lick our wounds and cut our losses."

He flinched at the barrage of words immediately hurled in his direction.

"I can't do that!" Kober bellowed.

"Impossible," Dena said. "We all have contracts. We can't break those."

"What would Max and I do with all our photography equipment? I'm sure we couldn't sell it for what we paid for it!" Evelyn rung her hands.

"None of us can afford that, Hugo. We've all sunk too

much money into this place. Even if we wanted to walk away, we simply couldn't." Skyler put her hands on her hips to make a point. "You couldn't either, could you?"

Hugo bit his lip and looked at the floor. He never wanted to admit this to anyone. Not now, not ever.

Kober stepped up next to Skyler. They looked with wide eyes at each other, then at Hugo.

Kober took another step closer to him. "Can *you* just walk away from this?" she demanded loudly.

Hugo felt like he was a rabbit facing a hungry pack of coyotes. "I wouldn't want to, but … yes, I could. I'm, um, rich."

"No way!" Skyler said. "If you're rich, why do you live in that tiny apartment?" She bugged out her eyes. "You could have your own washer and dryer!"

Hugo did not want to admit he lived in that tiny apartment with the communal washer and dryer in the basement so he could be near Skyler and was relieved—in more ways than one—when Dena said, "So it didn't matter to you when Norbert made you get a whole new sign for your chocolate shop."

He shook his head.

"Well, big whoop. You're rich." Kober looked like she wanted to strangle him.

"It is kind of a big whoop," Skyler said slowly. "It means he's the only one of us who didn't have a motive to kill Norbert."

Dena

EVERYONE SHUFFLED BACK to their shops, mulling over this new information.

Dena didn't know how she felt about Hugo's news. She thought about it while she continued with the never-ending task of pricing and shelving books.

A brainstorm—with nothing to do with Hugo—slammed into her like a bolt out of the blue and almost knocked her over. What if she didn't worry about putting a price on every book? What if she just had a blanket policy that her books were half the price of the original cover price of the book? That would solve her immediate problem of getting books out of the boxes and on to the shelves, plus would have the added benefit of not making her die a tiny bit inside whenever she tried to figure out a good price. Then in the future—assuming Hugo was wrong and that she actually had a future—she'd have a better handle on her cashflow and her customers and could make an educated decision, instead of the haphazardness of what she'd been doing lately.

She hurried over to one of her chalkboards and wrote:

ALL BOOKS HALF THE COVER PRICE. She added some dollar signs and hearts but then erased them. She wasn't a fourteen-year-old girl. She was an upper-middle aged businesswoman who now had a solid pricing plan.

She wedged the chalkboard in a prominent place so it could be easily seen by any customer who walked in.

Her pride in this solution was short-lived, however.

How in the world was she going to sell enough used books to the people of Sugar Springs, even if they actually showed up to the Marketplace for the Grand Opening?

Several weeks earlier, back when she was swollen with optimism, her accountant emailed her some projections about the sales she'd need to do every day, week, month, and year to break even. Dena had balked at the numbers and argued they couldn't possibly be correct, but the accountant walked her through everything line by line until Dena conceded the figures might be accurate. But they were still impossible numbers.

And now Hugo thinks we should all just walk away from everything? Maybe he could do that since he was apparently rich, just write all that red ink off his taxes, but Dena could not. She had sunk most of her money into this endeavor, just like everyone else here at the Marketplace. And she was still paying the mortgage on her house in Santa Fe, as well as for all the repairs and remodeling her contractor was doing.

Hugo had nothing to lose, though, it sounded like. No ties to anything or anyone. No wonder he was so mopey all the time, Dena thought with a pang.

Skyler was right. Hugo was the only one without a motive to kill Norbert.

But was he? Dena thought back to what Skyler had said about Norbert. Could Hugo have heard Norbert call Skyler *girlie* one too many times?

And what about Royce? Skyler said she'd gone out with Royce and that he'd invited her to spend the weekend with him in Gunnison over the weekend. Was Hugo's little crush on her more than a little crush? Dena never wanted to project her own fears on other people, but was Hugo a bona fide, dangerous stalker?

She kicked herself for ignoring that little knot in her stomach whenever she saw Hugo staring at Skyler. Especially after what had happened in Santa Fe. Dena vowed to be much more aware and proactive. She couldn't come right out and accuse Hugo of anything—could she?—but she could certainly tell Skyler what had happened to her in Santa Fe as a cautionary tale.

She'd tread carefully, however. There's a fine line between mentioning food for thought and scaring the bejeebers out of someone.

Maybe she needed more evidence against Hugo.

Dena peeked into the vendor room but Hugo wasn't there. Neither was Skyler. She snuck out the front of her bookstore into the promenade and tiptoed next door to peek into Skyler's cheese shop. Skyler stood facing the back of her shop, head cocked staring at her sign hanging on the wall.

Dena hurried past the photo studio to the other side of the Marketplace. When she reached Hugo's chocolate shop, she hugged the wall and peered stealthily around the corner. Hugo was concentrating on a tray of chocolates, drizzling glaze over them in precise designs.

She stared at him fussing over his candies. He sure didn't look like a stalker or a murderer. She watched him for a long time, his precise movements a bit hypnotic. Was he right about the Grand Opening? Was it destined to fail? How could they expect shoppers to come to the Market-place if it was the scene of a murder? With the second victim the employee of the first? With the murderer still at large?

Dena felt silly spying on her fellow tenant like that and walked back toward the bookstore the same way she'd come. When she reached Really Grate Cheese, she veered inside. "Skyler?"

She whirled around. "Oh, hi, Dena." She turned back toward her sign, pointing. "Do you like this?"

"You're still second-guessing your shop sign? Skyler, you really must move past that. It's too late to change it anyway. And it would cost a fortune, wouldn't it?"

"I suppose." She sighed and moved a half-step too close to Dena. "What's up?"

Dena took a half-step away. "I don't know. I just have a —" Dena wasn't sure what she wanted to say to Skyler. She didn't want to frighten her and she didn't want to come off like an overprotective mother. "I'm wondering—and it's none of my business—but I'm wondering about your, um, relationship with Hugo. He seems very … smitten with you."

Skyler laughed. "Yeah, I guess he is."

"Do you feel the same?"

"Oh, goodness no. He just has a little crush on me. He'll get over it soon enough."

Dena tried to keep her face neutral, but her eyebrows shot up anyway. "Will he?"

Skyler's face clouded. "Why wouldn't he? What are you trying to tell me?"

Dena placed her hand gently on Skyler's forearm. "I don't know. It's probably nothing, but I recently went through something … with a man …"

"Oh, Dena! Did he hurt you?" Skyler's face crumpled.

"Not physically, but he made me think. And question

people's motives. Maybe I'm over-reacting, but I'd really like you to pay more attention to Hugo."

"Pay *more* attention to him? I'm trying to get him to understand I just want to be friends."

"I didn't mean like that. I just meant to be aware of him and of his attention to you. If you ever feel the least little bit uncomfortable, get yourself away from him. Maybe even carry a whistle and pepper spray or something."

Skyler studied Dena's face. "I appreciate everything you're saying, but I don't think I need to worry about Hugo. I've never gotten a creepy vibe from him and trust me, every article, every social media post, every time I get together with girlfriends, this topic comes up one way or another. I was raised in the country. I was out in the dark worrying about boogymen ever since I was a little kid. I learned to carry my keys with my finger on the alarm, keep the earbuds out of my ears, and look into the backseat of my car before getting inside. Like you, I imagine."

Dena nodded.

"I just don't feel like I need to do that here in Sugar Springs." Dena started to interrupt but Skyler didn't let her. "I know what you're going to say. Bad things can happen anywhere and I get that, I really do, but I honestly have never felt that way around Hugo." Skyler leaned toward Dena and lowered her voice. "But you know who did kind of creep me out?"

Dena shook her head.

"Royce."

Dena

DENA LEFT Skyler and immediately called Sheriff Johnson. After exchanging brief pleasantries, Dena said, "Why did you say accidents aren't always accidents but then stop investigating Norbert's death when the coroner said it was an accident?"

"What makes you think I stopped investigating? Besides, I took one look at you and knew you'd be involved whether I liked it or not. Especially when I found out your daughter is a mystery writer."

"You investigated me?" Dena shook her head. "Duh, of course you did. And everyone else at the Marketplace. And you're convinced none of us killed Norbert or Royce?"

"Did I say that?" Sheriff Johnson paused. "Listen, Dena, I can't share our investigation with you, but I'll never say no to extra eyes and ears. Sometimes my hands are tied, though."

"Okay, then, here goes." Dena proceeded to tell her everything she knew about Skyler's relationship with both Hugo and Royce, just in case Skyler wasn't being truthful about having taken the information to the sheriff. She was pleased to find out Skyler had indeed confided to Sheriff Johnson. Dena left out the information she turned up about Quint O'Dell for fear she'd get him kicked out of the cabin he was squatting in. That was none of her beeswax. But she reiterated her concerns about Hugo.

"This is one of those instances where my hands are tied. From what I understand, Hugo hasn't done anything illegal or even pushed that envelope."

"No, he hasn't," Dena conceded. "But you should know."

"Absolutely. And now I do. And so do you and Skyler. Eyes and ears, remember?"

Dena mentioned her concerns about Kober's truthfulness and Sheriff Johnson chuckled softly. "I appreciate your concerns about Kober—"

"But you won't take them seriously."

"I take everything seriously." Sheriff Johnson took a long beat. "Again, I'm not going to share my investigation with you. Thank you for bringing me your concerns and information. I'm always here if you need me." With that, she disconnected.

Dena wasn't sure whether she should feel placated or brushed off. The sheriff seemed like she truly listened and heard what Dena was saying, but did she really? Regardless, Sheriff Johnson didn't tell her she'd arrested any murderers and she also didn't tell Dena to back off.

Eyes and ears.

Four things Dena possessed.

———

After her conversation with Sheriff Johnson, Dena read the online article about Norbert and Royce one more time.

She'd already read it so many times she'd practically committed it to memory, but she reread it anyway, hoping something important would jump out at her.

Nothing did.

Aja hadn't done any investigative journalism here. In fact, the article barely said anything new that they hadn't already heard around town. This "journalism" was no better than some fussy over-the-fence gossip.

But if Hugo was right and people weren't going to attend the Grand Opening because of this article, then maybe they could get some real information to Aja so she'd post a less defamatory article before the Grand Opening. It was a longshot, with barely any time to lose, but Dena felt like she had to try.

She gathered up the tenants for a meeting in the vendor room. She wished she could give them all a hefty dose of truth serum, but had to settle for hoping the threat of ruination of their businesses would be the catalyst she needed to figure out which—or if—any of them were guilty.

When everyone was sitting around the big circular table, Dena said, "I've called you all here—"

"Is this where you accuse one of us of murder?" Hugo laughed, but not in a humorous way.

Dena thought for a moment. She hadn't planned to confront them Hercule Poirot-style, but maybe Hugo was on to something.

She turned to him. "Okay, let's play this out. Hugo, you don't seem to have had a financial beef with Norbert, but did you, perhaps, have enough of the way he condescended to Skyler, calling her *girlie* and *sweetheart* all the time?"

Hugo snorted. "You think I killed Norbert because he

was a jerk to Skyler? Pretty sure Skyler can handle an oaf like him. I've seen her do it."

"Thank you," Skyler said. "But he really was mean, wasn't he?"

Nods all around the table.

"Okay, but what about Royce?" Dena asked him.

"What about him?" Color inched up Hugo's neck to his face.

"Did you feel the need to protect Skyler's honor with him? Or maybe you got jealous?" Dena said.

"Jealous enough to cut his brake line?" Kober added.

Hugo took a deep breath, glancing at everyone staring at him. "It's no secret that Skyler and I are friends, but for your information, I wouldn't have any idea how to do such a thing." He held up his hands. "Do these look like the hands of someone who has ever done any work on a car? I'm not always sure how to pump my own gas. I know there's a hose, and a tank somewhere, but after that, it can be a bit baffling."

Max let out a loud guffaw, which broke the tension in the room.

The real-life version of *Clue* continued.

"Okay, my turn," Kober said, turning to Dena. "You were furious with Norbert and then just happened to find his dead body." She glanced at the other tenants. "I accuse Dena in the second-floor vendor room with exposed wiring."

This was not going at all the way Dena expected. She took a moment to compose herself then said, "I was angry with Norbert, and I did find his body, but if I killed him, how would I get him to fix my lease?"

"Good point, dear." Evelyn jotted something on a notepad in front of her.

"Are you keeping score?" Dena asked incredulously.

"Memory's not what it used to be." Evelyn made a thinking face, then conferred with Max in whispers. "Our turn. We think it was Kober." She patted Kober's arm. "Sorry, dear."

"Okay, fine—"

"I was right?"

"No! I meant okay, fine, I'll play. Yes, I'm loud. Yes, I sometimes tend to stretch the truth a bit. Yes, I was yelling some choice words into my phone. But none of them were directed at Norbert."

"Who were they directed at?" Skyler asked.

"My husband. It's personal."

"You know," Max said, "my feelings are kind of hurt. Nobody thinks we could have killed him?" He put an arm around Evelyn. "I'm not dead yet. I could kill somebody if I wanted."

"Yes, dear. You're still a vital man." Evelyn looked at the other tenants. "And what about Balaam being up there? Didn't any of you consider that?"

Dena couldn't believe what she was hearing. What was this crazy game they were playing?

"Don't feel bad, you two. I said a long time ago that I thought you could have done it," Kober said kindly.

"Thank you, dear. That means a lot."

"Okay, okay. This is getting weird. Can we shift gears here?" Dena said.

Everyone shrugged or nodded.

"Unlike Hugo," Dena glanced his way and paused, "I don't have an unlimited supply of money. I've been saying all along that I think we need to solve Norbert's murder—"

"Which the police have determined to be an accident," Max said.

"But we know that's not true." Dena looked around the table. "Does anyone think Norbert's electrocution was an accident?" When nobody spoke up, she said, "That's what I thought. And now we have Royce's brake line cut." Dena snuck a glance at Hugo, whose face remained impassive. "All my energy and money has been sunk into my bookstore, and if the Marketplace fails before it even opens, I honestly don't know what I'll do. I think you guys—most of you—are in the same boat."

Everyone nodded then looked at Hugo.

"This is why I didn't want any of you to know I had money," Hugo whined. "And for the record, it's not technically my money. My parents are rich, so I'm just rich by … association. It would be just as bad for me if my shop failed. Maybe worse."

Nobody said anything, but they all shifted uncomfortably in their seats.

"Okay," Dena continued. "Let's agree we're all in the same boat. We *all* need the Marketplace to be successful. I propose we pool our information and see if we can find something—anything—for Aja to write about that might save the Marketplace from this bad publicity." Dena pointed to the whiteboard. "We have three days. Even though the print edition of the paper is going to come out just one day before the Grand Opening, we all know how fast the *Sugar Springs Courier* can get an online article circulating. Let's give her something she and Cap might think is newsworthy. They're all about the eyeballs on their stories, so let's find something juicy—" Kober held up one finger and started to speak but Dena finished her thought. "But truthful."

Kober lowered her finger.

"Let's walk minute by minute through the day Norbert was killed. And anything you know about Royce, too."

"That boy smoked like it was his sole job to prop up

the tobacco industry. Disgusting. He got rid of all his other vices except that one," Evelyn said.

"True," Skyler said, "but let's do what Dena suggested."

Dena wondered what, if anything, Skyler hadn't told her about Royce, but was glad to steer the conversation back to the timeline.

"Okay, I'll start," Dena said. "The morning Norbert was killed, I saw him drive up to the Marketplace."

"You actually saw him drive up?" Kober asked.

"I'm like ninety-eight percent positive. And the only reason I'm not one hundred percent sure is the fact his car was found over at the park. That makes no sense to me. But that morning I was looking out the window to the parking lot. I could swear I saw him park and get out of his car. He was carrying his toolbox so I knew he was going to do some work upstairs. Or I assumed he was going up there anyway." Dena cut her eyes toward Kober. "I want to keep this as factual as possible."

"What time was that?" Evelyn asked.

"Around eleven."

Evelyn nodded. "That makes sense because around eleven-fifteen, when Max and I were eating lunch—"

Someone made a noise, trying to suppress a laugh. It was a joke around the Marketplace how early and how often Max and Evelyn ate "lunch."

"Hardee har har. You just wait until you get old. You'll find A, you need to eat more frequent smaller meals, and B, you don't give a crap anymore about what anyone thinks."

"If you're hungry and you know it, clap your hands," Max sang.

As it was long past lunch, everyone clapped their hands, at first tentatively, then with more gusto.

Skyler jumped up. "I'll load up a cheese board for us. Keep talking! I can still hear you in there. I'll just be a sec!"

"So, as I was saying—"

"What?" Skyler called.

Evelyn raised her voice. "As I was saying, Max and I were at the little red bistro table—"

"Which one?" Skyler called.

"The red one in between the bookstore and the bakery," Evelyn shouted.

Max harrumphed and slumped backward in his chair, feigning falling asleep.

"I love that table!" Skyler shouted back.

Max let out a cartoon snore but smiled without opening his eyes when Evelyn swatted him.

"Anyway, that's where Max and I were when we heard Kober yelling at Norbert. They must have been back by her oven. She was slamming stuff around, getting kind of ... violent. At the time, we thought it was amusing, like watching the Netflix." Evelyn looked down at her folded hands on the table. "I'm sorry, dear."

Kober nodded, silent for a change.

Skyler bustled back into the vendor room carrying two cheese trays filled with slices and wedges. There were ample crackers of several varieties and two cheese knives on each tray. She set them down equidistant so at least one of the trays was in reach of everyone. "Oops. Forgot napkins." She hurried away then came right back in, passing out cute cocktail napkins with cheese puns on them.

Everyone laughed and read theirs out loud.

"Relax. Just take it cheesy."

"You brie-long with me."

"It's really gouda to have you here."

"I swiss you the best."

"I'm nacho ordinary person." Evelyn settled back into her seat, reached for a long slice of cheese and cracker to match. "Okay, where were we?"

"We heard Kober yelling at Norbert at eleven-fifteen." Max scooped up a hearty snack from the tray.

Skyler nodded. "I was putting new paint swatches on a piece of cardboard in here—remember how I was trying to decide between Autumn Gold and Autumn Splendor?" She looked at Hugo for confirmation.

"You mean yellow and yellow?" he said with a smile.

"There was a *huge* difference between those two and you know it!"

"I'm just teasing," Hugo said. "Yes, I remember that."

"That's when I saw Kober drag Norbert upstairs to see about the wiring. She was yelling at him, *if you won't fix it—*"

Hugo finished her sentence with her. "I'll fix you!"

Hugo and Skyler both looked at Kober. "We both heard you. Are you going to deny it?"

"Not in the least," Kober said confidently. "I did say it. But not to Norbert and I didn't drag him up there. You are definitely mistaken about that. I went up there to make sure that's what he was doing. Everyone here knows I've been bugging him to get my oven to work—that's no secret —and I was thrilled he finally was going to do it. I just can't believe it was only my unit affected, though."

"That oven of yours pulls the most energy," Max said. "Or maybe it has to do with the way the units are wired. Maybe we're all on separate circuits. Or a first-floor unit is paired with the second-floor unit right above them. The unit above the bakery is empty."

"I guess. At any rate, once I realized he might actually fix things, I left him up there while I came down and took a call from my husband," Kober said.

"You also said *men are pigs*," Hugo reminded her.

Kober looked down at her hands folded on the table in front of her. Quietly she said, "I already told you, I did not say that. I was annoyed at Nic because he told me he was stuck at the office. Again. Work problems. I might have thought it on occasion, but I didn't say it." She looked around the table at her fellow tenants. "And that's the truth."

She gave Dena the side-eye, which Dena took to be Kober's way of silently asking her to keep quiet about her marital problems. Dena kept her mouth shut, but that didn't mean she wasn't paying attention to the details. Or wondering where Kober's truth actually resided. Was her timeline and recollection of that morning to be believed?

Evelyn continued. "Max and I were just finishing up our lunch—must have been eleven forty-five or so—when you," she indicated Dena, "stopped by to chat with us."

"That's right." Dena nodded. "You told me there were fireworks upstairs with Norbert. I hurried up there to talk to him about my lease before he snuck away from me again. I passed Kober talking on her phone—"

"Like I said, to my husband."

Dena gave a curt nod then continued. "I went upstairs and he was standing on that ladder. I was trying to talk to him, but he ignored me completely."

"Maybe he was concentrating on the job at hand because he didn't know what he was doing?" Hugo said. "Maybe that could be something for Aja to write about."

"Maybe. But I didn't really get that impression. It seemed more like he was trying to ignore me. But I'll write that down." Dena jotted a note. "He told me my lease was on his desk back at his office and he'd get to it and I shouldn't worry. I made him promise he'd stop in the bookstore before he left the Marketplace." She shrugged. "But he didn't."

"That's why you broke into his office? To find that paperwork?" Skyler asked.

"I didn't *break into* his office. The door was unlocked and I walked in. Nobody was there so I was looking for him and stuck my head in his office."

"And that's when you stole it," Kober said.

"Stole what? I didn't steal anything!"

"Because Audra stopped you." Kober raised an eyebrow.

"That's not what happened." Maybe that was exactly what happened, Dena thought. Maybe she would have swiped the document if she'd found it. She shook the thought away. "But we're getting away from the timeline. So … Norbert was on the ladder and promised me he'd stop by before he left. It was probably noon by then. As I was coming down, Skyler was going up."

"You told me not to go up there. You held my arm to keep me from going to talk to him." Skyler's look was accusatory.

Exasperated, Dena said, "I told you, I wasn't trying to keep you from going up, I was trying to keep myself from falling down. You have the tendency to walk too close to people and we didn't both fit on that stairway."

"You do, dear," Evelyn said, patting Skyler's hand. "You're what I believe is called a close talker. You don't seem to have the same … uh … personal boundaries as other people."

Skyler's hand fluttered in front of her face. "I do that? Seriously?"

Everyone around the table nodded.

"I'm glad you're not a man," Max said. "If there were

seventy-five empty urinals in the men's room, you'd pick the one right next to me, I'm sure of it."

Hugo chuckled.

"Why didn't anyone tell me?" Skyler took a giant step away from everyone.

"We're telling you now, I guess," Kober told her.

"It's not a big deal," Dena said. "But that's why I was holding on to you."

"I feel so dumb." Skyler's face reddened. "That's the whole reason I thought you had something to do with Norbert's death."

"It's really not a big deal." Dena tried to reassure her and changed the subject. "But after that, I was working on my inventory stuff—a job I am just now realizing will never, ever end—and I could see Norbert's car parked right out front. I was sure he wouldn't be able to ditch me again, so I kept working. It must have been like one-fifteen by then. I honestly thought he'd do what he promised and stop in to see me before he left, so I didn't pay much atten-tion and got involved in my books. But when I looked up his car was gone."

"And we know now it was driven over to the park," Evelyn said, making a cheese and cracker sandwich for Max.

"But not by him," Hugo said with a low, ominous voice.

Dena nodded. "That's why I was racking my brain to figure out if I knew for a fact he drove his car, or if he was with anyone. Like I said, I'm almost positive I saw him drive up. And I didn't see anyone with him at any time that day. Did any of you?"

Everyone shook their heads.

"That's when I stormed over to his office."

"So, you were angry," Kober said, pointedly. "People get angry, don't they? It doesn't mean they killed anyone."

"Yes, I was angry. But I had cooled down on the walk over. When I got there, nobody was there but Audra came in a few minutes later with her lunch."

Everyone was quiet, waiting for her to continue.

Some loose thread was tickling Dena's brain, but she couldn't quite tug on it to find whatever answer she was seeking.

When Dena didn't continue, the others began recounting the aftermath of finding Norbert's body and being questioned by Sheriff Johnson and Deputy Chavez.

Dena's video chat alert chimed on her phone. Assuming it was Charlee or Lance, she opened it up without looking and was surprised to see her general contractor standing in the basement of her house in Santa Fe.

"Hey, I hope I'm not disturbing you, Miz Russo, but I just got here and saw this. I don't know how long it's been this way or if you saw it when you were here, but I wanted to make sure you knew it wasn't any of the guys I hired."

"I'll be right back," Dena said to the other tenants, scooting back her chair. As she hurried out of the vendor room she said into the phone, "Just a sec."

Out in the promenade, Dena squinted at the fuzzy image on her phone to see what her contractor was talking about. "What am I looking at?"

"The electrician you hired doesn't have the brains God gave a gnat. He's definitely substandard, and none of my guys," he paused for effect, "would have allowed that during any inspection. You're just lucky I got here before the inspector did. They are tough and would have dinged us for sure. Unless you have any objections, I'm firing him and putting my electrician on it instead." He pointed his camera at the breaker box, sans cover.

Dena shuddered. It was eerily similar to how the second-floor vendor room looked when she found Norbert. "You do what you need to. I hired that electrician before I knew what a big job this was turning into and found you. You're the professional. I trust your judgment."

"Thanks, I was hoping you'd say that. Nothing against the electrician if he's a friend of yours or something, but he doesn't see the big picture like me and my guys. We have to know more than the inspectors know, and they know everything. I'll keep you posted. Thanks."

Dena disconnected, but stared at her screen until it went dark. Audra had said something about inspections the other day when they were having lunch, how she had to learn so much, and even had to teach Royce some things, despite the fact he'd already gone through the course himself.

Audra knew her way around electricity. So did Royce.

Dena returned to the vendor room and interrupted the conversation swirling around her. "Evelyn, did you say that Royce was a smoker?"

"Like a chimney."

"What about Audra? Do you know if she smoked?"

"Hm. I never saw her smoke. Not that I can remember, anyway." Evelyn looked at her husband. "What about you, Max? Ever see Audra with a cigarette?"

Max shrugged then shook his head.

"What about anyone else?" Dena asked. "Have any of you ever seen Audra smoking?"

Nobody had.

"Why?" Kober asked.

"I'm not sure yet," Dena said. "I've just been assuming

some things, and now I'm thinking maybe I should rethink everything."

Hugo abruptly pushed back from the table. "I've got more chocolates to make. If you people insist that I give away candy this weekend, I may as well go out with a bang, right?"

"What do you mean?" Skyler asked.

Hugo walked toward the back door of his shop. "I mean, if only eight people will be coming to our Grand Opening, then I guess I'll bury them in truffles for their effort."

"Eight people!" Max scoffed. "That's twice as many as I predict."

Evelyn swatted him again. "Oh, Max!"

Kober groaned. "I guess I better get back to making the cake pops I'll be giving away." She turned back toward them before she slipped through her door. "Those eight people will be sick to their stomachs by the time they leave here, with all the cake, candy, and cheese we'll be loading them up with."

Everyone else went back to their shops, but Dena remained in the vendor room, tapping her pen on her notepad.

Dena

THURSDAY MORNING, the day before the doomed Grand Opening, dawned overcast and gloomy. The sun didn't look like it would break through the clouds any time soon.

Typical, Dena thought. She hadn't had much sleep last night and didn't particularly want to do what she knew she had to do today. The weather was actually a bit sunnier than her mood.

Her mood only got worse when she stepped out of her front door and saw a copy of the *Sugar Springs Courier* with Aja's article screaming TWO DEAD AT MARKETPLACE. "That's not even accurate," she muttered, scooping up the newspaper to take to the Marketplace with her. She'd fortify herself with one of Kober's pastries before she'd check to see if it was still the same poorly researched online article they'd posted previously.

Hugo's idea of telling Aja their theory that perhaps Norbert was concentrating on the job at hand because he didn't know what he was doing seemed ridiculously inadequate right now. It was the only idea they'd come up with yesterday, and still worthless and unsatisfactory.

Dena stood in the promenade in front of her shop and admired her Thrice Sold Tales sign. She was quite proud of it and how she articulated to the sign-maker exactly what she'd wanted to convey. It thrilled her that a casual, homey font and some soothing colors had the ability to welcome browsers and let them know they were welcome to stay as long as they wanted. She had gotten goose bumps when she saw it for the first time.

Today, however, she wondered what she'd do with it when her business failed. It would be a majestic reminder of her incompetence and misfortune. She'd probably burn it. Maybe smash it with a hammer. Hack it into tiny pieces and use it for mulch in her garden. Order some TNT from Wile E Coyote's Acme Company and blow it to smithereens.

After the security gate rolled up, she walked through the bookstore and unlocked her back door, fully intending to reread Aja's stupid, probably error-ridden article.

She needn't bother.

All the tenants were already in the vendor room, a plate of Kober's pastries in the center of the table.

"Did you see it?" Skyler asked glumly.

"Just the headline," Dena answered.

"No need to read the rest. It's basically the same, but with more adjectives and hyperbole." Hugo handed Kober a dollar and grabbed a raspberry-filled Danish.

Kober blushed at the bill in her hand, then stuffed it in her apron pocket.

Dena dropped her purse and coat on a chair and walked over to the whiteboard. She changed the sign to "1 Day Until Grand Opening" then erased the "5 Days Without a Murder."

"Goodness gracious!" Evelyn's hand fluttered to her face and covered her mouth. "What's happened now?"

"Oh! Sorry. Nothing. But I don't need this reminder and I bet none of you do either. Besides, what if one of our shoppers glanced back here and saw that? What would they think?"

There was mumbled agreement all around.

Dena left the haiku, which now read:

> Grand Opening might
> Be the thing that makes me want
> To get a real job.

"Who wrote this one?" Dena asked with a smile.

None of them confessed.

She didn't say it out loud, but Dena thought owning this bookstore might be the most real job she's ever undertaken. Aside from raising Charlee and Lance, that is.

Dena pulled the newspaper from her bag, fully intending to read it. But then she sighed loudly and dropped it on the table, instead pulling out her wallet. Following Hugo's lead, Dena handed Kober a dollar bill, then thought better of it and handed her two dollars before loading a plate with two pastries, one raspberry, one lemon. She took them into the bookstore and stood behind the front counter to eat them, holding the plate under her chin to catch any crumbs.

While she munched the raspberry Danish, she tried to reconstitute everything she'd learned about both Norbert's and Royce's deaths. So much information swirled throughout her brain and danced around the periphery. She couldn't quite put it in order. It felt like someone had dumped a 1,000-piece jigsaw puzzle in there but didn't give her the picture she was supposed to create.

Despite their raucous but weirdly good-natured game of *Real Life Clue*, Dena simply couldn't turn any of the Marketplace tenants into murderers.

It had to be someone else. But was it one murderer or two? What did Norbert and Royce have in common? The only thing Dena knew for sure was that they worked together. But was that enough of a link? And if so, what—or who—was the common denominator?

Audra? She knew about electricity. She took a personal day after Norbert's death to see old friends, and according to Royce, not because she was upset or grieving.

Dena thought about what she really knew about Audra, firsthand. She reconstructed the "Best/Worst" game they'd played that day while they ate lunch. Her best boyfriend had showered her with gifts, but she'd said their break-up was amiable. Her worst boyfriend had a crush on her older sister. It flitted through her brain that maybe one of these boyfriends could have been Norbert or Royce, but she rejected that idea immediately. Neither made sense.

Dena chewed a bite of her pastry. Her eyes widened and she inhaled sharply, choking on crumbs. She gripped the front counter and braced herself against a wave of adrenaline washing over her.

Audra's best boss was a park ranger, and her worst was when she was on a road crew.

Uh oh.

Dena

DENA SHOVED the rest of the lemon Danish in her mouth as she searched online for the issue of the *Arkansas River Valley Gazette* she had read while waiting for her tire to be repaired the other day. She scanned the article and jotted notes.

After she'd gone through it several times, and searched for any further articles, she found the phone numbers for both the state park and the construction company mentioned in the article.

She called both, but neither would confirm that Audra had ever been employed by them.

Dena tapped her fingers nervously on the front counter. She couldn't think of any other way to confirm any link between Audra and these other murders. She rubbed her jaw, unaware she'd been clenching her teeth.

It was all too coincidental, too circumstantial to take to Sheriff Johnson. But coincidences do happen and the sheriff had told her to be an extra set of eyes and ears, hadn't she? Dena picked up her phone then set it back down again. Twice.

Finally, she came up with a new plan.

Dena called Sheriff Johnson. "Can you meet me at Norbert's office?"

"Why?"

"I've been thinking about a conversation I had with Audra and I think she might know more than she's letting on. But I'm not sure and I don't want to … put myself in a position."

Sheriff Johnson didn't speak for a bit. "I can be there in about forty-five minutes. Don't do anything stupid."

Dena wanted to say how stupid everything was these days, but the sheriff had already hung up.

Dena checked the time, anxious now, after the sheriff's *don't do anything stupid* comment. Was this stupid? Was she wrong? What was going to happen? She wandered over to the bakery with an empty mug in hand.

"Is there coffee?"

Kober waved vaguely at the pot.

Dena pumped out a cup. Leaning against the counter sipping, she noticed Kober wasn't in a flurry of activity. Instead, she was simply standing, staring down at her prep table.

"What are you doing?" Dena asked.

"Not one darn thing."

They were quiet for a minute.

"Why not?" Dena asked.

"What's the point?" Kober picked up a batter-covered whisk and began to smack it rhythmically against the edge of the prep table. Flecks of batter flew in all directions. Kober seemed hypnotized by the splatter patterns.

"Whoa, whoa, whoa!" Dena grabbed the whisk from her and dropped it in the sink. "It's not that bad."

"Isn't it? I'm on the cusp of losing everything—my

kids, my husband, my business, my money, my pride." Kober narrowed her eyes at Dena. "So are you."

Dena rinsed off the whisk. "You don't know that. Especially about your family. We might be on a precipice about our businesses, but I'm not going down without a fight. I've got my store ready for tomorrow's opening, I've advertised everywhere I can think of." She reached over and touched Kober's hand. "And so have you. And look at all those gorgeous cake pops you made. You know, only time will tell about the Marketplace, but don't you dare tell me you're not proud of everything you've done. I mean look in your display case!"

Dena pulled her over and they both bent at the waist to assess the offerings. Perfectly golden mini-loaves of bread, iced cinnamon rolls, colorfully decorated cookies and cupcakes of all flavors, Danishes with generous dollops of jams and fillings, creamy cannolis, flaky baklava and croissants, even a gluten-free section. They all sat patiently in the case, like elegant debutantes waiting to be asked to dance.

Dena straightened and jabbed Kober in the upper arm. "You did all this. You. By yourself."

A grin spread across Kober's face and she nodded her head so hard that the foundation of her topiary of curls started to become undermined. The back of her hand hoisted it back into place. "I guess I did. Maybe I can face whatever comes next head on."

"I'm sure you can." Dena thought for a moment. "Hey, can you take a little break? I have to go talk to Audra and I could use a tough nut like you with me."

Dena

DENA DIDN'T TELL Kober everything she'd been thinking, just that Audra might have more information they could tease out of her to pass along to Aja as a correction to some of her terrible reporting. She didn't want Kober to know exactly what she was thinking, in case she was way off base. When they got to Norbert's office, Dena was surprised that Sheriff Johnson was nowhere to be seen. She checked the time. "We should wait until she gets here."

Kober had a quizzical look on her face but didn't say anything.

Even though the women were bundled up tight in their parkas—looking like two ticks ready to pop—they waited on the frigid sidewalk and did some deep Lamaze breathing to keep from shivering.

Minutes kept ticking by with no sheriff.

The door to Norbert's office opened and Audra stuck her head outside, calling, "What are you two doing out there?"

"Waiting for someone," Dena called back.

"Well, come here and wait inside. It's freezing out and you must be icicles." When neither of them moved, she added in a singsong voice, "I have hot coffee!"

Kober rushed toward her. Dena followed at a more reluctant pace.

Audra pulled chairs into the center of the room in a convivial little grouping. They settled in with matching white ceramic mugs branded with "Sugar Springs Marketplace is the Place to Market" in practically impossible to read red lettering on one side.

"Nice mugs," Kober said in a voice that clearly indicated she didn't think the mugs were nice in any way.

"I know." Audra groaned and pulled a defeated face. "They were delivered yesterday. Five hundred of them. Five *hundred*." Her eyes widened as she emphasized the number. "Norbert must have ordered them to give away at the Grand Opening. I wonder how many I can break before tomorrow."

"They're not that bad," Dena said.

"They're hideous."

"Well … yes, they are. But they're holding our coffee quite nicely," Dena said optimistically.

"True. They could be ugly *and* leak."

Minutes continued to tick by. The three of them sipped. Dena faced the front window of the office, keeping an eye out for Sheriff Johnson. Audra and Kober sat with their backs to the window.

"Who were you meeting, anyway?" Audra asked.

Kober began talking but Dena hopped to her feet and spoke over her. "We're keeping you from your work. We'll get out of your hair."

Kober didn't take the hint, remaining in her chair. Dena wished she'd completely filled Kober in on her plan, and not just the very broad strokes.

"What's going to happen here, now that both Norbert and Royce are … gone?" Kober asked Audra.

Dena dropped back into her seat with a jittery *whump*.

"I'm not entirely sure," Audra said matter-of-factly. "But I'm hoping to be able to keep running the office, maybe even buy the company outright."

Kober and Audra began chatting about how to find the best tax advice. Dena's eyes kept darting to the newspaper on Audra's desk. It was the same *Arkansas River Valley Gazette* issue that Dena had pulled up online not two hours ago.

Audra reached over and held out the issue to Dena. "It's from last week."

"I've actually already read it."

Audra cocked her head at Dena and looked like she might say something. Instead, she dropped the newspaper and turned to Kober. "How are your kids enjoying school this year? Did they have a fun winter break?"

Kober began telling her about the trials and tribulations of having four kids out of school at the same time she struggled to do everything necessary get the bakery ready to open.

Sheriff Johnson walked up and glanced in the window. Before she touched the door handle, Dena gave a small shake of her head and mouthed, "Wait."

With a jolt of bravery, Dena worried that if the sheriff came in, Audra would clam up and Dena wouldn't get her questions answered.

Dena interrupted Audra's and Kober's conversation. "Audra, do you still lead bird-watching tours at the state park?"

Audra's jaw stiffened and she stared silently at Dena. Finally, she sighed. "You know, you and I could have been great friends."

"We can still be friends."

"Not when you find out what I've done."

"I know what you've done."

"What'd she do?" Kober looked from Dena to Audra. Slowly, realization dawned on Kober and she recoiled in her chair.

Audra moved suddenly, causing both Dena and Kober to jump, but Audra was simply reaching for the newspaper again. "You don't need to worry. I'm done with violence. I've made my point."

"What was your point?" Kober's voice wavered.

Audra began to speak, but Dena stopped her. "Should we include Sheriff Johnson in this conversation?"

Dena

AUDRA PULLED over another chair for Sheriff Johnson and poured her a cup of coffee in an ugly Marketplace mug. Walking across the room with it, she said in a calm voice, "I've always leaned toward male-dominated industries. Construction interested me way more than teaching or nursing or being a receptionist. I thought if I was doing a man's job in a man's field, that should be enough. My mom was a highly trained and respected nurse in a big teaching hospital. Even though nursing has one of the smallest pay gaps of any industry, there was a study showing that male nurses—seven percent of those surveyed —still made more money than their female colleagues."

"That's infuriating!" Kober bellowed. "But what does that have to do … with … anything?" Kober trailed off quietly.

Sheriff Johnson and Dena both cut Kober a look, but Audra said calmly, "Everything, Kober. It has everything to do with it."

The earnest expression on Audra's face made Dena

realize that Audra had kept this story to herself long enough. She wanted to tell it.

"I found out Norbert was paying Royce more than twice what he was paying me," Audra continued. "When I found out, Norbert was over at the Marketplace working on getting the wiring fixed so your oven would function properly." She flicked her chin toward Kober. "Did you ever get it fixed?"

"Yes."

"Good. Anyway, I used my keys and went in through the emergency exit and straight up the stairs."

"Were you trying to avoid everyone? Did you know that something was going to happen with Norbert?" Sheriff Johnson asked.

It was obvious to Dena that the sheriff was probing Audra's intent, but Audra didn't seem to care.

Audra shrugged. "Something was bound to happen. All the way over there I was getting angrier and angrier. By the time I was up those stairs I could barely see straight. I reminded him how I trained Royce and taught him to do everything—inspections, how to sweet talk the building permit clerks, even how to turn on his stupid computer! I told Norbert, 'I've worked for you twice as long, and he makes more money than I do. How is that fair?'"

Kober was all wrapped up in the story. She leaned forward, "What did he say?"

"Norbert was cool as a cucumber and just told me that Royce had a family to support."

"Royce was married?" Kober's mouth dropped open. "He asked Skyler to go away with him for the weekend!"

"But you have a family too," Dena said. "Did you remind Norbert of that?"

Audra nodded. "I did. But he pointed out that I had a husband."

"And Royce had a wife. What's the difference?" Kober was hot and her voice showed it.

Audra continued, "I pointed out that half of American women who work were the primary breadwinners for their families, but Norbert didn't care, just kept fiddling with that electrical box. His only reasoning was that men needed to earn more because they were men. I really lost it then and yelled—"

"Let me guess … men are pigs," Kober said.

"How'd you know?" Audra asked.

"Because Hugo thought I was the one who yelled that."

Sheriff Johnson looked a bit apologetic when she glanced at Kober. "Then what happened?" she asked Audra softly.

"Then everything got really quiet. Like the whole universe was pressing in on me, smothering me." Audra looked at Sheriff Johnson with tears in her eyes. "He never got off that ladder or stopped tinkering the whole time I was talking. Like I was just an annoying child he could ignore." Audra stared into the distance for a moment. "But I decided I wouldn't be ignored, so I flipped that power switch on the breaker. He flew across the room. I knew he was dead before he even hit the floor. Sparks flew everywhere. On my blouse, on my gloves. I was swatting at my blouse, trying to yank off my glove when I saw flames. I panicked, worried I'd burn down the Marketplace. I smothered the fire, glad I just got a little burn on my hand. Everything happened so fast." Audra rubbed the back of her hand, healed now, just a small scar to remind her of the events of that day.

"Then what?" Sheriff Johnson prompted.

"After I got the fire out, I was thinking a bit more clearly. I checked on him, and just as I thought, he was dead. I took his keys and went back out the emergency exit, locking the door behind me. I didn't have to wipe my prints because I kept my gloves on the whole time."

"Why'd you take his keys?" Dena asked.

"It would be weird if everyone saw his car parked there for so long, so I drove it over by the park then walked back to the office. I knew Royce would be gone all afternoon, so I wondered how I'd bandage my hand myself." Audra smiled at Dena. "Then you showed up like an angel. You were so kind to me. Thank you."

"You're welcome," Dena said softly.

"I'm sorry I didn't get your lease fixed. I meant to, but then ..." Audra trailed off.

"What happened next?" the sheriff asked.

Audra thought for a moment. "Oh, before I got back to the office, I stopped by Corky's to get a sandwich for lunch."

"You are one cool cucumber," Kober marveled.

Everyone stared at her.

"I'm not saying that's a *good* thing—"

"That's sure how it sounded," Dena said with a frown.

"But she *was* calm!" Kober protested.

"You're right. I was. Cool as a cucumber. I was hungry too." Audra shrugged. "And it was nice having lunch with you and getting to know you, Dena. But over the next few days I couldn't stop thinking about all this."

"No doubt!" Kober said a little too loudly.

"I kept wondering if Norbert underpaid all of his female staff." She glanced at Dena. "That's why all those files were scattered all over Norbert's desk. I couldn't figure it out from those files, but then I began wondering if *all* my employers—not just Norbert—cheated me because I was a woman. So I went to visit them."

Dena paled. "The state park. The construction company."

Audra nodded. "I was afraid you'd figure it out," she said to Dena. "You're smart."

"What happened at the state park, Audra?" Sheriff Johnson asked.

"I went looking for my old boss and overheard someone on the walkie-talkie say he was out by the yurts because something was wrong with the power."

"Ironic," Kober said.

"I thought so too, but I went out there anyway. I needed to know. He'd taken his service belt off while he worked and left it over on a rock. I pulled his own gun on him after he hemmed and hawed when I asked about the pay gap." She looked pointedly at the sheriff. "I did not like his answer. I wiped off his gun and walked back to my car. Nobody even saw me."

"And at the construction company?" the sheriff asked.

"I was lucky and the owner of the company was in the construction trailer. I asked him where everyone was. On the job, he says. Even the girls? I asked. Then he got nervous and demanded to know what was going on. I asked if my salary had been the same as the guys. Sure, he says, of course it was." Audra's skin began to tingle and her breath came faster. "I told him to prove it and of course, he can't, so I say, 'I wish you'd given me the right answer' and I left. I didn't really know what to do. But then I saw the bulldozer and climbed up in it."

Kober's jaw dropped. "You bulldozed the construction trailer? I bet he did *not* see that coming."

"What about Royce, Audra?" Sheriff Johnson asked.

"What about him? I knew he was going over Monarch Pass so I nicked his brake line."

"That works?" Kober asked. "I thought that was just a movie thing."

"Not if you do it right," Audra said. "If you cut it

completely, the first time you tap the brakes it goes right to the floor and you know something is wrong. But if you make a tiny pinhole, the brake fluid slowly leaks out and when you're going over a mountain pass ..." Audra made a whistle sound like something sailing off a cliff.

"But why Royce?" Dena asked.

Audra sighed. "You know the saying *he was born on third base and thought he hit a triple?*"

Dena nodded.

"That was Royce. I had to do everything for him. He was practically useless but because he was a man, he just assumed he deserved everything he got, even when it was completely unearned. When I told him about our pay discrepancies he laughed, he actually laughed. Like it was all some big joke. And when I pointed out that I did ten times the work he did for less pay, he said, and I quote, *just get over it.* Get over it. Can you believe it?"

Dena felt prickly all over, hot and cold at the same time.

Audra saw the way the women were looking at her and frowned. "You see a monster, not a crusader. You have to understand, I didn't *want* to do any of it. I *had* to do it. For me, and for every woman who has ever been mistreated in the workplace, looked down upon, taken advantage of." Audra focused on Kober. "For your daughter." Then she looked at Dena. "And for your daughter too." Then the sheriff. "And for yours. She's only a kid, but someday she'll be in the workforce. I want it to be better for her. For all the daughters."

Sheriff Johnson stared at her for a bit before standing up and pulling out her handcuffs. "How does killing four people help my daughter?"

Dena

THE CLOUDS CLEARED, making the day of the Grand Opening even colder, although how that was possible was a meteorological mystery.

Dena dragged her feet, stalling at home until the last possible minute she had to leave for the Marketplace. May as well get this over with, she finally reasoned. *The sooner I fail, the sooner I can come home and shove that gallon of salted caramel ice cream in my gullet.* She checked the freezer to make sure it was still there and she hadn't accidentally polished it off in some middle-of-the-night frenzy of mindless depravity.

She drove to the Marketplace with two big sandwich board signs, intending to place them at two of the outside entrances to the Marketplace on the east side where the bookstore was. When she came around the corner to turn into the parking lot, she screeched to a stop, sliding a bit in the loose gravel.

The parking lot was filled with cars. Almost all the spaces were already taken, and she had to troll the aisles until she found one in the very last row on the west side of

"

the building. She left the signs in the back seat; they were obviously unnecessary at this point. Plus, they each weighed about seven-thousand pounds and she was happy to leave them be.

Dena pushed her way through the crowd until she neared the door to the Marketplace. "Don't worry! I've got a key!" she called through the crush of people. When she reached the door, she was surprised to see it already open. "Excuse me, can I get through, please?" The merry, high-spirited crowd shuffled and parted enough that she could squeeze inside. She was astonished to see there were just as many people stuffed into the promenade waiting for the shops to open.

She caught Hugo's eye where he peeked out from his back door. He grinned like she'd never seen him grin before. But seeing Eeyore smile was a bit unsettling.

Dena made her way around to the bookstore, unlocked the security gate and impatiently waited until it silently slid up into the housing at the ceiling.

"Can we come in?" a woman asked. "I've been *dying* for this place to open. Now I won't have to go all the way to Colorado Springs to shop for books."

Dena held up one finger. "Can you hang on one more sec?" Without waiting for an answer, she hurried through the store and flung open her back door to the vendor room. Everyone was there looking terrified and a bit hysterical.

"We're all here now. Let's do this!" Kober bellowed.

The tenants were run ragged all day, greeting customers, explaining about their shops, and giving away samples. Long after lunch time, Max came by to spell each of the tenants one by one, bringing them a peanut butter sandwich from the stack he'd raced home to prepare.

When it was Dena's turn, Max shooed her away to

take a break and eat. Instead of going into the vendor room, Dena went out the front of her bookstore and watched the chaos from the promenade where she leaned against the Marketplace window.

Suddenly Dena saw a young girl corner Balaam and reach down to pick him up. She shrieked. "Don't do that! He doesn't like to be picked up!" The crowd was too thick for Dena to get to her and too noisy for the girl to hear the warning.

By the time Dena elbowed her way through the crowd, the girl had Balaam up on her chest, his chin resting on her shoulder.

Balaam rolled his eyes at Dena and made himself comfortable.

"Today is full of miracles," Dena said.

"What?" the girl asked.

"Oh, nothing. I see you've made a friend."

"He's so sweet! I love him."

"He's our resident cat." Dena pointed to the photo studio. "Evelyn and Max own him."

At Dena's words, Balaam swished his tail angrily.

"I mean, of course, that Evelyn and Max are allowed to take care of him."

Balaam's tail settled down and he closed his eyes.

Dena left them to their cuddle and returned to the clutch of comfy chairs across the promenade from her bookstore. A group of women had settled into them exactly as Dena had imagined. A few of the skinnier ones had doubled up on the seats and several more perched on the arms of the chairs eating cake pops from the bakery.

Dena noticed they were all wearing matching t-shirts and asked them about it.

One woman tugged her shirt so Dena could read it.

"Nightmare Sallys?"

"We belong to an organization called Paranormal Festivities Tours. The Nightmare Sallys like to travel together," she said, smoothing her shirt.

Another one said, "We've stayed in Dracula's castle, overnighted at Alcatraz—"

"Don't forget the Shanghai tours in Portland," added another.

"And we've toured more haunted houses than you can imagine."

"It sounds like you have quite the itinerary," Dena said. "But why are you here, at our Marketplace?" She snapped her fingers and answered her own question. "Because of the Sugar Mill Curse."

"And the Marketplace Murders, of course."

Dena groaned. "Please don't say that. First, there was only one murder and isn't it a bit too soon for that?"

"I suppose." One of the women looked at Dena. "Do you know if that bookstore has a horror section?"

"I know for a fact it does."

"Okay, Sallys … finish those cake pops and let's go buy some books!"

One of them laughed and pointed at the sign. "I just saw the name of the store!"

Dena cringed.

"Thrice Sold Tales. What a great name!" The woman posed the Sallys as best she could in the surging crowd under the sign and took a photo.

Dena looked longingly at the comfy arm chair one of the Sallys had just vacated, but she knew if she sat down now, she might never be able to get up again. She followed the Sallys into the book store and pointed them toward the horror section.

She was surprised to see Quint O'Dell helping Max behind the cash register.

"Did you see?" Quint said as he handed a credit card back to a customer.

"See what?"

He pointed to the Colorado History section she and Quint had set up. It was decimated, every book gone.

"Where'd you move the books?" Dena glanced around the store.

"I didn't move them. They all sold!"

"What? All of them? Already? Are you sure?" Dena had been in such a frenzy all day she hadn't really even looked to see what people were buying. She'd have to check the shelves later to see which genres sold best.

Quint hooked his thumbs in his belt loops and stood tall, chest thrust out. "Told ya so."

"Wow. I'm speechless." Dena reached under the front counter and pulled out the inventory list they'd made as they arranged Quint's books on the table. She grabbed a calculator and punched at it for a few moments as her finger traveled down the list. She opened the cash register and counted out some bills, folding the wad and pressing it into Quint's palm. "You're well on your way to not squatting in some lady's cabin."

"I'm moving tomorrow."

Dena frowned and glanced at the money she'd just given Quint. "Not sure that's enough."

"He's moving into Royce's mom's house," Max said. "Evelyn got it all worked out. In exchange for looking after Janet, doing some cooking and cleaning and helping around the house, she'll let him have the spare room and the basement to store his books. He's even agreed to figure out how to install ceiling fans, something Royce had been trying to figure out."

"Of course! That's why Royce wanted those books about electricity and wiring." Again, Dena wished she'd had a longer conversation with Royce. She wouldn't have jumped to those conclusions about him.

"Will you be wanting me to bring you more books?" Quint asked.

"Does our agreement still work for you?"

"It does."

"Then yes I do."

———

After the last customer had left, long after the advertised closing time, Hugo locked the outside doors against any surprise wave of late shoppers and returned to the vendor room where they all sat. They looked like extras from a war movie—disheveled, numb, and shell-shocked, only missing the military garb.

Dena's mascara had migrated beneath her eyes. Kober's hair was more down than up. Hugo had chocolate smeared all over his normally pristine white apron. Skyler's usual perky expression looked precariously close to the edge of the hysterical spectrum. Evelyn had even shed her cardigan.

"That was spectacular!" Max said, beaming. "We did it!" He popped the cork on a bottle of champagne and filled a coffee cup for everyone.

Skyler went into her shop for a moment and returned with the saddest, loneliest cheese tray known to humankind. Four small lumps and two slices of cheese, eight olives, and three crackers—more crumbs than cracker—rolled around on a bed of torn and limp curly kale.

Skyler offered it first to Evelyn. "There's a tiny bit of feta, just for you."

Balaam came at a gallop.

The cheese plate continued its rounds, and everyone took something from that pitiful plate. Shellshock will do that to a person. Like soldiers happy to receive their MREs.

"People complimented my shop all day. I sold out of everything and everyone just loved that my cheese was all local. With all that praise and knowing I persuaded even Evelyn to enjoy my feta … well, the world is my oyster!" Skyler practically thrummed out of her skin. She waited expectantly for Evelyn to pop the bite of feta into her mouth.

Everyone but Skyler knew Evelyn still couldn't abide the taste of goat cheese but had been pretending she enjoyed it to keep Skyler from spiraling into despair. All along she'd been feeding it to Balaam.

The rest of the tenants scooted forward on the seats, waiting with anticipation to learn if today was the day one of them would win the betting pool. Everyone had made guesses as to when Evelyn would have to confess to Skyler. A dollar per guess. The pot had climbed to thirty-two dollars.

Evelyn held the crumbly cheese by two fingers near her mouth, as if trying to convince herself to eat it. Instead, she said to Skyler, "Maybe you better have a seat, dear."

Balaam hopped into Evelyn's lap and looked at her expectantly. Evelyn took a deep breath and held out the cheese to Balaam. He snapped at it greedily, then swished his tail in contentment.

"Skyler," Evelyn said wearily. "I still don't like feta cheese. Never have. Never will."

"Yes!" Kober raised a triumphant fist in the air. "I won!"

Skyler looked blankly at Kober then at Evelyn, clearly

not comprehending what was going on. "But I've been giving you samples all week!"

"Don't I know it."

"And you've just been giving it to the cat?" Skyler looked from Balaam's smug, contented face to Evelyn's guilty one, then to the other tenants. "And you all knew?"

Everyone nodded, ashamed-not-ashamed.

"And I'm thirty-two bucks richer," Kober said excitedly.

Skyler's face fell. She bounced back just as quickly. "No worries! Turns out I was worried about nothing. Everyone loved my cheese!" She pointed at Kober, then at Hugo. "And your goodies. And your chocolates." She looked at Dena. "What about you? Did you sell a bunch of books today?"

"I did," she said. "I hope today wasn't just a fluke."

"What about you, Evelyn?"

"Snapped the camera all day. People weren't even cranky about the wait."

"All the free chocolates I handed out today could have fed the entire Dutch population for a year," Hugo grumbled.

Dena wasn't sure if he was joking or not.

"Now everyone will always expect free samples," he said. "I'm sure we've created a monster. Who talked me into that, anyway?"

"That was Dena's idea," Skyler said. "It was also her idea to make the flyers and place those ads in the Colorado Springs and Denver papers."

"And she also solved Norbert's and Royce's murders," Kober said proudly.

Max refilled everyone's champagne. "A toast!" he said. "To Dena ... the new Marketplace manager!"

Everyone but Dena clinked cups saying, "Cheers!" and "Here, here!"

"*Hold on one minute*." Dena placed her mug a little too forcefully on the table in front of her. "What are you talking about, Marketplace manager? I already have a full-time job."

"The way I see it," Max said, "with Norbert, Royce, and Audra all gone, somebody needs to be in charge of this place, at least temporarily."

"Then why don't you do it?" Dena asked him.

"Because I'm old and cranky and nobody ever does what I say." Max drained his cup. "Plus, I don't have any good ideas."

"We've all been talking about it, Dena, and you're the logical choice," Evelyn said.

"You've all been talking about it?" Dena asked incredulously.

"And you're the logical choice," Evelyn repeated patiently.

"I think you're all off your rockers." Dena drained her cup and held it out for more. "I don't have any tech skills. And I'm fresh out of any more ideas."

"Don't need any," Hugo said. "You have people skills. Any idiot can work a computer."

"It's just until we get everything organized and can hire someone," Kober said.

"With Norbert gone, how do you even know what's going to happen with the Marketplace? Maybe it's going to disappear—POOF—like Brigadoon," Dena argued.

"Then your problem will be solved!" Max guffawed.

"Besides," Kober said. "It's preordained." She pointed at the white board.

There was no countdown to the Grand Opening, no body count. Just a haiku.

> Dena Russo is
> The Marketplace manager
> Because we say so.

This one was signed, however.
Evelyn, Max, Hugo, Skyler, and Kober.
Dena walked over to the white board to their loud protestations that she shouldn't erase it. But she never intended to. Instead, she picked up the red dry erase marker and thought for a moment. She counted syllables on her other hand while she wrote.

> I think I'm gonna
> Really like working with the
> Bunch of you loonies.

"Here's to many more adventures!" Dena said.
They all raised a glass with her.

Afterword

Thank you so much for reading my books! If it wasn't for readers, I'd be indistinguishable from a spider monkey banging away on a computer for no reason.

I hope you were delighted with your visit to the Sugar Mill Marketplace. If so, check out the rest of the series!

Your reviews help authors drive book sales *and* help readers find new books and authors. Please consider popping over to the BOOKED review page and dropping a few words. I'd really appreciate it!

Acknowledgments

The theme of BOOKED is "good vs evil."

We all have aspects of both in us, but I'm lucky to know so many people whose good far exceeds their evil. And so many of them helped me with this book!

Many of these stellar people hang out with me in my private Facebook group, Becky's Book Buddies. I slammed up against a brick wall of creativity so I put out the call to them to help me think of fake names for social media. Almost immediately, funny ideas started rolling in from **Sue Stoner, Pat Doyle, Christina Pontius, Heidi Prockish, Emily Scudder**, and **Mary Feliz**. I couldn't come up with anything I liked and you guys rode to my rescue, so thank you!

Big thanks to **Dan Cabrera** for helping me electrocute Norbert, and to **Tracy Brisendine** for showing me what that might look like.

And, as always, huge thanks to **Jessica Cornwell**, editor extraordinaire. I'm constantly telling her I make so many mistakes because I'm a good person and want to keep her busy. She remains unpersuaded. And very busy.

The Dunne Diehl Mysteries

Banana Bamboozle #1

Marshmallow Mayhem #2

Nonfiction

Eight Weeks to a Complete Novel—Write Faster, Write Better,
Be More Organized

About the Author

Award-winning author **Becky Clark** is the seventh of eight kids, which explains both her insatiable need for attention and her atrocious table manners. She likes to read funny books so it felt natural to write them too. She surrounds herself with quirky people and pets who end up as characters in her novels. Readers say her books are "fast and thoroughly entertaining" with "witty humor and tight writing" and "humor laced with engaging characters" so you should "grab a cocktail and enjoy the ride."

For entirely too much information about her, visit BeckyClarkBooks.com. While you're there, subscribe to her mailing list for **oodles of fun and free stuff**.

Follow her on Amazon and BookBub to get up-to-the-date info on new releases and sales. Join her private group "Becky's Book Buddies" on Facebook for shenanigans and fun. Put her books on your GoodReads shelf to make all your friends jealous.